CHAPTER 1

Monday 30th July 2018

Mr Phipps was in the gym.

It wasn't one of the best. He had memberships in different parts of the city because he always liked to work out before a gig and all he'd heard about that so far was that it was in North London. So he knew good gyms from bad. This one wasn't *serious*, more an add-on to the squash club. Basic machines, one rack of free weights. Still, that meant it wasn't busy, not just after it opened at 7 a.m. No one there, so he could play the CD he'd brought – they still had a stereo, crappy old thing but one plus to the place. He didn't like wearing headphones. He liked to hear when a door opened.

Lenny Kravitz sang about an American woman. Mr Phipps checked his stance in the floor-length mirror and slowly raised the twenty-pounders towards his reflection. *One. Two . . .*

A phone rang. Playing 'Blue Rondo à la Turk'. The phone he'd bought last night didn't play tunes so this call wasn't the one he was waiting for. This call was Sharon. The Ex. Always up early.

''lo?'

'Is that you?'

'Since you called me, I suppose it must be.'

'What? I can't hear you. Can you turn that racket down?'

Racket. What she'd always called his music. He went to the stereo, lowered the volume. 'Better?'

'What time are you picking Meaghan up?'

'Not sure. Afternoon.'

'Can you be more specific? Malcolm and I need to go to IKEA and we don't want to leave it late or the North Circular will be chocka.'

Chocka. IKEA. Malcolm. What had he ever seen in her? 'No. I'm waiting to hear about work. Early afternoon, I'd say.'

'Fine.' The way she snapped it meant it wasn't. 'Early as you can, please.'

She hung up. He looked at the phone. He didn't like minding Meaghan the same day he worked. But this gig, wherever it was, had come up sudden and he'd missed his day with his daughter for a gig the week before. He'd make it up to her, take her to the pictures, sit through some princess thing. Afterwards, over ice cream, he'd show her the hotel website in Mauritius. He'd promised to take her in February. Now she was five she could learn to snorkel. He'd cheer her on from the poolside. If the work kept coming this regularly, he'd upgrade them to business class. She'd like that. Took after her mum. Liked her luxury.

The door opened. He looked. A man came in. Ginger hair and beard, late thirties. No bag, and nothing in his hands. The man smiled, waved at the stereo. 'Mind if I turn this up?'

'Sure.'

ONE LONDON DAY

ONE LONDON DAY

CHRIS HUMPHREYS

Allison & Busby Limited
11 Wardour Mews
London W1F 8AN
allisonandbusby.com

First published in Great Britain by Allison & Busby in 2026.

A CIP catalogue record for this book is available from
the British Library.

First Edition

ISBN 978-0-7490-3335-4

Typeset in 11.5/16.5 pt Adobe Garamond Pro by
Allison and Busby Ltd.

By choosing this product, you help take care of the world's forests.
Learn more: www.fsc.org.

FSC
www.fsc.org
MIX
Paper | Supporting
responsible forestry
FSC® C018072

Printed and bound in Great Britain by Clays Ltd. Elcograf S.p.A

EU GPSR Authorised Representative
LOGOS EUROPE, 9 rue Nicolas Poussin, 17000, LA ROCHELLE, France
E-mail: Contact@logoseurope.eu

To Paul and Carole

Every kind of hunger . . .

PART I

FIVE DAYS IN LONDON

Carrot Top went to the stereo, turned the knob. Not as loud as before. *Fuck*, thought Mr Phipps, *please don't let him be a talker.*

The man was nodding at the stereo. 'I know this. Bachman–Turner Overdrive.'

'Lenny Kravitz,' Mr Phipps replied, then rolled his eyes – he was the one continuing the conversation.

The man didn't see the eye roll. 'Oh yeah. Good, isn't he? Saw him in—'

Mr Phipps ignored the drone that followed. When he didn't reply, just picked up his weights again, Carrot Top licked his lips and went to the treadmill.

One, two, three, four . . .

His phone went again. Still not his new one. Another tune. 'Für Elise'. Paula.

He picked it up. ''lo?'

'Where are you?'

'Gym.'

'Noisy. Can you turn the music down?'

'Not really. Other people here.'

'I see.' There was a pause. 'You promised to call.'

It was said sulky. Mock miffed. Except recently he'd been finding it hard to tell how mock it was. 'Been busy.'

'I'm sure.' A miffed pause, then, 'You coming over?'

'Can't. Working.'

'After?'

'I've got Meaghan.'

'Come when you've dropped her back.'

'I'll see.'

'Yes, well, why don't you do that?'

She hung up. *Two in two minutes*, he thought. Posh birds hanging up on him. Why did he get involved with hoity-totty? He supposed it appealed to the lad in him. Their educated voices. Their expensive scents. And he appealed to them. A bit of rough, Sharon had called him soon after they'd first met. Funny, he didn't think of himself as rough. He read, he worked out, he didn't drink. Even listened to Beethoven sometimes. But he could put the voice on if he needed to, along with his white plumber's overalls.

Another phone rang. Not the one in his hand, no tune. Dropping the one in the bag, he picked up the other. ''lo?' He spoke while crossing the gym, exiting.

'Severin. Joseph.'

'OK.'

'54 Allingham Close, N3.'

'OK.'

'Know it?'

'I'll find it.'

'The daughter leaves for school at eight-thirty. Wife takes the baby and goes for Mums and Babies Pilates at eight forty-five. So he'll be alone.'

'OK.'

'There's something else.' A slight pause. 'We need you to collect something from him first.'

Fuck. 'Yeah?'

'There'll be a bonus.'

'How much?'

He heard muffled voices, a hand half covering the other phone. 'One thousand?'

He heard the question in it. Thought of upgrades to Mauritius. 'Two.'

'Mr—'

'Oi!'

'Sorry.' More muffled talk. 'Very well. It's the books. He's an accountant. Get the books from him. He'll know what you mean.'

'OK. Drop 'em where I collect?'

'No. We need to see you. Let us know when you've got them. We'll tell you where.'

Unusual. 'Anything else?'

'Mr.' He didn't need to interrupt him this time. The caller wasn't going to say his name. He continued. 'My colleague asks: will you take a cheque?'

He hung up on soft laughter. *Very funny, Posh Boy*, he thought.

He went to the toilets, broke the phone up, flushed the pieces down the bog. As he watched to see if any floated back up, he thought, Allingham *Close*? He hated closes. And cul-de-sacs. Only one way in and out.

There was a half-decent Italian caff opposite the Tesco on Ballards Lane, so he picked up a skinny decaf latte, then crossed to the shop. Put on his overalls in a toilet cubicle. They were new, but he'd dirtied them up, washed them a few times. Slipped a red baseball cap on and kept his head low for the CCTV until he got back into his Mazda, parked where there were no cameras on Nether Street. Drove the five minutes to Allingham Close, found a space facing the close's entrance about fifty yards past the house, getting there just before eight-thirty, so he could watch the daughter leave.

She did, in a uniform, five minutes late and running. The wife followed ten minutes later. Not with a baby, as Posh Boy had said. With an infant, nearly two he looked. The kid wanted to walk but his mum was in a rush so she snatched him up and he started howling and kicking her. The terrible twos. Meaghan hadn't been so bad but even she'd had her moments. As the mum bent to strap the child into his seat, Mr Phipps noticed that she was pregnant. She was a big girl, but the bulge was prominent. When she climbed into her Sentra and drove off, he looked at the house again. Semi-detached but nice. Owned by the sort of people who would have full life insurance. Two kids and one on the way, she'd need it.

He finished his latte, got out of the car, opened the boot. His canvas tool bag was under some of Meaghan's rubbish — stuff he'd won for her at the May bank holiday funfair on the Heath. Two months and she still wouldn't let him chuck them. A giant stuffed alien. A white felt bear. Thank God they didn't do goldfish any more.

He pushed the shit aside, unzipped the duffel, reached beneath the pillow. He'd checked the Glock before he set out but he bent into the boot, checked it again. Round in the breech. Full mag. Putting it back under the pillow, he left the zipper open, picked up the bag, closed the boot, looked around. No one about. Pocketing his keys, he marched up to number 54, and rang the bell.

He heard Severin coming because he was talking loudly. Had they cocked up? Was there someone else? People in houses like this often employed Romanian or Albanian

14

cleaners. There were extra payments for bystanders – one fifth, usually, of the hit itself. He did 'em, but he didn't like it. The gig, the mark, he deserved it, but passers-by?

Then he heard words through the door, could tell they were being spoken loudly into a phone.

'No, please. Please, Lottie! I have to see you. Yeah, those as well, but I just really want to. I have to. Look, hang on, will you.'

The door opened. Mr Severin. Medium height, dark, Jewish, even had the cap thing. What was that called? He'd look it up, sort of thing that came up in crosswords. 'Morning, sir,' Mr Phipps began.

Severin held up a finger. 'Just a second.' He beckoned the man before him into the hall. Waved the phone at him, eyebrows raised, then turned away. 'Listen, I wanted to tell you—'

The man was speaking too softly to hear now. Mr Phipps went in. Always better but didn't often happen. Some rag, *Sunday Sport* or something, had called him 'the doorstep killer'. But they'd allotted about five gigs to him that had been down to others. Ridiculous. Besides, everyone killed on doorsteps if they could. It was like back in Helmand. Stand in the doorway. 'Shoot and scoot', they called it. Take out the bad guys, then crack on. All sorts of nasty things could be waiting inside.

He couldn't shoot and scoot today because of the collection. That's why the gun was in the bag not in his hand. He stepped inside, shut the door behind him.

Mr Severin was still murmuring into his phone, but the whine had gone, since now there was a bloke in overalls standing in his hall. 'Look, just ten minutes, OK? There's . . . no, listen . . . there's something I need to . . . yes, tonight. Not sure, I'll call. OK. Thank you. No, really, I'm—' He looked at Mr Phipps. 'Um, gotta go. The plumber's here. Yeah, I . . . well, you know. Me too.' He hung up. 'It's the kitchen one.' He gestured through a door at the end of the hall, to the back.

He'd had this once before, with another couple. Wife thought the husband had called the plumber or electrician. Husband thought the wife had. These houses, built forty-odd years ago, always something going wrong. 'Would you mind showing me, sir?'

Severin had his thumb on his phone, about to make another call. He sighed. 'Only one place for a kitchen sink, isn't there?' Still, he led the way past a telly lounge on the right into a long room with primrose walls. Cabinets and cookers this end, breakfast bar, a dining table and chairs the far end. French windows onto a long narrow garden. He crossed to the sink, which was full of half-scraped plates and some dirty pots.

'Oh, look, sorry,' Severin said, 'Aurelia's not in till ten. Could you just . . . shove 'em onto the side. I have to . . .'

He waved the phone, took a step back towards the hall. Mr Phipps let him get to the doorway. 'Kneel down,' he said.

Severin turned, blinked at him. 'What did you say?'

'Kneel the fuck down,' he shouted, stepping closer and pointing the Glock.

'Oh, Jesus. Please no, I—'

Severin dropped the phone and it bounced to Mr Phipps's feet. He kicked it away, stepped forward and put the muzzle

16

to Severin's head. The man dropped hard, arms going wide, knuckles banging into the door frame. Mr Phipps followed him down, gun to head, and held out his other hand. It had a hessian bag in it. 'Put this on,' he said.

'I beg you, I—'

'Put it the fuck on,' he shouted, putting weight behind the muzzle.

Severin obeyed. But he kept talking, his words soon muffled by hemp. 'Look, don't do any . . . I can help. I know who sent you. The Shadows, right?'

The Shadows. Mr Phipps shook his head. Fucking public schoolboys with their comic books, their Marvel Universe superheroes. Or maybe it was their retro geekdom? His father had had a 45 by a band called The Shadows. The song title was . . . some American Indian tribe. Twangy guitar shit anyway. His youthful employers probably had it too, since vinyl was *so* now. He'd preferred it back in the day when he was employed by old toffs with dandruff on their collars and numbers for their department name.

'You have something we want,' he said softly, putting the gun back.

'What? I can't hear—'

He took the muzzle away, moved around behind Severin then barked, 'You have something we want.'

'I do. Yes. I do but they, they're . . .'

He could almost hear the man's mind whirling through the bag. He had to know this wasn't good. That perhaps all that was keeping him alive was the fact that he still had something to sell.

Severin continued. 'They're . . . not here, though.'

'Don't lie to me!'

'I'm not, please. Please, don't . . . They're . . . they're with a *friend*.'

When he'd been with 3 Para in Belfast, he'd learnt to listen for nuance. For emphasis. Even if the Mick was blubbering under sacking in that fucking stupid accent, he'd listen, he'd hear. He'd been good at it. Now he heard the way this man said 'friend'. After a pause. He meant a woman. He meant a lover. He probably meant that girl he'd been blabbing to when he'd come to the door. What was it? Laura? Lorraine?

He believed Mr Severin. Civilians rarely lied in this sort of situation. The Shadows would know who she was. Or they would find out.

Mr Phipps moved around to where he'd started. He'd kept his finger off the trigger and along the frame the whole time. His first gig, he'd used a Smith & Wesson semi, took the safety off straight away and because he was a bit jumpy, the gun had gone off by mistake, took the fucker's ear off. The noise was horrendous. The Glock's safety was set into the trigger, one of the reasons he liked the gun. Now, he pressed it with the pad of his finger.

Maybe it was Severin's low babbling, lost to hessian, but Mr Phipps hadn't even heard the door. Just the voice. 'Forgot my mat. Now Reuben's decided he needs a poo. He—'

Mr Phipps looked at the wife at the front door. He saw what she was seeing: a man in white overalls and a no-logo red cap in the kitchen doorway with a gun in his hand, the man at his feet with the sack on his head in her husband's suit. She wouldn't believe what she was seeing, would look for some normal explanation; it's what people did. So he had

18

a moment to think about it, before the screaming started.

There were those small payments – for collateral damage, as the Yanks said. He'd taken them, when he had to. But the kid in her arms, tears forgotten as he stared at the gun? It wasn't much fun, being an orphan. He knew.

He made up his mind. Pointed the Glock at them. Shouted, 'Down on the floor. Faces on the floor. Eyes shut. Now. Now!'

To her credit, she obeyed fast. The kid started yelling but she grabbed him and shoved his head into her armpit. Then Severin started shouting too. 'Vicky! Help me. Help! Help!'

Mr Phipps reached into his duffel and pulled out the pillow. He shoved it onto the man's head, and fired twice. When the body was on the ground, he dropped the pillow onto his chest and fired twice more. He'd always had a knack for keeping track of ejected casings. Found the four fast, pocketed them. Then he put the gun back in the duffel, picked it up and walked from the kitchen. As he passed the woman, her face still to the floor, her son trying to squirm out from under, he said, 'If you move, or open your eyes, I will kill the boy.'

He left the front door open. He hadn't touched anything inside except for the bag and the pillow, and you couldn't lift prints from cloth. The woman might lie there for a minute or two. A mother's instinct, he thought.

He drove carefully. Despite it being his trade, his pulse always accelerated after a gig. Last thing he needed was to be caught on a speed camera.

Down Hendon Lane, joined the North Circ, headed east. Morning rush but he was in no hurry. He flicked on Magic FM.

Couldn't believe it when the third song up was . . . 'Apache'. Apache, that was it. Twangy guitar shit indeed.

Fucking Shadows, he thought, and laughed. Then spent from Henlys Corner to the A11 trying to remember the *friend's* name.

Laura? Lorraine?

CHAPTER 2

Five days before . . . Wednesday 25th July 2018

'No, three o'clock. I'll give it till twenty past. I know what she said, Oliver, but tough, she'll just have to come into the office like normal people. Yeah, I'll pop back, but later. I have to pick up Rachel at four so . . . no, that's OK, I'm done, you take it.'

Joe Severin hung up, put his phone next to the cutlery tray, picked up the inventory. Everything in the kitchen on the list was laid out on the counter so the leaving tenant could check it over, and the new one – Oliver was showing a few people around early evening – could see it was all there. Pots, pans, knives, forks, spoons. Electric frying pan. He couldn't believe that still worked; he'd bought it at Argos along with everything else needed to kit out his first rental property. This one, this one-bedroom in Tufnell Park, together with the two-bed above and the shop below. The beginnings of empire.

He looked around then shook his head. He so rarely came to this place, left nearly all the check-ins and check-outs to his employees. But actually it was kinda nice to be back because this one was special for sure. Seventeen years ago, when he'd come back from the States, his dad was so stunned that his fifth child was finally going to settle down, he'd broken a lifetime of 'I had to make it on my own, son, and so do you', by actually lending him the money to buy the building.

Seventeen years, and from this little acorn . . .

He owned five more buildings divided into flats – Finchley, Hendon, Golders Green – much like this, plus the one fancier one near Portobello he'd bought on a whim in the last financial downturn. Empty now, and too much left on the mortgage; he'd have to get someone in there fast, pay the exorbitant rent. Seven properties, and the twenty he managed for others. Hence the office, hence Oliver and Stacey and Max. But Stacey was seeing someone else into Hendon Central, Max was on paternity leave – Jesus, how his father's eyes had rolled when he told him that! – while Oliver was manning the office. He'd begged Joe to swap, let him check this tenant – what was her name? Joe glanced at the inventory form she'd have to sign and initial, made out to one 'Lottie Henshaw' – let Oliver check her out as he'd checked her in. 'Chaos on two legs,' he'd called her, adding, 'but what legs!'

It was the main reason Joe was there, not Oliver. Joe didn't like his employees flirting with the tenants. It was unprofessional. And in this day and age? Companies were being sued for such shit, and he had a reputation to preserve. Besides, the office was in Kentish Town so Tufnell Park made it easier for Joe to pick up Rachel at her school in Highgate and take her to meet her mum at the florist's in Hampstead. Choosing flowers for the bat mitzvah. Though why Vicky couldn't pick their daughter up he didn't know and hadn't asked. His wife's daily rounds were a mystery to him and he found it was best to just nod and pay off the Visa bills.

Joe looked at the counter. There was only one thing out of place – a plastic bag that the inventory clerk had apparently found wedged up the ornamental fireplace. Joe had peered inside when he'd first seen it. Papers. No, *letters*. He could see handwriting and a 'Dear . . .' someone. Who wrote letters these days? Well, this Ms Henshaw apparently – he could see her signature on the bottom of one, a mad scrawl of 'Lottie'. Odd, why did she have her own letters? Did she write them to herself?

None of his business.

He looked at his phone. Tsked. Three-fifteen. He'd give her five minutes and then he'd go. She'd have to come to the office in the morning. They were already doing her a huge favour by giving her the cheque today, rather than making her wait a week because Oliver was horny and she'd said she was desperate. Well then, she needed to learn to be punctual.

Since he had his phone out, Joe thought he might as well check his stocks. He usually only allowed himself to check at mealtimes because it could become obsessive – it was just too easy, pulling it up on his app, seeing how much he'd made that hour, or not. He'd done some trading while he was still at school, with two of his brothers, a little bit before he dropped out of college. But it had been so cumbersome then – studying the *FT* and Teletext, ringing his broker. Now, with a few flicks of the thumb . . .

His finger hovered. He burped. It *was* obsessive – yet it also made him slightly nervous. Gassy. He knew he shouldn't be doing this. That he was simply meant to be the bookkeeper for these people, setting down the figures: old-school double entry on paper. He knew he should have been content with the extra money this work brought in – monthly, cash – which was helping him pay all the bills Vicky was running up.

However, once he'd figured out where the money was coming from, where it was going – because his employers barely disguised the names of the companies they were investing in – it didn't take a genius to track them down, note their growth . . . and invest himself. Not too much – some of the Shadows' laundered cash. With a bit more borrowed against his properties. *Ride the wave*, he'd thought. It was little different from property speculation and he'd learnt that at his dad's knee.

He tapped, flicked. His portfolio was small. Three companies.

Phoebus Logistics, out of Limassol, had dropped slightly. Lynn Apparel, Manchester, had risen a little. But Bulawayo Prospecting and Mining P/L's shares had risen eleven per cent overnight. He'd read in the *Telegraph* only that morning that the world was short of coltan again. The South African company must have found some.

Three more flicks . . . and he'd sold some of the first two's shares and bought a lot of the third, adding some cash from his bank account. He belched again, but smiled.

He went down the corridor into the living room/bedroom. Hot in there because it faced the afternoon sun and July was baking this year. Shaping up to be the hottest since 1976, they were saying, which he didn't remember since it was the year he was born.

It was a nice room now, after a lot of work over the years.

Double glazing kept the worst of the high-street traffic noise out – and the heat in, he thought, feeling the prickle of sweat on his forehead. Freshly painted only last year. The fireplace was faced in faux marble. He'd done that himself, learning from manuals, and it still looked good. Faux was very big when he'd bought the place in 2001.

2001. That year he did remember well. Coming back from California, where he'd gone in doomed pursuit of Cassidy. Tall, blonde, impossibly American Cassidy with her perfect teeth and flawless skin. 'Goy goddess,' his mate Sol had called her when she first jumped down from the truck at the kibbutz outside Hebron the year before. 'Dull as ditchwater in bed, brother,' he'd added. And boy, was Solly wrong.

Cassidy had been carnality incarnate.

Joe heard horns outside and went to the window, watched a battered red MG trying to park in an unsuitable space right in front of the building. It went too wide on entry, pulled out, tried again. Cars backed up and a white van driver was leaning on his horn. Joe saw it all – but he was still thinking of Cassidy.

Full moon, and how they'd snuck past security at Masada, climbed to the top of the monument where, after a bowl of hash, she'd given him the best blow job of his life. Afterwards, feeling a bit guilty he'd said, 'You do know that my people sacrificed themselves here, don't you?'

'Well,' she'd replied, that grin on her face, 'so did I.'

The MG had made it in, though there was some bumper bashing. The driver stepped out. White Van Man paused to yell something. All Joe caught was, '. . . legs, darlin'.' He glimpsed long blonde hair, almost Cassidy length, a fur jacket – in July? – a blouse and a skirt that reached mid-thigh.

It appeared that Oliver's chaos on two lovely legs had arrived.

His phone went. He'd left it back on the counter in the kitchen. He headed there, as the buzzer sounded. That annoyed him, because it meant she must not have her keys, which she should be handing over. *Well*, he thought, *she's not getting her cheque without them.* He pressed the button.

'Sorry, I'm—'

'Come up.'

He buzzed her in. Went into the kitchen. It was Vicky on the phone.

'Joe? Where are you?'

'Flat. Doing a check-out.'

'Why?'

'I told you. I—'

Vicky started. The closer they were to the bat mitzvah, the more wound up she got. Which was not good for the blood pressure. A concern for her, pregnant at forty-two. Again. How they'd managed that – two years after Reuben, and him eleven years after Rachel, who they'd long assumed, after years of nothing, would be their only one – baffled him. Considering they only fucked on birthdays and the occasional high holiday. God's joke, he thought. Now, as usual, he let Vicky go on – she only needed to be heard, really.

He hadn't realised how competitive the bat mitzvah business was. Ever since they'd attended the one six months ago, for Suki Jacobs, Vicky had a look in her eye. There'd been a band, a sushi bar, along with jugglers, a fire eater, a mini trapeze, a close magician – it had been like fucking Cirque du

26

Soleil in that marquee off the Heath Extension. Ben Jacobs had told Joe that it had set him back twenty grand. Vicky was pushing him to go bigger so he wouldn't see much change from twenty-five. And with the Portobello flat still vacant after three months, fees at Channing for Rachel, Reuben about to go into Montessori crèche, he'd been a bit strapped.

So when, six months before, that bloke Nate who he barely knew at the synagogue had found out that Joe had been an accountant and had offered to put some work his way, he'd taken it. Old-school, like he'd been trained. Double entry . . . but only on paper, nothing electronic. Two ledgers, always kept together. He knew it was dodgy, the fact that he worked on paper and was paid in cash. But it was such lovely cash. The only problem was how to launder it. The business helped, but it was getting harder. Still, since Vicky appeared to be telling him that Naomi Jablonsky had told her that the caterers they'd settled on were in fact rubbish, and they needed to step up, cash would be very necessary. Again.

'Alright, love. Alright. I—' He heard clumping in the hall. 'Go through, Miss Henshaw,' he called. 'I'll be with you in a moment.'

Then he was back with Vicky, going, 'yup, yup, yup', agreeing to it all. While she talked, he tucked the phone against his shoulder, put his hand into the plastic bag, pulled out a letter. Read:

Dear Fuckface,

So you just get up and walk out with your cum running down my thigh . . .

He dropped the letter back in the bag like it was burning him. He didn't know what Vicky was saying to him. Maybe he hadn't made enough supportive noises because he heard her say, 'Joe? Joseph? Are you listening to me?'

'Uh, yeah, sorry. Look, tenant's here, I have to go if I am going to get Rachel to you in time. We'll talk then. No, then, love. Bye. Bye bye bye.'

He hung up, pocketed the phone. Then he picked up the inventory and, as an afterthought, the bag of letters, carrying them out of the kitchen and down the hall.

He wasn't sure why he took the letters. It was like a guilty reflex. *If she knows I was alone with them*, he rationalised, *she'll suspect I read them. So I'll brazen it out. Be casual. 'Oh, I, uh, found this bag, don't know what's in it, some papers. Here . . .'*

He stopped in the doorway. He didn't see her at first, partly because the sun was full-on streaming through the window now and dazzled him. Partly because she wasn't on the sofa bed, nor one of the chairs by the table. She was opposite it, by the fireplace. Kneeling before it, halfway in it, looking up the chimney.

He took in her legs below the short skirt. Saw her scuffed boots at the other end, Blundstones, no socks. But what he really saw, what he couldn't take his eyes off, what stopped the sentence he was going to casually speak about the bag – 'Looking for this?' – was the small of her back.

Her blouse, her short fur coat, both had ridden up because she was reaching up into the chimney and that stretch revealed . . . a shallow valley, sunbeams striking it, flaming the little hairs within it, golden against the tanned brown of her skin.

Without even thinking about it, Joseph Severin turned and threw the plastic bag down the corridor.

'Ow!'

He turned back. She'd come onto her knees, was holding her head and looking at him. 'I'm so sorry,' he said.

'You made me jump,' she accused, rubbing her head.

'I'm so sorry,' he repeated, stepping into the room.

''s alright.' She stood, pushed down her skirt. 'You're from Severin's, right?'

'Yes, in a way. Actually, I *am* Severin. Joseph Severin.'

'Cor, the man himself.'

She had one of those London accents, not her own, not the way she'd said 'you made me jump', which was like she was from a Winnie-the-Pooh story. So she was not London but from somewhere near outside, somewhere posh.

She stepped forward, offered a hand. 'Lottie Henshaw,' she said.

She came up to his mid-chest, and he was not that tall. When he took her hand she gripped him, hard. He must have winced because she laughed. 'Sorry. Pianist's fingers. Will you live?'

'Somehow. Joseph Severin. Oh, I told you that. You can call me Joe.'

'Oh, I think I shall call you Mr Severin. I mean, you're the big boss, aren't you?'

He shrugged, not sure if he was being flattered, flirted with or mocked. She glanced back to the fireplace. 'I was looking for something. Did your cleaners happen to find a, uh, a bag? Of papers?'

'I . . . don't think so. They would probably have made a

note on here.' He waved the inventory at her. 'I mean if it was on the fireplace they may have thought it was rubbish.'

'It wasn't . . . on it.' She tipped her head, and blonde hair fell over her left eye like a veil. The other, green like patterned jade, peered up at him.

'I . . . I can contact the company we use. Ask. For you.'

'Whatever.' She tipped her head the other way; the veil switched to her right eye. She reached up and wiped her hand under her small ski jump of a nose. 'Nothing vital anyway.'

She'd come close to shake hands – since her arms weren't very long, he supposed. She hadn't moved back – and now he could smell her. Scent of skin, it was a hot day and she had that fur on, which had seen better days – faux like his fireplace. There was a hint of coconut, tanning lotion, which accounted for her brownness. Tobacco, unusual these days and . . . leather, like the interior of an old car. Which she'd arrived in, of course, the MG outside.

His phone rang. He didn't take it out of his pocket. 'I should get this. Could you check that all's well in here?' He handed her the inventory and without waiting for a reply, pulled the door slightly to behind him and headed down the corridor. The bag of letters was halfway down it and he stooped to snatch it up. In the kitchen, he looked at his phone. His daughter. He let it go to voicemail and looked around, then opened the cupboard under the sink, knelt and shoved the bag into the cleaned, empty bin there, putting the lid, which had been to the side, back on top.

What are you doing? he thought, closing the cupboard. *What the fuck are you doing, Joseph?*

He stood as he heard her coming down the corridor, heavy

in her boots. She may have been gorgeous but she wasn't especially graceful.

'All good in there.'

'And in here.' He took the list from her. 'I, uh, checked before. You can go through it if you like.'

'No, Mr Severin. I trust you.' She waited, looking at him expectantly.

'I need the keys,' he said.

'Shit, yes, sorry, I left them at my friend's. Can I bring them round later?'

'Well, you could. But I'm afraid I can't give you your cheque till I get them back.'

'Shit,' she repeated, did the veil over the left eye thing again. Her voice dropped a bit lower, and she took her lower lip between her teeth briefly before she spoke. He recognised the look. Cassidy from Santa Cruz had been a master of it. The 'be a good boy and roll over' look. So he wasn't surprised when she said, in her normal voice, not her London put-on, 'I really need the money today, Mr Severin. I have . . . bills to pay. Your man said he'd make it to cash.'

'He did. We did. Hmm.' He cleared his throat. 'Look, I've, uh, I've had a thought. Where are you moving to?'

If she was surprised by the question, she didn't show it. 'My mother's. For a few days at least. Buckinghamshire.' She pronounced 'shire' like it was from *The Hobbit*.

'You don't sound very happy about it?'

'Happy? I'm delirious.' She clapped her hands together. 'What twenty-six-year-old doesn't *love* to be moving back in with Mummy?'

From the moment he'd seen the small of her back, he'd

only been thinking one step at a time. *Throw the letters. Hide the letters. Keep her talking. Keep her . . . somewhere near.* And then it hit him. A solution, as it happened, to several problems. 'Look,' he said, 'if you're looking for another place, I have—'

'I can't afford another place. I haven't got the deposit, or a month's rent.'

'You will have when I give you the cheque.'

'Nah, mate. Bills, I told you.'

She'd gone London again. 'Listen, I have a place. Near Portobello Market. Been empty a while. Two-bedroom. You could—'

'Two-bedroom? In Notting Hill? You're joking, right? How could I ever afford that?'

'Well, I could . . . could . . .' He reached up, scratched under his yarmulke. 'How about no deposit, and I let you off the first month's rent.'

'Hmm.' She took her upper lip between her teeth this time and studied him. There was laughter in her eyes. Curiosity too. 'Now why would you do that, Mr Severin?'

'Joe.'

'Why, Mr Severin?'

'Honestly?' He swallowed. 'You'd be doing me a favour.'

'Really? And would it be the only . . . favour I'd be doing you?'

'Oh. No, no. I don't mean . . . it's nothing like that, honestly.'

'Mr Severin, you're blushing.'

'I am not!'

'You are. No, it's cute. In fact, under all that' – she waved –

'Jewish paraphernalia, you're quite a sexy man, aren't you?'

Two thoughts. Sexy? No one had called him that since . . . a very long time. But also . . . 'You know you're not meant to say things like that, right?'

'Like what?'

'Pointing out my religious—'

'Why? I've never been much on what I am allowed to say or not. Besides, it was an observation, not an insult. And, in case you hadn't noticed, a compliment.'

He had noticed. And he felt like he was about fourteen. He thought his palms might actually be sweating. Which was ridiculous. He was the old hand here, the businessman. He'd been around.

He took a breath. 'There are no strings to this. And you *would* be doing me a favour. Have you heard all this talk of taxing vacant properties?'

She shook her head.

'I need the place occupied, starting tomorrow or I'll get clobbered.' He'd almost convinced himself. 'You can stay . . . till the right renter comes along. May only be a month. You interested?'

It was bollocks, but he'd said it confidently. He was the businessman once more.

She studied him again. Really looked him over, from his yarmulke down to his chest, level with her eyes. Finally she said, 'Yes, I am very interested.'

It was quickly sorted. He texted her the address, and they arranged to meet there at eleven the next morning; they'd swap keys then. She signed the inventory; he made a thing about making an exception when he gave her the cheque.

She left with a smile, clumping down the stairs.

He waited in the kitchen till he heard the MG start up – followed by lots of car horns when she must have pulled out. Then he got the bag of letters from under the kitchen sink and took it through to the living room. Sat at the table, and thought about how he would use the Portobello flat to channel £5,000 of the Shadows' cash per month. That would pay for a lot of jugglers.

He reached into the bag, pulled out the stack of letters. Each was addressed to the same person, Patrick, though sometimes he was 'fuckhead' and once 'you total cunt'. He wondered again why she had them. Had this Patrick returned them or . . . or what if they had never been sent? He had a few 'letters never sent' in his past. His one to Cassidy in Santa Cruz had been a classic. He'd burnt it, of course, when he married Vicky

He didn't start to read for a bit, though, just stared at the faux fireplace and remembered what he'd seen there. Brown skin, golden hairs, a cleft like a stone basin in some ruined Greek temple. And then he suddenly realised what he'd most like to do, more than anything in the world, was suck a shot of tequila out of it.

He'd set his phone to vibrate. It kept shaking on the table but he ignored it as he began to read. It would be his daughter, his wife, both. They'd figure it out.

CHAPTER 3

A few moments later . . .

Lottie pulled out as she'd pulled in, stopping the traffic, with angry drivers leaning on their horns. Daphne protested, not at the insults that followed, but just 'cos the old girl was not well. It was why she needed to cash the cheque, and get her to Dermot, who worked from a former coach alley in Belsize Park. The little man from Munster would work his magic and keep them on the road a little while longer. He might even fudge the air quality test for a smile and one of her special roll-up cigarettes.

But after she dropped Daphne? She'd planned to train it out to Bicester, get her mum to pick her up and whip her back to the manse at Barton Hartshorn; but that was more from necessity – being flatless and broke – than any real desire to see Peggy. They'd get into the gin, never her favourite method of inebriation. It would be fine up to a point – the point where her mum went from giggly to squiffy to maudlin to vicious in rapid succession. Some people shouldn't touch gin; it was a funny drink. Her mum was one of them. She'd start in on Dad, which was fair in one way seeing as how he'd dumped her for the 'floozy'. But Mum had had a gin problem long before he'd met Dorothea. Really, she was surprised Keith had stuck it out for as long as he had.

Besides, now she had to be in Notting Hill tomorrow at eleven and getting Mum with a hangover to drive her back to the station by 9.31, for the cheap ticket, was never a good idea. No, she'd have to find a place to crash tonight, to make her morning . . . what was it? Rendezvous? Assignation?

What are you about, Mr Severin?

She could guess the half of it. He'd been odd when they talked, disconnected, half looking at her, half not. She knew that look. But she'd meant what she'd said – he *was* quite cute. And ever since she'd lost her virginity to a Jewish lad – Israel Muzzet, one of the few boys in the sixth form at her boarding school – she'd had a fondness for them. 'Israel', she'd learnt from Izzy, wasn't just a country; it meant 'he who wrestles with God'. He'd certainly wrestled with her, the two of them just sixteen, and he'd often called on God, and even his son, towards the end of each round.

Stuck at traffic lights in Kentish Town, she leant down and said, 'Siri, how are you today?'

The man's voice came back. 'I'm very well. How you doin', Lottie?'

Lottie smiled. She'd switched to Australian Siri only that morning. 'Play my voicemail, please.'

'Certainly,' came the perky response.

The phone had rung when she'd been parking the car outside the flat. She was late enough so she'd let it ring. Besides, she'd seen it was Patrick; and she wanted to be calm before she spoke to him again, not super stressed.

'Hello, baby,' he began.

The voice was dark brown. When she'd called it that, first time they met when she played for him at his audition, Patrick had bristled, like Mr Severin had just bristled when she'd pointed out his Jewishness. But they were only observations, they were true and she meant them kindly. Her former landlord – and future benefactor – *was* Jewish. Patrick did speak – and sing – in the voice that went with his Ghanaian blue-blood background.

'How are you, baby? I've been missing you,' he purred on, like the great big black panther he was and she shivered, as she always did when she heard his voice again after a while. After a month, actually, since she'd told him she'd had enough of the games – the sex games, the drug games, the sex 'n' drugs games – that this time it really was over, this time she was done. She'd taken the letters she'd written him when he was in Los Angeles, and the three she'd written him when she was away playing with the jazz orchestra in Prague and he was back in London fucking who knows what. Taken them, and the few things she'd kept at his place in Stokey and gone back to her flat in Tufnell Park.

The purr went on. 'Listen, I'm sorry' – *yeah right* – 'and I want to make it up to you. So I did what you asked. I've invited her.' There was a little breath of excitement. 'Sonya that is. Remember? Her from the bar? It's on. Tomorrow night. You in? Gi'us a call, 'kay?'

He hung up. The Australian said, 'That's all your messages, Lottie. Can I do anything else for you?'

'That's it,' she replied, overtaking and accelerating through an amber, to more horns.

'G'day, Lottie,' he said.

As she turned onto Prince of Wales Road, she shivered again. This time, though, she was thinking about Sonya.

Oh, she remembered her alright.

It was a week before she'd walked out. They'd met her at Soho House, on Greek Street. She remembered the first sighting, walking in and seeing Patrick on a barstool, this absolute stunner on the one next to him. Had to be six foot, which usually would make Lottie hate her. As pale as he was dark, with a voice that was as rich as his, though not chocolatey, more . . . borscht, she'd thought at the time, which didn't do it justice. She had close-cropped auburn hair, grey eyes, cheekbones for eons – Slavic, she'd guessed, which was true since Sonya, it turned out, was from Russia. Lottie had her pegged as a model, which she sometimes was. What Sonya mainly was, though, what Patrick had established fast over his second, appropriate Moscow Mule, was an escort. As high-end as you get, he'd told Lottie in excited whispers when Sonya went off to the washroom. One thousand quid a night, more if you wanted extras. The way he'd said 'extras' made Lottie think, *Fuck, 'ere we go.*

When Sonya had returned, Patrick had asked the question, how much would it be for the two of them? Fifteen hundred she'd said. 'Less than usual,' she'd added, turning to Lottie, 'because you are so beautiful.'

But Patrick didn't have the money as he was between gigs, waiting to hear about a big movie. So he certainly wouldn't have the extra he'd need for coke, an essential accompaniment since his LA venture. He tried to sweet-talk Sonya into a discount but she just patted his cheek and whispered, smokily, 'You call when you have the money, sweetheart,' then finished the sentence looking at Lottie, 'because it will be beyond your dreams, trust me.'

Lottie had shivered then, and she shivered for a third time now, thinking about that look. Especially as, from his message, it appeared that Patrick had scored the role in the movie, and was flush again, or would borrow against the promise of it.

Lottie chewed at her lower lip. Though Sonya's breathed promise had excited her, their track record on threesomes wasn't stellar. The first time it had been boy-boy-girl and Patrick had got all territorial *and* hetero, even though he'd been the one who'd invited the young man back from the pub. Barely let the poor lad get a touch of her. The second time, girl-girl-boy, the other girl had freaked out and left. Which was alright by Lottie, actually. Despite the usual dormitory fumblings at Epsom College, she'd never been that into girls. Though she was reconsidering, remembering the way Sonya had looked at her.

'Move your bloomin' arse!' she yelled, at a zebra crossing on Prince of Wales Road, where the woman driver ahead wanted to wait for every school kid on the pavement to pass in case any of them suddenly decided to dart across the road. It made her think of Patrick again, 'cos it was a line from the show where they'd met, in the road company of *My Fair Lady*, him a colour-blind casting choice as Freddy, her on keyboards in the pit.

Then, they'd been all each other needed – and what a laugh it had been. Seedy digs in northern towns, thin walls, people shouting at them for all the noise they were making, only some of which was sex, most of which was laughter. She'd even thought, *Fuck, is this it? Or is it just a road thing?* But they'd laughed as much back in London. Until he got the indie gangster thing, which led to a bigger agent and the invite to Hollywood, coinciding with their two-years-but-still-not-living-together anniversary. In LA, his tastes had . . . broadened. She'd gone along with it all for a while. But they didn't laugh as much and she'd finally said, last month, no more games. It wasn't like she hadn't given him fair warning. Those letters?

Speaking of . . . where the fuck had they gone?

No more games, she'd said. Though Sonya? She saw them, the three of them, Patrick melded into the Russian, chocolate on . . . no, couldn't be borscht, that would be disgusting. Chocolate on . . . homemade vanilla ice cream! That was better; she'd like to watch that for a little – but not for long. Only until Sonya reached for her . . .

As she drove up Haverstock Hill, she said, 'Siri, call Patrick.' The rings came but after three there was the click. 'Hey! Good to hear from you. I'll get back to you.'

'Hey, P, 's me. I *am* in, actually. But not at yours. Can you spring for a nice hotel? Or' – she paused – 'tell you what, I'm moving into a new place tomorrow. Portobello. I'll text you the address, you text me the time.'

There was surprisingly little traffic. After a pit stop to cash the cheque at her bank in Hampstead, she made for the alley in Belsize Village. How Dermot could afford the rent in that neighbourhood was beyond her. Though she had a clue when she saw him, staring disconsolately at the engine under the hood of an Aston Martin. There was a Roller in the garage behind him.

'Ah, look there now. If it isn't Princess Di.'

She got out. 'I need it tomorrow morning, Dermot.'

'No fucking chance, lady!'

'Afternoon, then?'

'Still none.'

'What?' She reached into her bag. 'Not even if I roll you one of these?'

She stayed and smoked two with him, until he said yes. Then she walked to Swiss Cottage station to catch the Tube to Dollis Hill. She'd go to Sarah's. A swift text and a thumbs up back and she was set. Saar always let her crash at short notice on her couch. A trawl through memories from Epsom Sixth Form over a take-out biryani and a couple of bottles of pinot grigio was a small price to pay.

Her mind jumped again when she stepped onto the escalator, going down. *Sonya, Sonya*, she wondered, *I wonder where are you right now? Who are you with?*

CHAPTER 4

6.30 p.m., Wednesday 25th July 2018

Bernadette had been taking lessons.

Bitch, Sebastien thought, as his opponent shifted him off the T with a drop shot to the corner and then, when Sebastien only just made the return, beating him with a drive tight along the wall to the back of the court.

The squash match was not going its customary way. Bernadette's superior fitness, being also a marathon runner, would usually keep it competitive till game three, by which time Sebastien's deftness and general sneakery would win out. Years of playing – Bedales, Magdalen, the service – it was rare that he hadn't triumphed in four sets, had lost maybe ten matches in all those years, due to illness, hangover, luck.

Not going to lose today, he thought, as Bernadette went back to serve.

'Eight all,' came the call.

Two sets all. Game five, two clear points for the win. *One clear way to get those*, Sebastien thought, bending at his knees.

The finishing line in sight, Bernadette was overexcited. The serve wasn't as good, dropped shallow and short, allowing

Sebastien a back-hand flick that sent it without much force to just above the tin. Bernadette had to lunge, stretch, the ball returned easily to Sebastien's forehand, now back at the T. There was an easy kill. But an easy kill just meant he'd have to kill again. So instead of slamming the ball to the back of the court, he smashed it hard and straight – into his opponent's cheek.

'Christ!' came the scream, followed by the clatter of a dropped racket. 'Shit!'

'Oh, terribly sorry, old soul.'

'You fucker! That was deliberate!'

'Course it wasn't, old soul. Are you alright?'

'Do I look it?'

'Take your time.' Sebastien stooped for the ball, flicked it up, went to the server's box.

Bernadette, rubbing at the cheek, glared. 'What? You're taking that?'

'Alas, have to. Rules. You should have got out of the way. Eight all.'

It was soon over. A couple of fast serves, tight to the wall. The drop-shot-and-lob combo that had his opponent running back and forth. Desperate, Bernadette lunged, slipped on some sweat. Caught the ball but hit the tin with it. The glorious sound of the death knell.

'And that's match.' Sebastien stepped forward, hand out. 'Well played. So close. Didn't expect five sets. Swift shower or we'll be late for the chaps.'

Sebastien stooped for his phone, tucked into the corner. He'd put it on silent, so no dings but plenty of messages. A quick scroll – the shop, the wife.

Later, in the communal shower, Sebastien inevitably glanced at Bernadette's huge cock and pendulous balls. He really was a stallion – which had made his nickname at school all the more amusing. They were alone, in the large stall designed for five. 'So, going to tell me?'

'Not now,' Bernard grunted, still obviously pissed off. 'Don't want to have to repeat myself. I'll tell you with the others.'

'True cause for concern?'

'Perhaps.'

Sebastien felt his own smaller scrotum tighten.

'Oh, for God's sake, man, do you have to do that in here?'

'What?' Sebastien looked up from where he was directing his piss. 'All goes down the same drain, doesn't it?'

They left the RAC Club and headed along Pall Mall towards the Athenaeum. It hit him straight away, this absurdly hot summer, with the too-swift shower not quite removing the heat of the game. He felt instant sweat at forehead, armpits and groin.

The pavements were packed, parties of gawking tourists shambling along in their enviable shorts and sun dresses, requiring him to shift around them – on his bloody street! All off to Clarence House then on to Buck House, to attempt to get the busbied sentries at both palaces to crack a smile. When he'd been in the Blues, and assigned to royal duty, the colonel had insisted all his subalterns did at least a couple of days in a sentry box. He was one of those who thought his officers should experience the life of the ordinary soldier. Prat.

As they neared Duke of York Place, a party of Spanish teenagers, taking selfies of themselves with the Duke's statue in the background, blocked the way, forcing Sebastien to step wide. And there, just ahead, was a scrawny beggar he'd never seen before. This young man's – *schtick*, was that the right word, he'd have to ask Nate later – was to kneel on the pavement, his forehead to the stone, his arms thrust in supplication before him, with hands clasped around a polystyrene cup. Two steps away, he could see that it was half full of coins. Halfway to another fix.

Scum, he thought and, without breaking step, drove his right foot forward and kicked the cup hard.

Coins followed him as he continued up the street. The Spanish kids were yelling, scrambling. He'd caught a finger with the polystyrene, he was fairly sure. But oddly, the addict hadn't made a sound. Too stoned, no doubt.

'Fuck's sake, Sebastien,' Bernard muttered as they rounded the corner. 'You really are a sod, aren't you?'

They climbed the Athenaeum's steps and pushed through the doors. Another of their number awaited them at the porter's desk. 'Perry had already gone up by the time I got here,' complained Sadiq. 'And when they asked him to come down for me he said he couldn't, he was in a meeting. So they've made me wait.' He glowered at the porter. 'My own membership is still marked "pending", apparently. It's been that for six months.'

'Lots of closet racists here.' Bernard shrugged. 'Maybe you've been black-balled, old chum.'

'Well, he's been that since birth, hasn't he?'

'Oh ha-ha, Sebastien. You never tire of it, do you?'

'How could I?' He stepped past Sadiq to the guest book, picked up the pen. 'When I have such meet food to feed on as Signor Benedick?' He wrote in 'Sadiq Khan', then dashed his signature beside it. 'Your line at Magdalen in that all-male *Much Ado*, eh, Bernadette? Me as Benedick, you as Beatrice. In that mini skirt? Occasional glimpses of your massive tackle? Never quite recovered. Be still, my beating heart!'

Bernard shook his head. 'No, Sadiq, he never tires of it.' He gestured to the stairs. 'Shall we?'

'Shouldn't we wait for Nate?'

'Don't worry about him, old boy. He's already a member. They've let Jews in ever since Disraeli.'

They went to the bar. Perry was in the far corner, with a gaggle of his diplomatic corps friends. He waved, but went back to his conversation. They found a table. Sebastien and Bernard ordered their traditional post-squash pick me up, Black Velvet – champagne and Guinness. Sadiq, unusually for him, ordered a whisky soda. *Perhaps he believes*, Sebastien speculated, *that a Muslim that drinks has more chance of becoming a member.*

Bernard still refused to talk about why he'd summoned this meeting. 'Wait for the others,' he muttered. They attempted small talk – the ridiculous heat, the Schadenfreude of German disaster at the World Cup, the latest on refugees. Fortunately Perry soon joined them and put an end to all banalities.

'Sorry, chaps,' the little man said, using his MCC tie to wipe sweat from his forehead, 'bit of a buzz from North Korea today. That cowboy Trump might actually be getting them to disarm.' He hailed a waiter. 'I'll have what they're having.' He pointed at the Black Velvets. As the man went off, he lowered his voice. 'So what's the story, morning glory?'

As Bernard explained once again why he wasn't going to tell it yet, Sebastien sipped and studied his friends.

The Athenaeum wasn't short of brains. One of the first things you learnt on joining was that the club had more Nobel Prize winners than France – a joke that truly had everything. But there was a definite concentration of smarts that day around the table. He'd known Bernard since prep school; they'd met Perry at Bedales and all had gone up to Oxford together in '99, where they'd met Sadiq – and the awaited Nate – at Magdalen. They had discovered there – amidst the drinking and the leching – a shared passion for the movie *The Matrix*. Each had adopted a name from it. Bernard, since of course he was already Bernadette, had been forced to accept Trinity. Sadiq, with his Keanu-like dark good looks, was a shoo-in for Neo. Perry, who was a computer geek, was an obvious Cypher. While the tardy Nate had a steely affect that made him a perfect Agent Smith.

And he? Well, of course, he was Morpheus. The ultimate brains.

Though they went their different ways after Oxford – he to the army then on to Six, Bernadette straight to Five, Perry into the diplomatic, Nate into international trade and Sadiq into the City – they'd stayed in touch. All perfectly positioned in all required areas when, eighteen months before, an opportunity arose to make some serious dosh. Needed a name change, though. Needed to step back . . . into the Shadows.

He initiated it. At MI6, with his service in the Middle East, he was privy to all sorts of useful intel – especially the ripple-effect opportunities created by the war in Syria. Perry had been promoted to *chargé d'affaires* in Ankara, where he kept his ear – cauliflowered since some oaf from Cambridge trod on it during the Varsity game – to the ground. Sadiq, by now a partner at Goldman Sachs, knew just how to take all the money they made, legitimise and increase it, in high-return stocks and shares. While Bernard, at MI5, was able to monitor any domestic fall-out.

Something had obviously appeared on his radar. Bernard might have been annoying in refusing to say anything at all. But Sebastien had known the man since prep school. He was a steady Eddie, a little dull to be honest, even more introspective since his wife had died suddenly of cancer the year before. Little shook him – yet he was shaken now. And if *he* was shaken . . . Sebastien felt that tightening in his balls again. He needed to know, now. So he interrupted another Sadiq moan with, 'Look, fuck Nate. I think we should begin.'

Then he looked up and realised that a waiter was hovering at his elbow.

The man leant down and murmured softly, 'Mr Greenberg wishes you to know he has gone straight to the table, sir. Would you like me to take your drinks through?'

'No need. Drink up, all.' Sebastien hefted his own tankard and demonstrated. 'Time to move on to the wine anyway. I ordered two bottles of an acceptable Pomerol decanted four hours since.'

He'd reserved a table right in the middle of the room. The idea of being bugged at the Athenaeum was absurd. But ever since he'd heard the alarm in Bernard's voice when he called for this extraordinary meeting of the Shadows, he'd wanted to take extra precautions.

Nate was indeed already there. 'Kudos on the Pomerol, Morpheus.' As they approached, he swirled some wine in his glass. 'Good call, as the Yanks would say.'

He took a swallow that probably cost £50. Sebastien sat and looked at him. Agent Smith. The trader. Not only could Nate get anything shipped anywhere – beside the drugs and refugees, there'd lately been some valuable antiquities out of Syria – he had contacts with many fellow Israelites, ex-Mossad boys who saw that their shipments were well protected. They'd made a lot, in eighteen months. *You know,* he thought as he reached for the decanter, *if Bernard does have bad news, perhaps we can dissolve and reconvene. Too good a crew to break up.*

They ordered. The Bedales boys went for game – woodcock for Perry, grouse for Bernard and himself. Sadiq punished himself for the whisky by taking the vegetarian risotto, and drinking only water. Nate ordered a steak, well done. As the waitress walked away, Bernard began to speak.

'I'm concerned. We may be rumbled.'

'What? How?'

'Well, I don't fully know.' Bernard took a hefty pull at the wine. Sebastien was pleased he'd ordered two bottles decanted. It looked like they were going to need the second sooner rather than later. If it was bad news, there was no point hearing it on lesser wine. 'It's a rumour, for now, at the Box.' All knew what he meant. Box 500 was the postal address of MI5.

'How widespread a rumour?' asked Sadiq.

'Again, I don't know. Fairly wide, I would say, considering my source.'

'Who is?'

'Little number from communications. Junior. So if she knows . . .'

'Pillow talk? Knobbing her are we, Trinity?' Perry said.

'Certainly not! You know that I—'

Sebastien interrupted before he could launch into his usual song and dance about still being in mourning. 'What did she say?'

'She's new, wanted to check with me if she'd properly encrypted a couple of messages between departments.' Bernard picked up his wine, gulped again. '"Wild elephants in the Circus" was the phrase used.'

'We're almost certainly not the only . . . wild elephant at MI6,' Sebastien said. 'Why do you think this is us? Did she say more?'

'No. Well, I didn't ask. Didn't show any further interest.' He shrugged. 'I mean, if she *was* fishing—'

'So you asked elsewhere?'

'No. But I did do a little checking. On the QT. One of my cases right now is illegal immigration. I saw that someone called Ellerby was taking a special interest in one particular boat.'

'Which boat?'

'MVS *Thalia*.'

'Fuck.' The same word, from the four other mouths.

Nate now spoke for the first time. 'I told you. I said it was too risky. It was stupidity.'

'And yet you agreed.'

'I was voted down, as you know. Right in this room. Four sugar lumps to one.' He leant forward. 'Ari had told me,

50

in Haifa last month – the passage is getting harder. The fucking Libyans are sending boats out that are more rust than metal—'

'Rust is metal—'

'Fuck off, Perry.' Nate shook his head. 'It was bound to draw attention when it sank last week. Two hundred people dead? It was greed and it was stupid and we shouldn't have done it.'

'Would you like to transfer your forty thousand dollars back to the consortium?' Sadiq, the banker, said, leaning in. 'Since you have such a problem with it?'

'And you can fuck off too—'

'Shh!' Sebastien's hiss was a soft contrast to the rising voices. 'This table may not be bugged but there are souls about.' He gestured to other diners. 'Besides,' he continued, 'what's past is past, right? It's done; the money's banked. What we did doesn't matter. All that matters is what we do now.'

He turned to Bernard. 'Should we panic? Can they find us? I mean' – he waved at Nate – 'our friend here found a very adept member of his tribe to do our one set of books. Old-school. We'd agreed – the only untraceable trail these days is a paper one.' He waved at Sadiq. 'You're not questioning our black-balled friend's ability to hide the money, are you? If we simply—'

'Of course not, it's just . . .' Bernard interrupted. 'I looked into this Ellerby. A woman. Rising star. Very ambitious.' He grunted. 'Friend in her department says she passed on all her other open files to her colleagues, and is now only concerned with one.'

'Does it have to be our one?'

'No.' Bernard sat back and frowned. 'But I have a feeling in my waters.'

'Oh well, case proven, then!' Perry laughed and shook his head. 'Steady, you chaps. Let's find out some more before we do anything hasty. I mean, I've just ordered the fucking Morgan! And the wife's bought the full Aga for Faversham Hall!'

Sebastien looked at Bernard. He'd never talked about his waters before. He wasn't the type. There was something else. 'Trinity,' he cajoled. 'What aren't you telling us?'

His friend coloured. The red mark on his cheek, where the squash ball had struck him, crimsoned. 'Alright, one more thing. The Wolf's back.'

Sebastien flushed cold, leant forward. 'What?'

'Who the fuck's the Wolf?' asked Sadiq.

'My question as well,' added Nate.

'The Wolf . . .' Sebastien paused, considered, spoke. 'Maurice Wolfden. A bit of a legend. Moved between 5 and 6 depending on the, ah, need. A sniffer out of rodents. Or wild elephants. Also said to be the man who used to do internally what we contract Mr—' He broke off without saying the name. Suddenly he felt things needed not to be said. 'What we use our freelancer for.' He turned again to Bernard. 'I thought he was long dead. Back for a visit? Or back to work?'

'I don't know. He was at the Box twice last week.' Bernard drained his glass, immediately refilled it, emptying the decanter. 'Could be coincidence. Or he may not be a threat. I mean the bastard's older than God, isn't he? Still . . .'

Sebastien nodded. He also felt something in his own waters now. 'Well, gentlemen. Given that, I think we may need to take some precautions. Fold up the tent? Slip back into the Shadows? For the nonce, anyway?'

'Oh, come on!' Perry, his new sports car and country house cooker clear in his eyes, threw himself back in his seat. 'Some old animal visits and you all bleat like sheep in the fold? At least wait until the end of the week. We've got that shipment of heroin base coming through Turkey. Our biggest yet, on its way to the lab in Bosnia.'

'What would that be worth, Sadiq?'

The money man sucked at his lower lip. 'To us? At least half a mil.'

'Not so much, then,' said Bernard, 'so not worth riski—'

'Apiece.'

The four other men simultaneously sucked air between their teeth.

'Well, gentlemen. Perhaps we shouldn't be overhasty – on a feeling in Bernadette's waters.'

'I still think—'

'Sugar?' suggested Nate, interrupting Bernard.

'Look, let's discuss further first—'

'Sugar,' agreed Perry, and reached for a lump.

Each man took one, Bernard reluctantly last. Each pulled out a pen, cupped their hands over the lump, stabbed down – or not. Sebastien held out a bread plate; each looked away – and dropped their lumps onto it.

They all looked then. One lump had a clear blue mark on it. But after turning the others over, it was clear that there was only the one.

Bernard grunted. Sebastien spoke. 'So we think about dissolving. But not till after this week. For now. Each to their own . . . field.' He turned to Sadiq. 'How much do you think we have left to share out?'

'I'd need to see the books.'

'Ah yes, the books.' Sebastien looked at Nate. 'Your friend has them safe, I trust.'

'Why wouldn't he?' Nate shrugged. 'I'm going to his daughter's bat mitzvah on Saturday. I'll confirm.'

Sadiq leant forward, lowered his voice. 'But this is something else I have to report – I have learnt something disturbing about our bookkeeping friend.'

Everyone frowned. Sebastien put down his wine glass. 'What?'

'As you know, I invest our profit – legitimise it and make some good interest on the principal. I have been focusing on three companies – obviously all a little shady to be honest, hence the high returns. But I have also been monitoring who else is investing in them. Confirming my choice, etc. Hedge funds, some big brokers . . . but I noticed this rather odd, regular investment, day traded but very small sums. So I got our young hacker chum, Vladislav from Minsk, onto it. Guess what he found?' He looked around at the others, none of whom replied, so he went on. 'It's our friend, the bookkeeper. Following my bets. Making some extra money for himself.'

Nate leant back. 'So? Proves he's smart, doesn't it?'

Sebastien hissed. 'We didn't want smart. We wanted steady. That's what you promised us.' He turned to Sadiq. 'Is this dangerous?'

'Well, it's a trail. An electronic one, which we wanted to avoid – which is why we hired a man to do double entry on paper in the first place.'

'So it *is* a danger?'

Sadiq shrugged. 'Possibly.'

'I think this calls for our friend Venom, don't you?'

'Wait a minute.' Nate leant forward. 'You mean just to collect the books, right? You don't mean—'

'Oh, I rather think I do. If we do need to dissolve – for now – we'll need a proper tidy-up.' He looked around at the others. 'Don't you agree?'

'No, no!' Nate raised both hands, palms forward. 'This man is from my synagogue; he has a family—'

'We all have families, Nathan.' It was Sadiq who spoke.

'And when push comes to shove, I prefer mine to his,' added Perry.

'Oh come on! You asked me to find someone to do the books. You never said he'd ever be at risk.'

'Well, now *he's* the risk.'

'You can't—'

'Sugar?' Bernard said.

'Sugar,' Perry and Sadiq agreed.

'No, not yet. Let me reason with you—'

Sebastien reached forward and picked up a lump.

The others did as well. 'Fuck,' Nate muttered, but he reached as well.

When they looked at the plate only one had ink on it. It fell apart as Sebastien turned it over, so hard had Nate driven his pen nib into it.

'Well, fuck you all.' Nate pushed back his chair, stood.

'Sit down, you fool.'

'No. I'm off.' He turned away, turned back, leant down. 'I hope you can live with yourselves. His daughter is getting bat mitzvah-ed. He's got a two-year-old, another kid on the way.'

'Calm down, Nathan. And for God's sake sit down, and I'll tell you what I'll do.' Nate still stood, so Sebastien sighed, and continued. 'I'll . . . investigate your friend. Be interesting to find out why this Eddie is not quite so steady, eh? And see if he's . . . unsteady anywhere else, hmm?'

'And you won't . . . do anything hasty?'

'Not until we've found out more.'

'And then?'

'Hopefully all will be fine. If not . . .' Sebastien gestured to the sugar lumps. 'Well, we have a mandate, don't we?'

'I want to be consulted again. Before anything.'

'Of course. Look, the food's coming so stop being a clot, sit down and eat.'

'You know' – Nate looked at them all – 'I believe I've lost my appetite.'

As he turned again, Sebastien murmured, 'Nothing stupid now, Agent Smith.'

Nate passed the waitress approaching with their plates.

'Shall I go after him?'

'No, Sadiq. Leave him. It's just a . . . tribal thing. He'll come around. He has as much to lose as anyone here, after all. Which he'll realise when he gets home, and tucks *his* kids into bed. Ah!'

The waitress had arrived and put the grouse down before him and Bernard. It was bloody, just how he liked it. The woodcock she placed before Perry, the risotto before Sadiq, the steak where Nate had been. Sadiq immediately scooped it up and dumped it onto his rice.

'Oh, you can bring the other decanter now, sweetheart,' Sebastien said. As she went off, Sebastien beamed at them.

'Eat hearty, all.' He paused, his first forkful halfway to his mouth. 'Sadiq, what's the chap's name again?'

'Joseph Severin.'

'Happen to know where he lives?'

'Near Nate, if it's the same synagogue,' Bernard replied while chewing. 'North West London.'

'That'll do.' Sebastien smiled as the waitress returned and poured a splash of the wine into his glass. He swirled, sniffed, tasted, nodded. She filled up the others. He noticed that Sadiq did not refuse this time. Sebastien raised his glass. 'Here's to the finale of our first venture. And to the overture of many more.'

They clinked, then set to on the food. The rest of the meal passed in trivialities.

Sadiq compensated for his earlier restraint by hitting the wine hard. They had to order another bottle. Gigondas, not decanted, still acceptable. Outside the club, on Pall Mall, they hailed then helped him into a taxi. As it drove off, Perry called 'Cheer ho!' then climbed the steps of the building next door. The Travellers Club was the foreign services' external 'office'. More of Great Britain's foreign policy was conducted over post-prandial port in its reading rooms than in Whitehall. Rumour was that they'd admitted their first woman onto the premises in 1982, and Mrs Thatcher had decided to take back the Falklands over a large Sandeman's Tawny.

They watched him disappear. 'Hmm. Could have asked us in for a snifter,' muttered Sebastien.

Bernard shrugged. 'He'll be on business now. Didn't you notice how little he drank?'

'Well, Sadiq made up for him. Share a cab?' Sebastien asked.

'Not going home. Going on.'

'Oh yes? Where to?'

Bernard blushed. The squash ball strike flared again. 'I, uh, I'm seeing, uh, Sonya tonight.'

'The Russian whore?'

'I wish you wouldn't say it in that tone. I told you, she's only working to earn money for—'

'Yes, yes. All sorts of good causes, no doubt. You really are such a soft touch, Bernadette. Fall for any old claptrap.' He clapped his friend on the shoulder. 'Still, if it helps you to forget dear Eloise. Oh, look, cab. You take this one. Love's wingèd chariot and all that.'

Bernard climbed in, and off he went. Sebastien watched the taxi merge into traffic. He was sure his friend regretted the bottle of Macallan two weeks before that had loosened his tongue, lowered his guard, and caused him to mistake Sebastien's sympathy for honesty. He'd blurted out this connection with this prossie, this Sonya. More ammunition for a tease later. Though he didn't blame him – it had been the matter of moments to track Sonya Ivenetza down. Visa photos were notoriously underwhelming. So she truly had to be a cracker.

Another yellow light was approaching from Trafalgar Square. He thrust up an arm and the black cab pulled over.

He was about to get in when he noticed the coin at his feet. One pound. It had almost certainly come from the cup he'd kicked earlier. The owner of that had gone – fixing up in some squalid Soho alley, no doubt.

As the cab pulled in, he stooped and picked it up. *A profitable night*, he thought, spinning it up into the air. Half a million quid more apiece if all went well in Turkey this week . . . and this pound in his hand. For just a moment, he couldn't work out which sum gave him the greater pleasure.

CHAPTER 5

The next morning . . . Thursday 26th July 2018

Some clients wanted it normal. Some wanted it different. Some very different. Sonya was up for most things, on a sliding scale of payment, so long as her base rules were observed: condoms, courtesy and no pain – for her. Pain for them? Fine. Negotiable as to degree and rate. She wasn't a dominatrix, but knew . . . the *ropes*. English was such a funny language. In Russian, a system was a system, a rope was a rope and bondage was . . . *zavisimost*. They were not the same.

Sometimes a client wished to talk. No, truly, some clients wished to be listened to. She could do that. In the army, she'd taken a course on interrogation techniques. Knew what questions to ask to provoke the answers. She'd also learnt about inflicting pain, though this wasn't the sort of pain her clients were interested in. Mostly.

This man, Bernard, wasn't ever after anything different. They'd usually meet for a late supper in the hotel restaurant – though last night he'd already eaten so only she did. He'd do most of the talking. Later, in the hotel room, they'd fuck briefly, simply, missionary. Afterwards he'd cry, and she'd hold him till he fell asleep. He paid her to spend the night, which she didn't do for many. But he paid her extra so she stayed. In the morning they'd have a room-service breakfast and then they'd leave. He'd lost his wife one year before, ovarian cancer.

He was snoring now. It was what had woken her, though she'd barely slept. She looked at her phone. Six-thirty. Breakfast would be there at seven. They were three hours ahead back home, so Maria would be getting ready for school, as it was Thursday, which had a late start. It wasn't one of their days, so it would be nice to surprise her. Also she had texts to check, clients – she hoped – to answer. She kept the phone on silent when she was with Bernard; it was part of the deal, part of the illusion, like the sealed envelope of cash that was always laid out below the television and was now in her bag and never referred to.

Even though he had turned onto his side, his back to her, he had an arm stretched back, resting on her hip. She lifted it, slid from under, laid it down as she stood. He muttered something, didn't wake up, pulled his arm in and a second pillow close.

She wrapped the hotel dressing gown around her, tiptoed to the bathroom. Closed the door before flicking on the light. Took her glasses from her washbag and looked in the mirror. Whistled between her teeth. Bernard liked her not made up when they went to bed, hair back, was fine that she took out her grey contact lenses. Another part of the illusion, as her true eye colour was brown.

I am not so fine, she thought, studying. She knew that no one looked great under hotel bathroom lights. But this mirror showed the truth of her to herself. She knew she was thirty-seven, even though she told everyone she was twenty-nine. In a bar, under those lights, with good make-up and after some drinks, men would not notice the lines around her eyes. Later, by candlelight, or hotel-room lamp, they would not notice that her breasts were perhaps larger than they'd imagined, but not quite so shapely. One businessman, City type, all club tie and rugby playing, *had* noticed but said later that he hadn't cared; he'd had his 'beer goggles' on. More funny English.

She dropped the dressing gown off her shoulders, lifted her breasts, pushed them together. She'd thought of having them done but it was expensive and she needed all the money she made for Maria's procedure, not her own. Besides, after tonight, she was a little less than £7,000 short of her target. Earn that and she would not need to keep working. Let her breasts go where gravity wanted. Get fat and transform into her mother.

She looked at the line of scar above the right nipple, a finger's length of jagged white against her sunbed tan. She told the men who asked that it was a childhood accident, falling through a tree, a snapped branch gouging her. But as she lied she always saw the flash of knife as it cut her, as Ivan raised it to her throat and said that if she didn't do what he asked, the next cut would kill her. But as he was drunk, he made a mistake by trusting her weeping and put the knife back in his belt. Georgiy had laughed when she told him later, and claimed the victory, as he'd trained her in unarmed combat. 'You also trained Ivan,' she'd countered, 'and look what happened to him.'

Georgiy. It was 6.40 now and she should call, or her husband would be taking their daughter to the bus. She swept a brush through her hair, washed her face, put her glasses back on, pulled up Signal, hit 'Home'. She put down the toilet lid and sat, as the phone rang.

She heard her voice before she saw her. 'Mamochka,' Maria shrieked; there was some jiggling and then she was there. She held the phone up, and Sonya could see Georgiy behind her by the sink, silhouetted against the sun, chopping something. 'Why are you calling, Mamochka? Are you OK?'

'I'm fine, sweetheart. Just wanted to hear your voices.'

She heard Georgiy's then. 'Set the phone up, Marusya. Finish your cereal. We are late.' His voice was tired. But it was also a little slurred, and Sonya took a shorter breath.

More jiggling and now Sonya was looking up at her daughter, who picked up a spoon and started shovelling food in, talking all the while. It was prattle, exactly what she needed to hear: a trip to the zoo, school friends, a hip-hop class they were starting that Papochka said she could do when she was stronger, and the top she'd bought to wear when she was. After a minute or two, though, Sonya found she was watching her husband's back more than her daughter's face. The way his shoulders moved.

He turned but the sun he'd blocked streamed full in now and she couldn't see his face. She heard his voice, though. 'Bathroom, Marusya, teeth.'

'I want to talk to Mamochka!'

'If you hurry, you can say goodbye. Hurry. Hurry!'

'I'll come back, Mamochka. Don't leave!'

'I won't,' Sonya called, as her daughter put both hands on the tabletop, pushed herself up, took a breath, then turned and moved very slowly out of view.

Hurrying.

Georgiy stepped closer. He blocked the sun again now and she could see his face. He was unshaven, the stubble like his hair, more grey than black and spread over jowls that seemed to have got fuller, even in the three days since she'd last called. But it was the bags under his eyes that alarmed her most. They were also fuller, and pasty white.

'You look tired, Gosha,' she said.

He shrugged. 'I'm not sleeping so good.'

She bit back her response – that he'd sleep better if he didn't drink so much. But she didn't want him angry. She wanted to hear about their daughter.

Maybe he sensed her concern. 'Petya and Artem came round last night to play cards. We had a few beers.'

It was a lie. His old army comrades would have brought vodka. In one way she didn't mind. If that was all they were doing . . .

Perhaps something showed in her eyes. His hardened, and moved over her. 'Where are you?'

'Nowhere. Hotel.'

'Hotel Nowhere.' He licked cracked lips. 'Have a good time?'

'Don't, Gosha.'

'"Don't, Gosha".' He peered. 'The gown looks expensive. Is it?'

He almost never talked like this. He knew what she was doing and why. The why in the other room, going as fast as she was able, so not very fast. And she knew what he was doing now too. Preparing excuses for when he fell. Then he'd say again what he'd said once before, when he'd got drunk, the week after she'd got to London. 'What do you expect? My wife is a whore.'

He didn't say it now. Instead, 'I hope you are sending money today?'

'Some. Later today.'

'Some? More than last time?'

She bit back a yes. If the look and the pain in her husband's eyes meant what she feared, more would only go one way. And soon enough they'd be back to the beginning, where Marusya could not afford to be.

'The same as last time. For groceries, rent. It's been slow—'

'Then fuck faster,' he snarled, his face contorted with rage. Then it sagged; all the fury left it, and his voice too. 'It's so hard, Sonechka,' he whispered. 'She's . . . she's . . .'

'Tell me.'

'Getting slower. The painkillers are not working so well. At night she—'

Her voice. 'I'm done, Mamochka.'

Georgiy's face masked over. 'Quick goodbye, Marusya. Don't want to be late for the bus. I need to pack your lunch.'

He turned, became a silhouette against the sun again. She and her daughter did their farewell – three kisses, two in the air, one right on the screen, lips to lips. Then the screen went blank. Sonya always let her daughter ring off.

She pulled the phone to her chest, did not move, eyes unfocused. For the moment, she wasn't in a hotel bathroom but back on the parade ground. That first time she'd seen Georgiy.

In his dress uniform, with the chestful of medals he'd won in Afghanistan. His black hair, lean face, the fire in his eye.

Seen him, not spoken to him – did that for the first time three weeks later when he was her instructor in unarmed combat. He was twenty years older but she didn't care. He didn't either – she made him laugh; he was proud of her. She won her own medal that year – she was the fastest Kalashnikov stripper in the whole Russian army! Crazy! Kneeling, he'd proposed on the podium. She'd hesitated only because of one thing – the scars on his arm, not got in a war. Well, perhaps because of the war. But he told her he was five years clean and done with it for ever.

For ever had lasted nearly a decade, till the first fall, when Marusya was nine and the tumour was found on her spine, and the army discharged him, and the economy tanked, and there was no work, and his wife took the decision that needed to be taken. He'd tried again. One year clean this time, she thought, since she'd left for London and he was a single parent. But she could see the signs now. The slow slide had begun. The drinking first. The choice of comrades – Artem especially. Anger as excuses.

When they were so close. Less than £7,000 to go, for the flights to Baltimore, for the best surgeon at Johns Hopkins, for the recuperation. She thought she could earn that in two weeks. But not if he started using again. She didn't know what the current price of heroin was on the streets of Moscow but it couldn't be cheap. Her two weeks would become three, four. Their daughter would get slower. And then there were the stories that street drugs were even more dangerous now. Tainted. Something else in them, that was killing people quick.

She had a flash of Georgiy, dead in some back alley. A problem solved. Then instantly teared up at the image. She

66

loved him still, even through all the shit times. His addiction, their daughter's cancer, both would have finished them long before if she didn't.

'Fuck faster,' he'd said. How much fucking ended in £7,000? How soon?

She shook her head. The first sixty had come easily enough. She didn't spend much, only on the clothes, the uniform she needed, and even those she bought in higher-end charity shops and altered herself, her mother's daughter. Lived cheap, in an immigrants' ghetto in Walworth. The last ten, though, had been harder because the pound had crashed with the Brexit shit, and the City types who were her main clients were jittery because of it. Smaller bonuses, less frivolous. And the Yank doctors wanted dollars, each pound buying less of them.

Fuck faster.

She looked into the mirror again. *With these breasts*, she wondered, *these lines around my eyes?*

Noises came from the bedroom. Room service had arrived a little early. She could hear Bernard's voice. He paid her £1,000, which was top rate but she owed rent, tax on the job she didn't have. Her membership fees at the two clubs that were her prime hunting grounds were coming up soon too. And Bernard was only a once-a-month client. Though last night at dinner he'd asked about her daughter, and when she'd told him that Maria wasn't getting any better, that she needed to earn more, quicker, he said he'd recommended her to a couple of friends. It was the first time he'd ever done that – even though she knew it detracted from the fantasy he'd made up for her. He was kind, Bernard. Gentle. Unlike many.

She put the phone by the sink, lifted the toilet lid, peed. As she was doing so, she picked up the phone again to check texts.

The first was from her daughter, on the school bus. Only a GIF, a girl dancing to hip-hop. The second was from someone called Patrick.

> *Hey! It's me, from Soho House, remember? It's on. Tonight. Venue TBA. Let me know if you're free and you got this. I'll send coordinates. Oh and P.S. Lottie's very excited.*

It was Lottie that brought it back. Patrick was the handsome actor she'd met a while back at Soho House. Lottie was perhaps his girlfriend. There was something about her, in her smile, that had made her name stick.

A threesome, she thought. How much had she quoted him? *£1,500*, she thought. *More than usual. To be earnt tonight.*

That would leave £5,500 or so to go. Her jaw tightened and she nodded to her reflection. Doable, she decided.

As Bernard called her from the bedroom, she texted a thumbs up and a kiss to Patrick.

CHAPTER 6

Later that day . . .

Joe Severin sat in the residents' parking bay outside the Portobello flat. His guest permit was on the Audi's dash, clearly displayed, but the warden had to be short-sighted and have memory loss, because every time she passed she leant into the windscreen to peer at it. It made him even more nervous. It made him feel guilty. Even though he had nothing to feel nervous or guilty about.

OK, he'd made a mistake. A hot day, a pretty girl, memories of Cassidy, all the pressure in his life, he'd blurted an offer to let this Lottie Henshaw stay in the flat, rent free. He'd have to honour it; he kept his word. But he could bend it a little. He thought he'd told her a couple of months but he'd drop it to one. Give him time to find a suitable tenant to pay the ridiculous rent – five grand a month. A month to hide that latest five thousand he'd get from the Shadows for doing their books, in his own books.

He didn't truly know what he'd been thinking. He wasn't an adulterer. Fifteen years of marriage, barely a glance elsewhere. Kinda like drugs. He'd had his time fucking around. He'd settled down. He was responsible. That little thing he'd bought last night in the Indian shop just down from the Tufnell Park flat would remain in his briefcase. He'd put it on his desk when he got home. Laugh at it. A reminder of fleeting madness.

This Lottie, though? Clearly *not* responsible.

He'd read her letters the previous afternoon, all ten of them. He was still undecided whether they'd ever been sent, or were just her . . . venting. Quite the vent. For a girl from the Home Counties – the way she'd said 'Buckingham*shire*!' – she had a pretty foul mouth. Well phrased, though, she was well educated – mentioned Epsom College, her time at the Guildhall School of Music and Drama. Her fury with this 'fuckhead', this 'total cunt', this 'Patrick' was beautifully rendered in a mad, right-slanting cursive that at first he'd found hard to decipher but, like a code cracked, he had suddenly got.

He looked at his phone. 5.17. When she'd rearranged the meeting from the morning – sudden audition, she'd texted – she'd said five. Late again. He'd nearly cancelled, especially when Vicky gave him grief for missing the interviews she'd set up with three potential new caterers. But he kept his word to tenants, to anyone. It was who he was.

He was tempted to open his trading app, check again. His mining shares had jumped another five per cent in the last three hours alone. Coltan was the new gold. But the excitement still gave him the pip. Burping, he tucked his phone away and reached for the plastic bag on the passenger seat. He'd decided he would give the letters back, tell her that his inventory company *had* found them. He wouldn't say he'd read them, of course.

His hand was on the bag. He reached in, pulled the bottom one out. It was, he'd decided, his favourite. The very last one, according to the date. They were all dated, which helped him keep them in order. With a place named too. Properly laid out. He wondered if his daughter at Channing was taught how to write a proper letter, rather than correct emoji use, ways to deal with online shaming, or how to raise her emotional intelligence, whatever the hell that was. He'd heard that most schools didn't even teach cursive any more. He didn't know why he felt that was just so wrong.

Shaking his head, he laid the paper on his thigh, bent, read.

Venice Beach, CA.
22nd April 2018

Dear Wanker,

So I'm off. I thought I wouldn't like it here and how right I was. Hate it, in fact, for all the reasons you love it. The view to the boardwalk and all those roller-blading beauties with the perfect bellies under their sports bras. The casual eccentrics and the true casualties. Venice just edgy enough still to make you think you're real. But you're not, mate. Real is Tufnell Park on a Saturday night, stepping around the puke. Nah, scratch that, this isn't about nasty.

Try this instead: real is us on the road, living off our touring allowance, staying in crap digs to save our pennies for our upcoming conquest of London. For the place we'd get together.

Never happened, though, did it? The play at the Donmar, the low-budget indie that wowed the festivals, the agents begging you to come here. The excuses that followed. 'Later, Lots. After.'

I just wish you'd had the balls to tell me straight, not drag me out here. The Patrick I knew had balls. I remember them well.

So I am going, before new shitty memories totally replace the old. Besides, there's only so much spirulina a girl can eat. I'll leave you to the parties, the powdered nostrils, the toned-borderline-anorexic bodies that fall into your grasp. The Patrick I knew liked a bit of heft, a bit of belly.

I'll leave you with this memory.

We'd played Birmingham, had the Sunday off. Drove to Shropshire for a walk in the hills. Late October, but weirdly warm, some breeze from the west. That pub for lunch, the landlord with the one eye, which he kept on us, we were giggling so much, must have thought we were high. But we weren't, unless cider counts. High on life. Fondling each other beneath the table. You were hard from the moment we sat down and roast beef au jus, Yorkshire puddings and two pints of Strongbow did little to diminish that. I thought you were going to kill me when I asked for the dessert menu! Finally done, drove Daphne up the narrow lanes, parked but I was out the car before you could grab me, running up the footpath. You caught me at the top of the hill, we laughed, wrestled, fell over. A view of some turf ramparts, no one about and one of the best blow jobs ever, you claimed, though I just thought it was one of the swiftest. Your recovery time was impressive, no coke

*needed to sustain you then. You led me off the path, not far,
you laid me down in the gorse where you were not swift
at all. Afterwards we lay silent and staring at these wild
clouds, boiling across the sky. Lay there till the sheep found
us, and we shrieked, panicked, ran.*

*Best fuck of our many fucks? Maybe. Would Edinburgh
run it close? Backstage at the Crucible, for sheer bravado?*

*Better than anything here in this City of Dreams and
Angels.*

*So see you, mate. Have fun, if you call it that. And
remember Shropshire, 'cos that was real. You were real.*

You're not real now.

L

Joe looked up, startled by a figure pausing near the car. The
myopic traffic warden again, glancing at him. He shrugged
'what?' at her, she moved on and he looked down at the letter
again.

What was it about outdoor sex? Some genetic legacy from
hunter-gatherer days? That sense of freedom? When had he
last made love outdoors? Never with Vicky; she was very
much a soft furnishings and low light kind of gal. So when?
He couldn't remember.

Until he did. Of course – it was the last time with Cassidy.
On that beach near Santa Cruz. Christ, eighteen years ago? It
had been terrible, too. No wonder he'd blocked it out.

Farewell fucks, in his small store of experiences, were
nearly as bad as first ones.

He heard the car before he saw it, same growl he'd heard
pulling up outside the flat in Tufnell Park. Saw a flash of red

as it passed him, saw her manoeuvre into the space ahead. She bumped his bumper – cheeky cow, he was sitting right there! As her door opened, he remembered the letter, and shoved it back into the bag. Out of order, on top. He didn't want her to see it till he was ready. So he pushed the bag behind his seat, grabbed the parking pass for her, got out of the car.

She started when she saw him. 'Oh,' she exclaimed, 'there you are.'

She was wearing the same clothes she had yesterday – blouse, skirt to mid-thigh, Blundstones on bare feet, though she was holding the faux fur.

'Do you always park like that?' he said, aggrieved, looking at his bumper.

She laughed. 'It's what they're for, right?' Then, before he could respond, continued, 'Sorry I'm late. Dermot had Daphne done early so I had to collect her.'

'Who?' he managed before she carried on.

'Dermot. Mechanic from Ireland. Daphne . . . my only true and constant love!' She said this sweeping her hand over the MG, then held it out to him. 'Sorry, Mr Severin.'

'Joe,' he mumbled, taking her hand, prepared this time for her grip. Pianist's, she called it. She may not have changed her clothes but she'd showered, she smelt different, of vanilla. The coconut gone, the tobacco and leather interior still there, but fainter.

She kept his hand while she looked up at the building. 'Lumme,' she said, but in her posh voice, 'is this it?'

He disengaged, handed her a visitor's parking pass. 'Put this on your dash. There's a traffic warden itching to clamp. I have the form for the council for a month's pass. You take that down to the council offices with the rental agreement I give you, they'll issue you one.' He gestured to the stone steps. 'Shall we?'

'Let's.'

He demonstrated the keys for the front door's double locks. The lift was small and she grinned up at him as they rose. The flat's front door was almost opposite the lift on the landing. He produced more keys, and used them. 'After you,' he said, pushing the door open, stepping aside.

She walked down a short corridor's end, then halted. Whistled. 'Wow!' she gasped.

He'd thought the same, in the same spot, when he first saw it two years before. Wondered what his life might have been like if he'd lived in a place like this, in an area like this, and not in a semi-detached in Finchley.

The short corridor gave onto a single large room, with tall windows to the front, the middle one of which was a French door, opening onto the balcony that ran the length of the frontage. To their left was a brick fireplace with a marble mantel above it under a tall, wide antique mirror. In front of a long, deep, oatmeal Heal's sofa stuffed with cushions was a white rug, a low glass table on that. To the right was a cherrywood dining table, six tall wicker-backed chairs around it. A rectangular opening, with wooden frames folded into its edges, gave onto the kitchen. 'Want to see in there first' – he gestured – 'or the master bedroom?'

'Bedroom, please. I'm not much of a cook. Whereas . . .' she paused just long enough then added with a chuckle, 'how I do love to sleep!'

He led the way. The bedroom was in keeping with the rest –

minimalist, off-whites, richly furnished. Walk-in wardrobes in dark wood lined one wall. The king-sized bed was pre-made with rich linens. She sat on it, bounced. 'Nice,' she murmured.

The bathroom was opposite the cupboards – chocolate tiling, separate walk-in shower with multiple heads, a high-sided tub, an old sink like from a Loire Valley farmhouse with a vintage faucet.

They went to the kitchen. A smaller bathroom was opposite it, just a shower and loo in there, with a smaller bedroom beside, single bed, desk. 'Office,' he said.

She glanced around the kitchen, dutifully admired the double oven, the stove built into the countertop, the twin sinks. But she didn't want to linger, pushed past him in the doorway, back to the main room, dropped her coat over the back of a dining chair, which she then sat on. Reaching into the fur's pocket, she pulled out a packet of rolling tobacco – Drum, he noticed. 'Do you mind?' she asked.

It wasn't a hotel. And the flat was usually rented to Greeks or Arabs and they nearly all smoked. He shrugged, went into the kitchen, came back with an ashtray.

'Ta,' she said, when he put it down. He was going to tell her all the other stuff: how to work the heating – not that you'd need it right now – where the fuse box was. But he was interested in what she was doing, the precise way she was preparing to roll her cigarette – the paper extracted, smoothed, laid down, a filter set on its end. He sat, to watch. 'So, Mr Severin,' she said, not looking up, pulling a pinch of brown strands from the bag, 'what are we doing here?'

She said it softly, without weight. So rather than take

what he thought she meant, he took her literally. 'Oh yeah, the papers.' He flicked open his briefcase, brought out the rental agreement, the inventory. When he looked up she was studying him but he couldn't tell what was in her jade eyes. 'So if you could just read this carefully through then sign?'

She laid the tobacco on the rolling paper, rubbed her fingers, picked up the top sheet. Her eyes shot wide. 'Five thousand quid! You're 'avin' a laugh.'

'That's the price. What I can get. Usually. You're not paying that, of course.'

'Bloody right, I'm not.' She laughed, laid the paper down, studied him for a long moment. 'But, uh, why am I not, again?'

He began to explain – about empty flat tax, waiting for the right rich renter, but she waved her hand. 'Come on, Mr Severin. The truth now. I always like the truth.'

'It . . . is . . . partly true. You would be . . . helping me.' He thought of the Shadows, hiding their money, not anything he was going to share with her. 'But also' – he shrugged, and looked her straight in the eyes – 'I like you.'

She took her lower lip between her teeth, and dropped a veil of hair over her left eye. 'Hmm,' she murmured, appraising him. 'And how far do you hope to take this, uh, liking?'

'Oh, not far. I mean' – he swallowed – 'I am married. Happily married.'

'I wonder if I know what that means. I wonder if you do.' She studied him a moment longer, then flicked her hair back, and reached again into her tobacco bag. This time, though, she didn't pull out more strands but a small brown lump. 'Do you mind?' she asked, slightly differently than she had before. A challenge in it.

It had been a while – but it wasn't something you forgot. 'Now look,' he began.

'You do? Oh.'

She held the hash above the bag, didn't let it go. And suddenly he thought, *Fuck it*, and said, 'Fuck it. Look, do what you want. But smoke it on the balcony, eh? There's an Indian family in the penthouse above.'

'Of course.'

Reaching into her coat pocket again, she pulled out a Zippo lighter, struck flame, scorched the edge of the hash, crumbled it in, deftly rolled the joint. He smelt the acrid sweetness.

'Join me?'

'On the balcony, not to—' He gestured at the paper cylinder in her fingers.

She led the way. There were two deck chairs, but she lit the joint then leant on the parapet, looked down at the street. There was a corner shop, a pub almost dead opposite. She dragged, let out a waft of smoke, inhaled the cloud through her nostrils. 'You sure?'

She held the joint out to him. When he'd been on the kibbutz, and then all through India and Thailand, he'd smoked a lot. It had almost been his life. Now, how long had it been? His brother Tony's bachelor party in Amsterdam, ten years before, and that the first time since he'd married Vicky, four years previously. He hadn't liked it. Had persuaded himself that he no longer liked it.

Fuck it.

He took the joint, inhaled deeply. Coughed hard. The nicotine hit him first, made him sway. Then he felt the other drug, underneath. Felt it in the throb at his temples. In the loosening at the back of his neck. He took another, more cautious hit, and his shoulders dropped.

'That's better,' she murmured. 'Isn't it?'

'Much,' he replied. He looked down into the street. What a great street it was, so . . . alive. He suddenly and deeply fancied an afternoon in that pub, several lagers. See if his shoulders could loosen even more.

Then he noticed a familiar dark shape, ambling, peering into windshields. Into *his* windshield. He pointed. 'Look at her.'

'Who?'

'The traffic warden. Desperate to nab me, to have me clamped or towed. Silly cow!'

Lottie leant over the balcony. 'Oi! You!' she yelled. 'Silly cow! Silly old moo!'

'Don't!' He giggled, putting his arms around her, pulling her away. Laughed, couldn't stop, coughed again, couldn't stop, laughed some more, let her go. They went back inside, and while she got him some water, he went to the fireplace, stared into the old mirror, fascinated at first by the patterns the corrosion made in it, until he noticed his face, and became more fascinated by that. This was not the man who looked back every morning when he shaved. This was . . . who he'd been. Who he was, perhaps. Under all the rest.

She came and stood beside him, handing him the glass. He looked at her now, really looked at her, but in her reflection. Remembered the letter. About what was real, and what was not. Decided.

'There is something else, actually,' he said. 'I *am* a married man . . .'

She supplied the missing word. 'But?'

He told her. Of the moment back in the flat in Tufnell Park. What he'd seen. Her eyebrows – thick, he noticed now, unruly – rose. 'That's it?' She shifted from looking into his reflected eyes to his real ones. 'That's all there is?'

'All there is.'

'Well.' She smiled, drank some more water, set her glass down on the mantel. 'That's a very small favour indeed in return for' – she looked around – 'this.'

She turned away from him then, dropping to her knees on the white rug. Leant down on one hand. Then, reaching behind her with the other, she slowly pulled up her blouse. The sun wasn't hitting it as it had yesterday. But he could still see the faint filaments of hair, golden in the cleft of her back.

Joe gazed for a very long moment, taking in every small detail. Then he put down his glass, went to his briefcase, and pulled out a miniature of tequila reposado.

CHAPTER 7

Sebastien kept the telephoto lens resting on his rolled-down window and pointed at the balcony. But Severin and his tart had disappeared inside a few minutes earlier and he suspected, from the hugging, that they weren't going to emerge anytime soon. Also, they'd smoked a blunt.

Stoned sex, he thought. It had been a while. Since Magdalen actually, what, eighteen years before? That Rhodes Scholar from Somerville, Canadian, couldn't remember her name. Her wildness had freaked him out a bit, he remembered that. He thought he'd slapped her but he couldn't be sure. Maybe she'd wanted him to? But the sex had been . . . consuming. So it seemed unlikely he'd be seeing the bookkeeper anytime soon.

He noticed a shadow approaching on the pavement and pulled the lens in. It was that fucking traffic warden again. Fat West Indian cow had been sniffing around him since he arrived. Peering in at him. Staring suspiciously at the 'Disabled' sign hanging on his rear-view mirror. She peered again now, stared at him; he shrugged his shoulders at her. She sniffed, moved on. Bitch.

He went back over some of the shots he'd taken.

The tart was quite cute, in a slatternly way. Charlotte Henshaw was her name, known as Lottie. He'd discovered that by having Miles, back at 'Legoland', run the plates on the MG. His assistant had sent the name and, soon after, a mini bio. Twenty-six, a pianist in show bands, she was a registered tenant of Severin Properties – not here, though, over in Tufnell Park. The property listing on 45 Clonmarle Gardens showed it as a two-bedroom, furnished and vacant. Had the bookkeeper brought her to Portobello for a quick shag? It didn't fit at all with what Nate had said about his fellow Yid, the quiet family man and husband. The vetting brief Miles had also sent, that they'd run when the Shadows had been deciding whether to back Nate's nomination for bookkeeper, was brief, certainly, mainly because there was nothing to find out – Joseph Severin was ordinary to the point of dullness. Following him from his home this morning on his rounds had only confirmed that. He'd visited two properties, he'd picked up his blimp of a wife and taken her to a catering company, he'd stopped for a bagel at a Hendon eatery.

The only vaguely interesting thing happened when Sebastien had dropped into the company office, on the pretence of seeking rental accommodation for a fictitious nephew. He'd dealt with a bovine lump called Oliver but only needed to give him less than half of his attention. He'd watched as Severin fielded calls, shoved paperwork around, could tell his heart wasn't in it. Occasionally the man would swipe and grin, and he'd wondered if he was on Tinder – or perhaps, horrors, Grindr? But when Oliver went into the back room to photocopy some property specs Sebastien had faked interest in, Severin had got up to go to the loo, and Sebastien had been able to get to the phone just before it locked.

It wasn't Tinder. But it was proof, if proof were needed, that the man was indeed dabbling in stocks, the very same stocks where Sadiq was hiding and increasing the Shadows' money. He knew he didn't have much time, so he just checked messages after that. *Trouvez la femme*, he'd thought, as he saw the texts from one 'L' – full of emojis and txt on her part, more restrained on his. He'd memorised her number and laid down the phone, just as Oliver came back.

He knew where Severin was headed when he'd set out, from the messages, but he tailed him anyway. His 'target'. It was part of the job he'd enjoyed when he joined Six straight out of his short service commission in the Blues. Field work, he'd always been quite good at it. Bernard, who was jealous because he'd gone into mundane data work at Five, had mocked him as a low-rent James Bond. But it had certainly been different, and he'd learnt his stuff in Zagreb, Beirut, Tokyo. They'd kicked him upstairs a few years back – but he seemed to have retained the essentials. Probably over-egged it, seeing as Severin was about as clued in as a nun at an orgy. Still, it made a change from driving his desk and computer.

Did he need to stay any longer? In his camera he had what the Russian oppo termed *kompromat*. Compromising material, enough to convince Nate of his choice's frailties – not that evidence was really required, seeing how the sugar vote had gone. Absurd the rituals they went through, rather than a show of hands. But he, Bernard and Perry had done sugar lumps since Bedales, the reason now lost to the mists. Something to do with Perry's brief obsession with Dungeons & Dragons, he thought. Still, Nate was a key member of the Shadows, his contacts in the Middle East unsurpassed. Best to keep him onside.

5.59. He'd stay till half six, in case anything else came up. He turned on his radio, to listen to Radio Four news. Sat there, shaking his head at all the fatuous nonsense people were spouting about Brexit. *Just fucking get on with it*, he thought.

Sadiq had done a study for them – with their connections, Brexit was a goldmine. All those EU regulations gone, the Eastern Europeans scrambling to cut new deals, British nous – English nous really, because the Jocks would probably soon be gone, and the Micks tearing each other apart again – set to dominate and exploit. He was seriously thinking of getting into the private sector. His cousin Gervase – a belted earl, no less – had been keeping a seat warm for him at the family's merchant bank. He grinned. *All the more reason to enjoy this field work while I can*, he thought.

At six-thirty, he got out of his Volkswagen Passat – taken from the Six pool, non-descript but with a souped-up engine – and started to stroll down the street, on the opposite pavement to the house. Out of the air conditioning, the heat hit him straight away. He was in the third of his disguises, which meant the reversible jacket, which guaranteed more sweat. His shirt was short-sleeved and silk, though, and he was wearing shorts, trainers, the blue LA Dodgers baseball cap. Bernard called it his American tourist outfit, and Sebastien had profited from his time in Washington to pick up an acceptable accent. And even though this street with its pub and shop was not the Palace of Westminster or the Tower, you never knew what Yanks were into. Several of the houses sported plaques so he hefted his camera and snapped them. Some Rastafarian poet, who had lived three doors down from Severin at number 39, was honoured with a blue one. In pink, nearly opposite at number 30, was a feminist, Elizabeth Dingwell, Suffragette.

He'd never taken his eyes off number 45 for more than a few moments. Now he turned, crossed the street to its side and walked slowly back towards it.

He was about twenty yards away when Severin came out the door. Without hesitating, Sebastien lifted his camera and snapped. It could have been a mistake, a breaking of cover, but the target was too set on his car to notice, hurrying into it, driving off fast. For a moment, Sebastien thought about following him, then thought better of it. Truly, he'd got all the evidence he needed on Severin. He thought he should spend a little more time on this Lottie Henshaw before calling it a night. If Severin had only just rented the property to her – or more likely, given the state of her, set her up in his love nest – she'd probably have to rise from her 'enseamèd bed' – what was that, *Hamlet*? – sometime soon to get some groceries. He'd ask her directions in his fake American. He'd like to hear what she sounded like.

He was thirsty, though. And there was a gastropub almost opposite the house with a window that gave onto the street.

He went in, ordered a pint of some strong European lager, sat on a stool at a shelf that ran the window's length. Street life passed by – including that fucking traffic warden, who stopped and peered at his windscreen, actually made a note of something, walked on. Really? What had this country come to? No pity for the disabled?

Nothing moved in the building opposite. He took the odd shot of the balcony as he sipped his beer, made sure he'd compensated for the pub window. Then, as he drained his pint and was just about to leave – it seemed the lady was not for stirring – he saw a young black dude approach and stop before number 45, staring up. Sebastien hefted his camera, set it to multiple frames, as the man turned. Caught his face – and instantly knew he'd seen it before. As the man ran up the stairs, pressed the third buzzer – hers – then went in, he stopped shooting and flicked back to one of the man's full face.

I know you, he thought, studying. Criminality came first to mind, and why not? People yelped about racial profiling but it was a simple fact that there was a far higher chance of a black man being a dealer, or carrying a knife, than a white one. Had he seen this man in a mugshot briefing he'd had recently? Drug smuggler? Terrorist? But then, when he realised where he knew him from, he laughed. Then immediately frowned. 'Another of these,' he said, turning, and lifting his glass, 'and the lamb tagine,' he added. He'd settle in for a bit, watch. The newcomer was a complication they didn't need. Like an STD Severin was spreading around, people were getting infected. People who could attract attention.

The barman set the pint down in front of him. Sebastien took a sip, then got out his iPhone and googled the name he'd also remembered.

A whole string of headlines came up for Patrick Ogulu.

CHAPTER 8

'Very fine, Lots. Very fine indeed.'

Patrick was standing on the rug in front of the mirror in which he'd already checked himself out. She didn't blame him. He was, Lottie admitted, looking very fine too – a hot and vivid contrast to all that cool and minimalist white.

He was dressed for the beach. Antigua, though, or the Seychelles, not Margate. And more for the après rather than any actual sun or surf. Wayfarer shades, a tipped-back Panama hat, but not airport bought, the kind you probably *could* roll into a cigar cylinder. An old, long-sleeved linen shirt, folded up to the elbows, burnt sienna with a faint frond pattern, open to mid chest. Hemp culottes, tapered to just below his knees. Vans skateboard shoes, forest green with yellow laces, thick-soled. No socks and plenty of skin exposed everywhere, ebony glow on muscles that, if they didn't bulge like they had when he'd played rugby sevens for England Under 18s, were still prominent and taut.

Yeah, still pretty fucking gorgeous, she thought, scoping him as he scoped the room. *Pity he's such a tosser.*

She thought back to how she'd first seen him, when she was accompanying at the auditions for the tour of *My Fair Lady*. Not cool, nervous as hell, still at Central drama school, his hands actually shook when he handed her the sheet music. Asked if she could transpose it down a major third. She could, did; he sang a bit of Che from *Evita*, old-school for an old show. Not brilliantly, not bad, and better the second time when the MD pushed him to sing it in the right key. Truthfully, it wasn't a great voice but it was good enough. And he had the charm for the role of Freddy, that was for sure. She could sense the creative team leaning forward, that moment when people recognise that someone different has entered the room, someone who is . . . going places. Plus colour-blind casting was all the rage, so he was in.

Lottie smiled to herself, thought: *Right then and there I knew I'd 'ave him. Made my play before any of those anorexic dancers even saw him, and devoured him. Wrote my number on top of his sheet music before handing it back, tapping it so he saw. He was surprised – but he called three days later. And he looked at no one else the six months of the tour, was so sweet, so naïve, with me all of three years older, the seasoned pro. What larks we had. What japes, as I took him in hand. As I took him . . . everywhere.*

Look at him now, four years on. The boy all gone. Ecce homo.

He took off his hat, put it crown down on the coffee table, dropped his shades into it. He'd cut his hair, a close crop on the top, shaved up the sides. He grinned at her. 'Bedroom?' he enquired.

She led him through. He nodded at the bed, the mirror, whistled at the bathroom with its huge walk-in shower. She could see him already planning it – the bodies entwining, white on black on white, hot water cascading down. For a moment, she saw it too, and she felt her whole skin flush.

They returned to the living room. Patrick pointed at the Veuve he'd set down on the coffee table. 'Open one, other in the fridge?' he asked.

'I'll fetch the glasses,' she replied, bending to pick up one bottle, while he lifted the other. She was wearing a summer dress, Laura Ashley, old-school: yellow, patterned in bluebells, buttons down the front, undone almost as far as his. No bra. She took her time, knew he clocked her breasts by the quality of his sudden stillness. 'A pocket Venus' he'd called her, that first time she pulled a dress over her head, by candlelight in Tufnell Park, second week of rehearsals. Small in height she may have been, but he was right, she was in perfect proportion. 'How tall are you?' he'd asked, on their first date.

'Five foot 'n' a fag paper, mate,' she'd said, in her faux London and made him laugh, as she discovered she always could.

She rose, not fast, and his eyes rose a fraction behind hers. She smiled at him, and he smiled back.

She went to the kitchen, stashed the one Widow, searched in the cupboards, found an ice bucket, filled it from the spout on the fridge, grabbed three flutes. The place had everything. Came back with it all, and saw Patrick at the mantel, cutting a line on the marble. 'Can't that wait?' she said. 'I'm thirsty.'

'Sorry, love,' he replied, dropping the credit card. 'Coming right up.'

He bent to the bottle, ripped off the foil, the wire, thumbed the cork out, turning at the last moment to the open French window to launch it, with a suitably awesome pop, over the balustrade. He poured, they waited for the froth to die down, he raised his flute. 'To an interesting night,' he toasted. '*Skål*. No, wait,' he added before sipping. 'She's Russian, Sonya, right? So we should say, what is it . . . *nostrovia!*'

'*Nostrovia!*'

They clinked. They both gulped, then he put his glass down next to the coke. 'Want some?' he asked, rolling a twenty-pound note.

'I'm good,' she replied.

He bent, placed, snorted, just the one line. A modest beginning, Lottie thought. When they first met, and on the road, it hadn't been part of the repertoire; he'd been content enough with her special roll-ups. LA had changed that, his stint there. She'd gone along with it for a bit, 'cos he liked it. But she'd never reckoned it was the sex drug he cracked it up to be. Coke, in her limited experience, made everyone too selfish. Plus Patrick, who could go on for ages anyway, was rarely able to come when coked up. 'It's alright, love,' he'd said, flopping back the third time it happened, 'it's very millennial to withhold one's jism.'

They'd drained their first glass so he refilled the champagne and they took it onto the balcony. The street alive with people, out for early evening fun. She smoked the ciggie she'd been rolling when he'd buzzed. Not special, just tobacco. She wanted to keep a clear head for what was to come, at least initially. Given their less-than-illustrious three-way track record, it seemed like a good idea that one of them did.

They chatted about this and that – mainly the role he'd just scored. Superhero, major Australian director, exotic locales.

Then he asked the question he'd obviously been aching to ask.

'So, Lots . . . who'd you have to fuck to nab this palace?'

She thought then of Mr Severin – she still couldn't think of him as Joe, despite his pleading. Despite the tequila on her back. Only an hour before, and he'd panicked and run straight afterwards. Back to his wife, no doubt. 'No one.' She picked a tobacco strand off her tongue. 'Landlord at Tufnell Park needed someone in here fast, otherwise he'd be paying loads of tax for an empty pad . . .'

'. . . that wouldn't stay empty for long. It's gorgeous.' He sniffed, ran a wrist knuckle under his nose. 'You can't afford this. How much you paying?'

'Same as Tufnell Park,' she lied.

'Bollocks!'

'I told you, it's helping him out.'

'Who is he again?'

'Just the landlord. Mr Severin. Jewish fella,' she added; she didn't know why. Perhaps because the vision came of looking back at him bent over her back, sunlight glistening on the polished leather of his yarmulke.

'Ah, righteous Jah people,' Patrick said, in the spot-on Jamaican-London accent he'd acquired for the Yardie movie *Payblack*. Then he added with a smile, in his normal voice, 'Just as long as you're not Bathsheba to his King David.'

'How did that go again? I only know it from the Leonard Cohen song.'

She asked to distract him from his cross-examination – and to distract herself from hers. OK, she admitted it, it had been weird, with Mr Severin. She'd wondered then, and wondered again now, if it was going to get any weirder.

91

But Patrick, with all the focus of cocaine – while on which she'd heard grown men obsess for twenty minutes on the relative merits of square tea bags versus round – was off. Unlike her school, where they were all heathens, Patrick had attended the Oratory, a Catholic boarding school near Reading. He'd hated it, ran away at sixteen, but he'd absorbed the stories. Preferred the Old Testament, he said, because it was full of sex, battles and revenge.

He was juicing up the Book of Samuel, in a most irreligious way, lingering on the voluptuousness of the naked woman bathing on a roof – 'Bathsheba was a lot like you, my love,' he said – when the door buzzer sounded.

He broke off, and Lottie went to the door, pressed the button. 'Yes?' she said.

A moment's pause and then a voice. As soon as Lottie heard it, even through the buzzer distortion, she instantly recalled the face that went with it.

'It is Sonya.'

'Third floor. Come on up.'

She turned back. Patrick was grinning at her. 'Game on,' he said, drained his champagne, and headed for the kitchen to fetch the second bottle.

CHAPTER 9

Sebastien was just finishing his lamb tagine when the Audi A8L pulled up opposite number 45. He snatched up his Nikon, snapped one of the licence plate, and then trained it on the back door. This model was on the luxury end, not quite full limo, but classy, used for chauffeur work. He suspected whoever arrived would be getting out from the back. Might have nothing to do with the flat he was watching. Might.

He took a couple of shots of the driver – a broad, pudgy face – as he got out, before he turned and opened the door for a woman. He shot as she stood, immediately confused by her face because he knew he'd seen her before. She was attractive, so his mind went to actresses, since Patrick Ogulu was now in the mess. She turned away, and crossed the road . . . to the steps of number 45. He telescoped to the bank of buzzers. He saw her hand heading for Flat C before her back blocked the actual shot. A moment of waiting, the door opened, she was gone. He sat back, went through the frames. Who was she? He knew her, but from where? It didn't come. He began to regret that second pint.

There was one shot, just as she was turning away from the car, in which she was angled more towards him. He zoomed down to her face. Attractive, yes, beautiful even – but not quite as young as he'd first thought. There were crow lines around her almond eyes, and though the zoom had blurred them somewhat, he could see age in the expression, too, as if she'd seen a lot of life. A . . . resignation there, perhaps? Then, in the later series across the road, which he played like frames of a film, he'd caught her looking up at 45 and then . . . setting her shoulders, as if preparing for something. For a role? It said 'actress' again, and he raked his Staropramen-befuddled memory. Still nothing came.

Then, when it did, he said, 'Shit!', loud enough to make the couple on stools at the other end of this same ledge turn around. He'd seen a photo of her before. Not that long before. She'd looked less attractive in that one – on her Visa application.

'Sonya Ivenetza,' he muttered. He felt a chill, nothing to do with the over-air-conditioned pub. What the fuck was this? Their bookkeeper with a blonde in a love nest who's welcoming . . . Bernard's Russian whore?

He shivered, stood up, raised his glass for the last inch of lager, then put it down without drinking. He went to the bar, paid cash for his tab. Field work was over for the day. He needed to go to Vauxhall, to his office, and do some serious investigating

Outside, he glanced up at the flat. As he did he heard a faint pop, and something sailed over the balcony. A champagne cork landed not ten feet from him in the street. Celebrating a sting? It didn't make sense – a musicals pianist, an actor, a whore . . . what? She was Russian so perhaps she was an FSB op, honey-trapping Bernard. Or worse – this Sonya working for that bitch he'd mentioned at Five – Ellerby, was that her name? – probing the Shadows?

He stopped at his car, clicked the electronic door, but did not stoop to open it. Because another thought had come.

Could this all be a coincidence? Just a coincidence?

He hated fucking coincidences.

'Excuse me? Sir?'

The strong voice came from close by, and he was so lost to his thoughts that Sebastien jumped. He turned. *Speaking of bitches*, he thought.

The traffic warden was there. She had her hand stretched towards him. 'Can I see your disabled papers, please?'

'You what?'

'Your papers, please. You have a doctor's certificate, yes?' She pointed at his windshield. 'For disabled licence.'

Her voice was African, not West Indian. There were even scarification marks on her cheeks. He flushed, hot again outside in this ridiculous summer, hot again inside from what he'd just learnt. 'Look, lady, why don't you just fuck off?'

Her dark eyes narrowed but her voice stayed neutral. She moved her fingers in a 'give me' gesture. 'Licence,' she repeated.

Sebastien thought. Six kept those licences in the glove compartment of the car that was registered for the disabled. But he'd snatched the sign from an old, battered Astra and hung it on the Passat's mirror because he'd decided that if he was going to play James Bond for a day he might as well have some poke under the hood. This car wouldn't have any licence at all.

She was still standing there, hand out. 'Fuck off, Sheba,' he said, and walked around to the driver's side.

She followed him fast. Actually put her hand on the driver's door, leant her considerable weight onto it. 'You show your licence now . . . sir!'

He looked at her. He probably gave her 40 pounds. The last thing he needed was to be caught up in some fracas in the street. Not when he needed to be at his desk. 'I beg your pardon. Certainly.' He opened the car door, slid in, made a show of reaching over to the glove compartment. She'd kept the door open.

So much the better, he thought.

With his foot on the clutch, he pressed the start button and the engine started instantly. 'Hey!' she cried, but he ignored the open door. Already in first, he hammered down the gas; the engine took him out of the parking bay and away fast. He swerved slightly as he reached and slammed the door, forcing an oncoming car to brake hard. It hooted him.

He glanced into his mirror. The African Queen was on her knees in the road. Two bystanders were already rushing to her. A car had stopped and the driver was getting out.

Serves her right, he thought. The Bond theme music was playing in his head and made him smile. Though that quickly went as he thought about the evening ahead.

First, change the plates on the Passat. Do it himself, not for the first time. Return the disabled sign to the Astra. It would take days for the enquiry to come through, the up-ending of a traffic warden near Portobello. Of course he'd not signed the car out in his own name anyway. It wouldn't be high priority for Six to investigate and he'd slow it further. Give him the time he needed.

Bernadette, you fucking prat, he thought, as he turned briefly onto Bayswater Road, before cutting down Kensington Church Street, heading south. Not only a call girl but a Russian at that? Shades of Profumo, for God's sake!

Still, it *could* all just be a bloody coincidence. They happened after all. According to a friend he'd had at Magdalen, Jonathan, mathematician, people shouldn't be surprised, because they happened all the time. Sebastien considered possible overlaps, the Venn diagram of it all. Bernard had a passion for trendy bars, was a member of several. There was one, what was it called? Soho House! Actors went to it. So did hookers.

No need to panic. He'd investigate, find out everything about this Sonya Ivenetza. Indeed, more fieldwork might be required. That made him smile again – because she really was quite gorgeous.

As he took Queen's Gate, headed for the Chelsea Embankment, he began to hum the Bond theme.

CHAPTER 10

On the buzz, Sonya pushed the heavy front door open. It clunked solidly behind her and she leant back against it for a moment.

She was still tired. On the rare times she did stay over with a client she never slept much. Plus she'd only managed a few hours' sleep that afternoon, in her own place, the walls thin on the Aylesbury Estate in Walworth and with kids out in the central yard, yelling. Besides, her mind was too active. Seeing Georgiy's face, what he was hiding behind it. Hearing what he said again, about their daughter.

'She's getting slower. The painkillers are not working so well. At night she . . .'

Only one way to help with that, she thought, pushing away from the door. At least there was a lift, waiting; she climbed in, pressed 'C'. As it rose, she looked in the mirror that was the whole upper rear wall, accessing herself. She dressed for clients, but since these people were new, she'd had to make a guess. It was to be a threesome; she suspected that wasn't their normal thing, but people didn't want normality when they were exploring something different. They wanted a little danger, they wanted to lead – but they also wanted to be led. Her pale pink silk blouse was neutral, unthreatening, though it opened enough over her cleavage and her vintage scarlet Schiaparelli upthrust bra to entice. Her panelled skirt, also dark red, was cut to just below the knee. Above that she wore open-crotch knickers and a garter belt to hold up her black, deco-patterned stockings. If, after some conversation, she discovered that these people were more conservative, she had simple cotton underwear to change into in her bag. If they were not, her red leather bag also contained . . . accoutrements. Handcuffs, ropes, blindfolds. She never used drugs herself, but she carried them: powdered MDMA, some vials of amyl nitrite, Viagra, a pre-rolled joint of Colombian sinsemilla.

I will just have to see, she thought, as the lift arrived at the third floor with a *bing* and she looked into her eyes. They did look tired, despite the grey lenses, the make-up and drops. But she'd discovered, because so many men had told her this, that it was partly her heavy-lidded eyes that made her the Slavic beauty of their fantasies. 'Sloe-eyed' one client had called her, in a gushing note he left her and she'd had to look it up, thought he'd misspelt 'slow', which had confused her. Until she found, 'the bluish fruit of a blackthorn'. Her eyes were brown, though grey now with the contacts, but she supposed he meant the way they drooped, like plums from a bough.

She straightened, pushed her shoulders back. 'Show time,' she murmured, and opened the lift door.

The young woman was standing in a doorway just along

the landing. Sonya remembered her when she saw her. She'd called her beautiful, which she was, even if in a very different way to herself. An English way, with an oval of a face, pale skin and even features though the eyebrows were crazy and thick, another contrast to her own plucked and painted lines. She'd had her blonde hair down when they'd met at the bar; now it was up, rolled and held by a chopstick. 'Sonya,' Sonya said, stepping closer, offering her hand – there was no need to rush into kisses; she had an immediate sense that this woman would want it taken slow. Not . . . sloe.

'Oh, I remember,' came the reply, together with a grip on the hand that was stronger than most men she knew. 'Lottie.'

'Oh, I remember,' she echoed, with a smile.

'Won't you come in?' Lottie said, and gestured her to go past, still holding the door, adding, 'Patrick, look who's here.'

Sonya entered. A short corridor gave straight onto a living room, stylish, uncluttered, very white. In the middle stood a man, very black. She recalled him now as well; she'd talked with him a while at the bar at Soho House. Handsome, with a nervous energy to him, like other actors she'd met, which he'd told her he was. He'd been trying to impress her, with show names he must have thought she'd know. But she didn't have a TV, and she used her computer for business and for Skype.

'How *are* you, Sonya?' His voice came back to her, as distinctive as his look, mellow, deep.

'I am very well, Patrick. And you?'

'All the better for seeing you. Glad you could make it.' He had a bottle of champagne in his hand, was just undoing the wire. 'Would you like some?'

'Thank you.'

Lottie pointed. 'May I take that? It's a lovely bag.'

'Oh, I'll leave this here.' Sonya put down her bag, leaning it against the back of the sofa.

Patrick aimed the bottle and the cork exploded out over the balcony. He poured into the empty flute. 'Come and sit.' He held up the glass like a lure. She moved around the sofa, took the champagne. He kept it for a moment, their hands linked by glass. 'Oh, and there's also—'

He gestured to the mantelpiece with his free hand. She could see the unfolded paper there and the rolled note. *Fuck*, she thought. Men could go a long time on cocaine, especially through the compulsory condom. Also with three people involved, and at this price? This could be a long night.

Perhaps something showed in her eyes. 'Maybe later, eh?' Releasing the glass to her, he sat.

The sofa was a square U, with short sides, around a glass table. Lottie came to the right end of it; Patrick was opposite her on the left, leaving Sonya in the middle between them. *As will be later*, she thought.

They talked a while. She learnt a little of them, they almost nothing true of her. When she worked, she kept her own truth, and any hint of sadness, far away. She enjoyed the champagne, Veuve Clicquot, one of her favourites. She let them drink most of it, though; she was already sleepy enough. Patrick made one trip to the mantelpiece, accepting her second refusal with a shrug. Lottie put some music on from her phone, on Bluetooth. A good speaker system brought the sounds to the room, sealing it off from the outside. The street noises receded as the jazz took control.

A break in tunes. A silence in conversation. Sonya put her

half-drunk glass down on the glass tabletop. 'A moment of business, please. Do you have . . . ?'

'Of course.' Patrick went to the mantelpiece again. An envelope lay there, which she hadn't noticed before. He picked it up, sat again and reached it to her. She took it, and he said, 'Count it?' and she replied, 'No need,' and leant over the back of the sofa to drop it into her bag.

She turned back, to their eager faces. Placed her tongue against her upper teeth and stared long at Patrick. Without taking her eyes off him, she said, 'Lottie. Will you come here?'

Lottie drained off her champagne, put the glass down, got up, came over, stood above Sonya. She looked nervous. 'Where do you want me?' she asked.

'Here,' Sonya replied, taking her hand, opening her mouth, pulling her down into it.

Much, much later . . .

White on black on white. *Though actually*, Lottie thought, *it isn't.*

The black was a deep, dark brown, while the whites were not pure white at all. Sonya's was a pale rose, the colour fading or damasking depending on the action, the friction, the stimuli. While she was brown, latte brown, a colour gained from hours of nude bathing at the Ladies' Pond on Hampstead Heath. Only the faintest of tan lines scarred the uniformity, at breast, at upper thigh, whenever decorum had demanded a cover-up. But she'd been grateful for those at times that evening, when tongues and fingers used the lines as trackways to greater pleasures.

Earlier, with twenty fingers and two tongues, Lottie hadn't known where to turn, how to yield. Until she realised after the other two, certainly after Patrick, that salvation was to be found in surrender. In the realisation that there was nothing to give up, only something to accept. This time, unlike those two other times, Patrick wasn't territorial and, despite the coke, he was also generous. Half his fun appeared to be watching her have fun too. There was an equal desire in the room.

In the *rooms*. Because they moved, of course. Took advantage. Someone initiated, someone led, the others followed. But that wasn't just locational. It was the core of the matter. The cock of the matter. The cunt of the matter.

It was quite late on, and in the bedroom, when the final revelation came. Lottie had led the way there, seeking an easing for a back that had spent too long bent over a sofa.

'Very nice,' Sonya purred, taking a long look around before placing her hands on Lottie's shoulder and easing her onto the bed. The Russian was down to an amazing bra, and crotchless knickers. The English girl was down to nothing at all.

It was then that Lottie discovered there was something the Russian could do with her mouth that no man had ever done. She'd had a hint of it before, on the dining-room table. But now, while Patrick was back at the mantel, fuelling up, also taking a break because he'd been fucking so hard, fucking them both, equal opportunities fucking. Though he said he hadn't come, and that he didn't care. At least not yet.

Sonya stood for a moment above her, eyes moving all over her, then bent to spread her legs, before kneeling between them, laying her mouth, her whole mouth, so softly against

Lottie. Held it there before she began to move. And though Patrick came in sniffling, gave a wee cry, knelt in his turn, put on another condom and pushed himself slowly into Sonya, the pressure on Lottie didn't alter; the tongue kept true to its course.

The pace was stately, and Patrick, taking note of the rhythm, adjusted to the speed, a slow withdrawal, a slower re-entry. He brought his hands over, laid them on Lottie's breasts. He had always known how to work her nipples, gently, but not too gently, using the calluses gained from lifting weights, a sweet chafing, a slight distraction, sideshow to the main event, where the speed was slowly building, the probe lingering, the touch lightening, getting faster. Lottie realised she'd been moaning for a while when Sonya began to moan too, the vibration of her moans sending an extra pulse through Lottie, goading Patrick, whose pace grew in parallel. Then, and suddenly, there was a hardness within her, one finger, two fingers curled in, up, pads finding a spot within, one hitherto undiscovered, *terra incognita*, discovered now, the finger pads pressing into it, stroking it . . .

. . . as the tongue moved on her, as the fingers circled within her, Lottie opened her eyes to see Patrick even closer, moving faster. It was as if he was in them both; Lottie felt that they were all fully joined for the first time, three with three, the noise each made blending. The tongue, the pressure, the fingers, the fucking, all of it came together, and they all came in a row, she first, loud and long, Patrick shortly afterwards in a lingering shudder, Sonya, she thought, a few moments later as she withdrew from Lottie – thank Christ! – to push herself back and draw Patrick's final spasms deep within her,

her fingers clawing into the bed's white blanket.

He fell back against the door, Sonya sank onto the floor, Lottie had to use her hands to get her legs together. Then – she didn't know who began it – they were all laughing. It was crazy laughter, absurd, uncontrollable. Lottie pulled her knees up to her breasts and slapped the bed, again and again and again.

Wobbly legged, all three walked to the shower; soaped each other down, held each other as water struck them on all sides. Then Patrick must have recalled his first plan for this location, because he ran his hand down Lottie's side, moving it towards her sex. She slapped it away, felt that if either of one of them touched her there she would die in the explosion. But Sonya accepted his touch, touched in her turn. Lottie extracted herself, sat on the bidet, washed herself, staring at the shapes fading into steam. When all was lost to mist and moans, she rose, dried herself, then slipped into her Chinese silk gown. She returned to the living room, sat and rolled herself a special cigarette, took it out to the balcony to smoke. She could see a clock on the wall in an office above the pub opposite. It was 11.17. *Jesus*, she thought. She let the jazz, which she'd never turned off, take her, let her mind go blank. Took a while before she remembered what she held, and lit it.

'So that is where you went.'

The voice behind her, she didn't turn to it and a moment later Sonya was leaning beside her, wrapped in a bath towel. Lottie held up the joint, Sonya sniffed the smoke, shook her head.

'Where's Patrick?'

'In a bubble bath, with headphones on. He says he'd like to slow down. But with what he's had?' She shrugged, pointed at the joint. 'Maybe he should have some of this?'

'Nah, he's only a speed king these days.'

'So, I think he is maybe preparing for another round?'

The way she said it, not fearful, certainly weary, made Lottie turn and look at her more closely. Between the sex and the shower all her make-up was gone, her hair still wet, plastered down. She looked young – yet old too, especially around, and in, the eyes.

'Why don't you go?'

There was a moment of hope in those eyes, which came and went. 'No. He paid for a night. I stay.'

'I paid too. Well, I provided the venue. I'm an equal partner. And I say you're done.'

'You . . . are sure?'

'Yup. But if you don't want an argument, you had better move fast.'

She did. Towel dropped, clothes on, bag shouldered. Within two minutes she was out on the balcony again. 'Goodbye, Lottie.' She offered her hand. 'It was a pleasure.'

Lottie smiled at the formality. Took the hand. 'The pleasure was mine.' Sonya tried to withdraw her hand but Lottie held it. 'But was it only mine?'

Sonya stared at her, something else going on in her young-old eyes. Finally she said, 'You know, Patrick thinks it was him that made me come. I tell you a secret – I do not, often, with clients, though I pretend, of course. But truly? It was you. The way you . . . gave to my touch. I like this. Yes. This I like very much.'

She pulled Lottie slightly to her then, kissed her on both cheeks. As she stepped back, Lottie whispered, 'Will we meet again?'

'You have my number.'

'But I'm a broke pianist. Don't be fooled by this place.'

Sonya pulled away. 'For special friends – maybe a special discount?'

They held each other's eyes for a moment. Then both heard Patrick call from the bathroom. 'Hey, you two. I've had a really great idea.'

'Go,' Lottie whispered.

She went. A minute later the house's front door opened and she emerged. Lottie watched her walk down the stairs, onto the street, start walking south. She heard the familiar diesel hum of a black cab, and so did Sonya, who hailed it. As she got in, without looking up, she raised a hand in one brief salute.

CHAPTER 11

Friday 27th July 2018

Ellerby woke just before 5 a.m. Again.

She wasn't sure how long she'd slept, tossy-turny from the moment Terry had kissed her goodnight and turned off the light. As usual he was asleep in moments, that regular gentle breathing somehow more aggravating than snoring, which, to be fair, her husband almost never did.

She'd tried all the usual tricks. The meditation through every part of the body, from toe to crown. Moved on to headphones, first sounds of waves, then an actor reading something incredibly boring in a soft Scottish Borders dialect. Still awake, she found herself scrolling, the worst thing. At least she avoided re-reading her messages. There'd been two dozen at least, from the time she'd got home at seven, to the bedtime story. The rule was sound off, no checking during family hours but she couldn't help her eyes flicking each time the screen lit up, trying to read upside down without appearing to glance over. As Terry dished out dessert, she'd excused herself to the bathroom, sat on the loo seat, read. It was a shitshow at work, updates coming in fast. And being in charge she was expected to be on top of them, react, answer. The office might pay lip service to work–life balance but that's all it was. Doubly so if this was your first big deal.

Fuck. She ground her teeth. Her mind had gone there again, to the place where sleep wasn't. Should she just get up, seize the opportunity of the quiet house, everyone else asleep till the first alarm went off at six? The presentation she must give in the morning meeting needed to be full and comprehensive. No one could leave the room at the end without knowing exactly what they had to do.

She rolled onto her side, folding the pillow over an ear to block out even the faintest sound of her husband's breathing. She was back to resentment now, jealousy's close cousin. His day involved no briefings, no key decisions, no colleagues' false smiles. Double maths in the morning, followed by coaching football in the afternoon, both of which he loved. Work–life balance right there!

She opened her eyes. Speaking of . . . today was the twenty-seventh day of the month. Which meant . . . date night. Why they'd ever settled on that, rather than a sensible last Saturday, she didn't know! No, she did: Terry, the statistician. The romantic. 'I met you on the twenty-seventh of May. We made love for the first time on the twenty-seventh of June. I married you on the twenty-seventh of November. So . . .'

So. Tonight there should be romance. A babysitter, Italian or Thai in Kentish Town. Love should be made. Except with her no doubt late because of work, the shitshow, and now exhausted from lack of sleep? They'd missed a few lately too. He'd be . . . expecting. And it wasn't that she didn't enjoy it still, didn't enjoy him. But with the day she had ahead?

He flipped over. An arm came across her. His chest pressed against her back. One leg ran the length of hers, and she thought, *Yeah but . . . it is the twenty-seventh* all day, *isn't it?*

'Hey,' she whispered.

Nothing.

She reached back, squeezed a bony hip. 'You awake?'

It took a few moments. 'Am now.' He sighed. 'What time is it?'

'Dunno. Five-thirty?'

'Fuck.' He snuggled in a little closer. 'Sleep more.'

'Yes. Or . . .'

It took less time. Perhaps because she'd accompanied the word with a nail dragged along his thigh. 'Are you . . . ?'

'I think I am.'

'Oh.' He reached around her, passed a palm over her right breast. He lifted weights; the skin was a little chafed. It scraped her – but not in a bad way.

Au contraire, she thought. 'And after all, it is the twenty-seventh.'

The hand, which had slipped from breast to belly, stopped. 'Date night?'

'Yes.'

'Does that mean tonight . . . ?'

'I may be late.'

'Ellerby!'

'I know. But remember that *Guardian* article? How we should be more spontaneous?' She took his hand, moved it further down. 'Isn't this spontaneous?'

'Oh, hello. You're very wet.'

'I know. Still, if you insist on waiting till late . . . I mean, very late tonight.'

He laughed. 'That might be a problem because, uh, you see?'

'Oh. I don't see. I don't need to.'

They'd tried things over the years, of course. More *Guardian* articles giving tips on spicing it up. Though the fact of the matter was, and though she wouldn't admit it to her sister, who planned her sex life like a military campaign, she simply liked the routine. The familiarity of his touches. The steady progression. The increasing pace. As he liked all the usual things that she did to him. All the way to their certain, mutual destination.

Which he reached first, as ever, and she held him deep within her when he did, loving his shudders, the vibrations they caused within her. She would be pretty close behind, as ever.

'Mama!'

'Baby? What's the matter?'

Terry was out and off in a moment. But Ellerby knew Mona wouldn't have noticed anything. She was short-sighted, and never put her glasses on till breakfast. Silhouetted in the doorway against the early sun coming down the hall, she was rubbing her eyes with one hand, the other clutching Tootoo, the seal, by one flipper. 'Bad dream,' she moaned.

'It's alright, my darling!' Terry was up, had his dressing gown around him in a second. 'Let's go the kitchen, get you some milk.'

''kay.' Mona shuffled away.

Terry turned, bent over the bed. 'Well, that's a pain. Tonight?'

'I hope so but—'

'Oh right. Work. Shit.' He took his lower lip between his teeth. 'I hate for you to go off without . . .' His gaze moved to her bedside table. 'Unless . . .'

She followed his gaze – and his thought. 'You wouldn't mind?'

'Mind?' He grinned. 'Not as long as you promise to tell me later. And, of course, be thinking of me.'

'Sure. Both.'

He bent lower, kissed her hard on the mouth. 'Coming, darlin',' he called to the voice down the hall.

It didn't take Ellerby long. Her sister had recommended the Rabbit and she'd been spot on – as was the device. Terry *was* in her thoughts for a bit. Though that actor off the Netflix crime series popped in too. As did Kendrick Lamar. As did, briefly, alarmingly, the new driver in the car pool.

Her family were all out the door at ten past, with their varied kisses as they passed her where she still sat over her cooling Earl Grey – son's embarrassed, daughter's clinging, the last the most lingering from Terry as he also gave her a wink to show he knew exactly why she was so flushed.

Ellerby showered, then dressed with care. As always there was a balance to be struck between ball-breaker boss and empathetic woman. Why did men never have to worry about that shit? There was also this summer's ceaseless heat to deal with. So a white shirt and suit were out – sweat stains would give away her nerves. She settled on a burgundy blouse, a dark cotton skirt cut to mid-calf. Practical shoes. There might be some walking involved.

She walked to Kentish Town Tube, waited for a Morden-via-Bank train so she just had to cross over to the next platform at Euston to get the Victoria line – the North Londoner's trick. Got off at Pimlico. Sometimes she'd stop at Tate Britain; she was a member. Look at the Turners, steady her mind for the day ahead. Not today.

By the time she walked through the door at 12 Millbank she was glad she'd chosen dark, this dragon of a summer still raking London in flame. Half an hour in her air-conditioned office, looking over her notes, cooled her down. So she was ready for what she had to do, as she went down the corridor to the meeting room at 9.29 a.m.

Her immediate superior, Siegfried, was at the door. Either he was nervous or his air-conditioning was broken because his bald pate glistened with sweat. Nervous, because his slight stutter was more pronounced. 'A w-w-word, Ellerby, if I may?'

'Yes?'

Her coolness didn't calm him. 'There's a n-newcomer inside. S-secondment from Six. J-j-joining the team.'

She frowned. 'Without me interviewing them?'

'N-no, indeed. Wrong phrasing. Sorry! Not joining. He's h-here to help?'

He. She glanced through the glass door. Her team were gathered at one end of the table. Conspicuously alone at the other end – her end – was a tall old man, with a shock of grey hair.

'I'll-I'll-I'll introduce you.'

Ellerby took a deep breath. 'That's alright, Siegfried. I'll introduce myself.'

She swept into the room. Murmured 'morning's greeted

her. She walked to the end where the man sat. Her first impression from outside was amplified closer to. With his pallid wrinkled skin, and that hair, he looked close to eighty. She extended a hand. 'Good morning. And you are?'

He looked at the hand, then rose slowly to his feet. He was very tall, at least six-six, she guessed. 'Maurice Wolfden,' he replied, shook her hand once sharply, began to lower himself.

The name rang a faint bell. 'Ah, that's mine, Mr Wolfden.'

She gestured to the seat and he grunted, moved around to a vacant chair.

Ellerby sat. 'You've introduced yourself to my team?'

She waved a hand at the man and two women – each one, she guessed, less than half his age.

'Not really,' he replied – drawled, it was that sort of voice, upper-class but of an older era, vowels extended, like a 1960s newscaster.

Well, if he hadn't she wouldn't. 'And you are here to . . . ?'

'Supervise.'

'Supervise?'

The colour she gave the word made him look at her a little more closely. 'Advise, then.' He coughed. 'I've had dealings in this sort of area before.'

Wolfden! She remembered now. A legend at Six from the icy depths of the Cold War, when there was one clear enemy to fight – the KGB. Predictably he was called the Wolf. The rumours were he was as vicious as one. Though as her son would tell her, having done a school project on them, wolves weren't really that vicious at all.

She considered. Make a fuss and certain people would say she was too rigid. Let him muscle in, and she'd lose respect among her team – and those above her. She'd worked too hard to earn that and, besides, this was her operation and she was fucked if she wasn't going to keep it that way.

'Well, Mr Wolfden, we look forward to your experience in all our dealings.'

He stared at her. There was something else in his rheumy eyes. Something she recognised. She'd seen the look before. Especially with men of a certain generation. Surprise. Some resentment.

Sometimes it felt to her like they'd never seen a black woman before.

'Have you been fully briefed, Mr Wolfden?'

'Fully? No. Got the gist. Fear of a rogue op at Legoland. Links to the Box. Appreciate a catch-up.' He coughed at the end of the sentence, as if asking for favours got stuck in his throat.

'Indeed.' Ellerby turned to the woman to her left. 'Jenny, since it all really began with your DIU, perhaps you'd begin?'

'DIU?'

She looked at Wolfden. 'Sorry, fairly new designation. Digital Intelligence Unit. Don't you have them at the Six?'

'I'm sure we do. Can't keep up with all the bloody acronyms.' He waved a hand. 'On, please.'

Jenny opened her laptop. The others did too and Sam, the young surveillance officer, shifted his so Wolfden could see. The older man pulled glasses from a front pocket, put them on, leant in.

'Slide one.' Jenny pressed a key, and a photo of a ship appeared on all their computers. 'The MVS *Thalia*. Sank last week in the Mediterranean, not far from Lampedusa,

Southern Italy – the island where so many refugees try to arrive, as it is the closest point of Europe to North Africa. Most of these, sadly, didn't make it. Two hundred dead. Fifteen survivors. One of whom was . . .'

She pressed again, and another photo came up, 'This man. Khadir Abdul Mohammed. Egyptian-born, Tunisian passport. He was half-drowned when they pulled him out. Had appeared on our radar before. People-smuggler, fairly low in the ranks. But we'd been tracking one of the phones he was known to use. Just before the ship went down, he used Signal to send a message to a number in Agrigento, Sicily – closest Italian landfall to Lampedusa. This was then re-routed to a phone in St Albans, Hertfordshire.'

She pressed a third time, and a copy of two pieces of paper came up. One gobbledygook, one in English. 'What you have here is the original message, and its decoding.' She bent, read. '"Not amused in Sicily."'

'Devil does that mean?'

'We didn't know either, Mr Wolfden.' Ellerby waved a hand. 'Until my colleague here called in some favours from her countrymen. Bella, would you?'

The hitherto silent woman sat straighter. 'No problem.' She was clearly Italian. 'A . . . friend in Immigration recognised Mr Mohammed from an international warrant. Pulled him aside, took him somewhere. *Talked* with him.' She gave 'talked' a strange emphasis unconnected with her accent. 'He's small fry, didn't know much. But he did reveal that his message was a kind of joke. Or perhaps more like a crossword puzzle clue. A-mused. A muse. Because Thalia—'

'Is the Greek Muse of comedy.' It was Wolfden who spoke

116

it. For the first time his eyes appeared energised. 'So he was warning someone here that the ship had sunk, eh?' On Bella's nod, he continued, 'And the number in St Albans?'

'A one-off phone. Not used before or since. However' – Ellerby leant over her computer – 'we traced where it was bought. Two weeks ago, in a motorway service station in Wiltshire. And they had CCTV.'

She clicked a key. A photo appeared on all their screens.

'But . . . but I know him! That's . . . that's whoozimiflip. It's—'

'His name is Sebastien Grant.'

'That's the chap!' Wolfden gave a low whistle. 'He's a senior covert intelligence officer at the 6.'

'Indeed he is.'

'Fucking idiot.' Wolfden stared at the photo a moment longer, then sat back. 'So we think that, what? That he organises refugee boats?'

'Amongst other things, yes. Several other things. Fingers in many pies.'

Ellerby picked up a biro, began clicking it open and closed, a ridiculous habit she'd realised annoyed others. She put the pen down. 'Jenny and her team investigated the *Thalia* and its connection to London. It was the centre of a web, the spokes radiating out beyond people-smuggling into, oh, Chinese fentanyl? Stolen antiquities from Syria? Heroin base from Afghanistan moved to, ah, somewhere in the former Yugoslavia? Up to eighteen months ago it all appeared to be random. Lots of different players. Then suddenly much of it seemed to be more, uh, coordinated. Which is when a single quite odd word kept popping up. More often than could be coincidental.' She turned. 'You say them, Bella. You're a much better linguist than me.'

The Italian dipped her head. 'The first that came was in Turkish: "*gölgeler*". In German, it's "*Schatten*". The Italian is "*ombre*". In Hebrew, of which there were quite a few mentions, it's "*tzlalim*". Then there's—'

'Yes, I think I get the point. What's it bloody mean?'

'Shadows.' Bella smiled. 'In all those languages it means "shadows", Mr Wolfden. Or, "the Shadows".'

'I see.' The Wolf leant back. 'And have you started to investigate Mr Grant and his dealings?'

'Some. We only drew all these ideas together in the last two days. A surveillance team was assigned just yesterday. Still, some interesting things were discovered. Sam?' She gestured to the other man there. 'Sam is on our surveillance team.'

'Looks like he's barely out of nappies,' muttered the Wolf.

The young man smiled. Unlike the others, he wasn't in a suit but was wearing a dirty, off-white T-shirt and ripped jeans. The trigger finger of his right hand was encased in a neoprene-and-aluminium cast. 'Sure.' He pressed the key to his computer. Six faces appeared on all their screens. Six men. Five of the shots appeared to have been taken against the same backdrop – white Corinthian columns.

'Sebastien Grant you already know. As you say, he's at Six. This gentleman is Nathan Greenberg. He's what they call an International Commodities trader – buys cheap, sells high. On a very big scale. The man next to him is Perry Lascelles. A rising diplomatic star, currently *chargé d'affaires* at our embassy in Ankara. This man is Sadiq Khan—'

'The Mayor of London?'

'No, sir. Apparently it's not an uncommon name. This one's a partner at Goldman Sachs. And this fellow' – he leant forward and tapped his screen – 'is Bernard Crouch. A colleague of ours here at Five.'

'Jesus. And they are all connected?'

'Indeed, sir. They all were at Magdalen College, Oxford together.'

'Where were these photos taken?'

'They met for lunch two days ago at the Athenaeum Club. It's on—'

'Pall Mall. I am a member myself.' Wolfden turned to Ellerby. 'And you think these men are, what, these Shadows chaps?'

'Well' – Ellerby smiled – 'if I was to draw together a team to make a great deal of money illegally from all the options we just mentioned, using intel gleaned from our secret services, I can't think of a better group to make it, then hide it.'

'Hmm.' Wolfden turned back to the screen. 'And this last fellow? He's not against the same backdrop, is he?'

'No.' Sam leant in. 'His name is Joseph Severin. And I took this photo of him yesterday almost at the same time that Sebastien Grant did.'

'How's that?'

'Grant was running his own op, tailing this Severin yesterday,' said Ellerby.

'Why? Who the hell is he?'

'No one.' Ellerby shrugged. 'He's a rental property owner and manager. Though he began life as an accountant. Wife, two kids, one more on the way. A normal life. He was arrested for smoking cannabis on Hampstead Heath when he was seventeen. That's the extent of his criminality. He wasn't even charged.' She tapped the screen. 'The only connection, apart from Grant following him, is that he goes to the same synagogue in North London as Mr Greenberg.'

'Interesting.' Wolfden sat back, steepled his fingers. 'How can I help?'

Ellerby took a little breath. This was the moment. She was damned if she was going to hand over the running of her operation to anyone. But Wolfden had power, could command resources. Resources they needed. Such as . . . 'Budget cuts mean we are fighting others for essentials, especially personnel. We'd like to be following all these people. So far we've got only Sam, and Aisha, who is still out in the field. Get us half a dozen bodies, sir' – she noticed Sam clench and unclench his hand low against his chest, indicating ten – 'or perhaps ten, so we can tail them all in shifts. Then we'd like to put taps on their phones—'

A grunt interrupted her. 'Fat chance there. Home Secretary has to approve. And he's a Magdalen man himself.' He stared at her for a long moment before nodding. 'However, I can get you a few chaps and chapesses from Six – since one of ours appears to be involved. Surveillance and intel.' He raised a hand against her murmured gratitude. 'Not that many, though. Four perhaps? So concentrate on Grant and his chums. This Severin is peripheral, I feel sure.' He stood. 'I'll go and make the calls.'

He moved to the door. He had his hand on the glass when Ellerby spoke. 'Just to be clear, sir. This is Five's op. My op.'

He looked back. The eyes that had appeared rheumy were

now clear, bright. 'Absolutely. Told you. Here to give advice.' He stared at them a moment then stepped back. 'And this is my first piece.'

He lowered himself from his great height to rest his palms on the table then looked at each of them in turn before he spoke. 'Never underestimate the intelligence of these men. Magdalen College does not graduate fools. The Athenaeum does not admit them to their number. To catch them is one thing. To successfully prosecute them will be something else again. To do so, you are not only going to have to be smarter than them, you are going to have to be luckier too.'

He stood straight. 'You'll hear back from me by noon. Good day.'

He swung out. Ellerby waited till the door settled before she looked again at her team. 'Right. You'll divvy up whoever he sends – but make it clear you are in charge. Digital for you, Jen. Covert for you, Bella. And you lead the surveillance team, Sam.'

'Me?' The young man appeared startled. 'I thought they'd bring in—'

'You. This stays here in the Box. But count me in if you are short. For this one, I'd like to be back out in the field.'

'Absolutely.' Sam gazed at the photos on his computer. 'But Sebastien Grant is mine.' He tapped the face with his splinted finger. 'I owe him.'

'Oh, and Sam? I think Mr Wolfden is wrong. Severin? He *is* important.'

'Gotcha.'

They departed for their respective cubbies. Ellerby, though, had an office. When she was behind her desk, she looked at the framed photo of her husband and kids. 'Sorry, darlings,' she murmured, 'looks like I will be late home tonight, after all.'

She said it with a smile.

CHAPTER 12

Friday 27th July 2018

Joe was trying to concentrate on what Vicky was saying. He truly was. But it was as if her voice was a badly tuned radio, or a mobile in an area with poor coverage. His wife, her meaning, kept drifting in and out.

Except it wasn't her. It was him. Him and his phone, on silent.

It was in his trouser pocket. It vibrated now with a text message. He got texts all the time. It could be Oliver or Stacey from the office, his daughter, his mate Saul to give him the time and venue for the five-a-side, which he was going to need to cancel anyway. It needn't be her. It was unlikely to be her. Still, he didn't pull it out to check.

Because what if it was her?

He swallowed, tried to listen. Vicky deserved his full attention. She wasn't talking about the bat mitzvah for once. Was being very funny actually, about another mother in the tots and Pilates class, a newcomer who didn't get the North London boho-chic aesthetic, had come dressed in full Lululemon.

He smiled now at his wife, his lovely, funny wife. Her humour had been the first thing that had attracted him when he'd returned from California, for a brief stopover en route back to Thailand – or so he'd thought at the time. But Vicky, who he'd met at the welcome-home party Saul had thrown for him, had greeted him with: 'Oh, so *this* is the wandering Jew?' as soon as they were introduced, had teased him in a way he'd forgotten, having spent the last two years around seldom ironic Americans. The sort of banter only the English did, and those of his North London tribe did especially well. She was the type of girl he'd known all his life, the type who'd fuelled most of his adolescent fantasies. He even discovered he'd lost his virginity to her cousin, Becca – a fact that provoked even more mockery.

Vicky had travelled herself, had studied art in Italy, lived in New York. She seemed different. Different certainly from shiksa Cassidy, who'd recently taken out his heart and stomped all over it. Yet in the end, Vicky had turned out to be not so very different after all. Yet neither had he, for all his posturing, his woven traveller's bracelets, his Buddhist practice. For now here they were, in the same Finchley kitchen where he'd spent his childhood, in his parents' home, sold to him at a discount – not much of one, because his dad was funding his retirement. The only difference being that the kitchen was remodelled. Unlike his life.

He focused, listened, laughed as she went off on another one, this time about his sister, Nomi, her terrible clothes sense, her terrible choice in men. But when his phone vibrated again, he couldn't help himself. He pulled it from his pocket, looked at it. And it *was* her, at last.

So he said, 'Oh, sorry, love, crisis at the office.' Lying for the fourth time that week, twice more than he'd lied in their fifteen years of marriage. Lying in a way he thought Vicky must surely guess the lie, though she just waved at him, and picked up her own phone.

He went upstairs to his home office, shut the door. Studied the screen again, tried to mine meaning from the simple words.

But of course, Mr Severin. Tequila? LOL. Just tell me where and when. X

He held the phone to his chin, stared out onto the close. In the pollarded sycamore, a blackbird sang. He hadn't really listened to a blackbird for a long time, remembered now that when he came back from his travels in Israel, India, South-East Asia, America, he'd realised that a blackbird, all English birdsong really, was one of the main things he'd missed. He listened now to the wild swoops, trills and runs and he thought, *You fucking idiot, Joe. You fool.*

He'd sent her three texts since 'the incident of the back', as he'd come to think of it, the day before. The first, last night, falsely casual and cool:

Hey, thanks for the shot.

The second, an hour later, apologetic.

I hope I didn't put you in a difficult position. Sorry if so.

She'd replied to neither, which was a kinda relief because he'd thought, *Good, good, that's good, it was just a moment, me unused to hash after all the years, nothing important.* But at other moments, especially waking in the night, the memory tore at him, literally made him sweat. He wrote and erased three more messages. Until the one he'd sent at midnight, left his bed and a lightly snoring Vicky to send from the kitchen. Simple, unambiguous.

Drink?

He re-read her message now as if deciphering hieroglyphs. He could hear the way she'd called him *Mr Severin*, in that teasing Home Counties voice. *But of course?* Did she think a meeting was the natural follow up to 'the incident'? Had she been expecting it, this offer? *Tequila?* Was that an offer of more? Of more than just the drink? Then she wrote *LOL*.

He'd read once that the former prime minister, David Cameron – that wanker who'd fucked the country with his referendum! – had texted that to some newspaper editor but had thought it meant 'lots of love' not 'laugh out loud'. So was Lottie laughing about the incident? Dismissing it? Had it meant nothing to her, then? When it had meant so much to him?

Fool, he thought again. But *Just tell me where and when?* That was unambiguous, surely? She'd meet him, she was happy for them to meet. Keen even? Maybe. He'd only find out when they did.

Then there was the *X*. Their first kiss. They hadn't when he left the flat, not even cheeks. Their only physical contact had been those two fierce handshakes, grabbing her shoulders to pull her off the balcony after she'd shouted at that traffic warden – and the moment his lips touched the cleft of her back when he sucked tequila from it.

126

He sat down in his office chair. Flopped into it, his knees suddenly soft. Saw, not a blackbird in a tree, didn't hear its wild song – saw light brown liquid in that tanned valley, the golden hairs in it dampened now, heard her slight gasp as the tequila filled her there, and a second gasp, this one with a giggle in it when his lips tickled her as he bent and drew the liquor slowly into his mouth.

When was the last time he'd shot tequila? That dinner party that had got a little out of hand at Saul's a year before. This was nothing like that. That had been about the drink. This was about . . .

What? *What?* He put the heels of his palms into his eyes, rubbed. He was a fool, he was a fucking idiot and he could do no other than he did – pick up his phone and text her back.

Union Tavern. Pub garden on canal, Westbourne Park. Noon? Shall I pick you up?

He couldn't hesitate or he'd be lost. He hit send, then dropped the phone onto his desk as if it had burnt him. He sat, listened to the blackbirds, two of them now, one a distance away. A vocal turf war.

Thirty seconds later, his phone moved.

See you there.

He laid the phone down, carefully this time. She was meeting him there. 'Fool,' he muttered, but through a smile.

He looked at his computer clock. 9.13. He had time to do some work. Shadowy work.

He kept their books in his safe – even though the bloke who'd recruited him had said not to have them at home. The

127

numbers of the combination were his children and Vicky's birthdays, which was probably also dumb.

He pulled them out now, laid them side by side on his desk. Two plain ledgers. He opened one. His father had insisted he learn old-school, handwritten double entry. He'd baulked at the time, thinking it so dated. He'd even briefly worked in the field, for a printing firm, before he took off travelling. He was glad now.

He'd only had one meeting, with a man named Sebastien, along with Nate, the man who'd introduced them, the one he barely knew from the North London synagogue. It had been a slightly unnerving encounter, since the younger Englishman already knew quite a lot about him and probed for more detail. Unnerving and yet . . . exciting too, in a way he hadn't been excited since his years on the road. Little detail came in return – a secret government organisation within the intelligence services; operations on behalf of Her Majesty that needed to be kept quiet and certainly needed to be kept off any drives, hard or flash.

At the end of the meeting, accepted, Sebastien had given him these ledgers, some information already inked in, debit and credit. There were a multitude of accounts to be reconciled: a capital account, a premises account, various bank accounts with capital letters that did not indicate country but he'd figured those out because of the exchange rates. They had accounts in Luxembourg, Kazakhstan, Russia, Japan, several in the Bahamas. He'd figured out some of the transactions too, what they had to be. Regular payments from suppliers into those countries' accounts, many quite large, in the €100,000 to €200,000 range. Governments, businesses, individuals, he'd guessed, greasing British intelligence's wheels.

In return for . . . ? He didn't need to know. He'd kept up as much as anyone did, with the Wiki revelations, Snowden. Had felt stirrings of outrage, his old, more Kibbutzim self. Swiftly suppressed when some of the entries he made were payments to himself. Cash to the 'Star of David', which seemed a little too obvious. But the £5,000 cash in figures beside it, the first of many envelopes he collected along with more receipts and deposits from a PO box in Camden Town, made his concerns go away. This was patriotic work, he'd been assured. Snowden could go hang. Would, of course, if the Yanks could get him out of Russia.

There were monthly outgoings to different accounts, mainly the Bahamian ones. There was one that puzzled him – semi-regular payments of £20,000 to £30,000, into a Swiss bank under the heading 'Venom'. An informant? Perhaps. One of the things this Sebastien had told him was not to spend too much time considering anything but the figures themselves.

But of course he had. At first it had seemed like a game, to decode the entries that looked like investments. It hadn't taken long, the names simply anagrams with a few letters removed. He'd found Phoebus Logistics, Lynn Apparel, Manchester, Bulawayo Prospecting and Mining P/L. The ones he, like the Shadows, now invested in. He felt a little guilty doing it. But the extra money he was making, especially in the mining company, took away the guilt.

Time for work. He'd collected two envelopes – one held his cash, the other a single printed sheet – typed, he could tell – with new debits and credits. The first sat in his home safe now, and he'd use its contents to pay off various suppliers for the bat mitzvah galloping closer, just a day away. The sheet was open before him, so he pulled out his father's old electric calculator, opened the ledgers and did his sums.

Absorbed, he only grunted a farewell when Vicky called up that she was heading out. Glanced at his clock, realising that she was collecting Reuben from his tots' playgroup. If she stuck to form, she'd be meeting other mums at a coffee bar in Totteridge. She'd made a whole new group of friends, all younger than her, in their mid–late twenties most of them, with their firstborns. She loved it, playing the wise old bird. And was a source of wonder with her belly swelling again at forty-two.

It was ten-thirty. She'd be back by eleven-thirty-ish, unless she decided to go on for lunch. But he'd not risk seeing her before his . . . rendezvous? Assignation? He didn't want to lie to her again about where he was going. He knew he wasn't very good at it.

Knowing how he could get lost in numbers, he set an alarm on his iPhone for 11.10 and picked up a pen.

The Union Tavern had changed since he was a student at the Central London Poly, shared a flat nearby and used to come there. Then it had been kind of ramshackle and threadbare, a jukebox, a pool table, darts, out to attract the local estate residents of Westbourne Park. Now it had, like so many places, gone full gastro. In place of burgers, pizzas, chips you could get braised sea bass, lamb tagine, quinoa salad. They still did good beers – probably better than they used to, since craft beer was so in. Yet now they also had a decent wine list, and Joe had a bottle of Pouilly-Fuissé in an ice bucket before him on the wooden table. Two glasses.

The back garden hadn't changed much, though. New wooden tables, nicer umbrellas, some open, some folded for those who wanted the summer sun to reach them. He tended to avoid the sun these days, after all the warnings, unlike in his wandering youth when he'd rub himself with olive oil and bake. He'd been mistaken for Indian before, when he was down there. Sephardic genes, he knew. The table he'd chosen was full in it, against the back wall, and for once he'd kept the umbrella furled, enjoyed the sun on his face. It felt . . . right.

He looked at his phone. 12.15. She was late again, of course she was, he knew it was going to be something to expect. He'd got there early, ten to, had sat nursing the white wine – nursing memories too.

He'd brought Cassidy here, just once, when they were on their way to California from Thailand and he wanted to introduce her to his mates, and his parents. The former had been envious ('She could be in *Baywatch*,' was his friend Dave's envious comment). His parents had been appalled by the goy goddess and barely disguised it. He'd been delighted, of course. This would show them.

Cassidy had been scathing about this, his old haunt. 'It's got a water view,' he'd protested, waving at the Grand Union Canal.

'It's got a view of a sewer,' she'd responded. 'Look, cue the fucking rat!'

He looked at the water now, not seeing it, seeing other water for a moment – Big Sur, waves surging in, her walking away from him, from them. It was so strange. He'd barely thought of Cassidy in years. Since meeting this Lottie, he'd thought of her every day, several times. Remembered moments.

'Penny for them, Mr Severin?'

She was there, backlit by the sun; he was dazzled, couldn't see her face. He raised a hand, then she moved her head to block the light. She had her lower lip in her teeth, and her eyes were smiling.

He stood, slightly awkwardly with the back of the bench against his knees. He didn't know what to do, but she leant in and kissed him quickly, both cheeks, before slipping to the other side of the table. Dropping a capacious carpet bag onto it, she sat, her back to the canal. She wasn't wearing the blouse and faux fur any more, just a simple pale blue summer dress, buttons up the front, old-school.

'Wine?' he offered, taking the bottle by the neck.

'Please. Ooh, looks nice. What's the occasion?'

He poured. 'Felt like the right choice. For a day like this.'

'I like the way you think.' She raised the glass, tipping it towards him. 'To days like these,' she toasted.

They clinked, she drank off half the glass, he sipped. She reached into her bag, pulled out her fixings for a cigarette. 'You mind?'

'Oh, no, carry on. But it's not one of the, uh . . .'

'Naw, mate. Straight nicotine. Though in Westbourne Park I doubt anyone would object.' She grinned at him. 'You want I roll you one?'

The instant refusal stalled on his lips. There was something in her eyes, a touch of challenge. Besides this place of memories, of student days, pints, fags. 'I'd love it.'

'Good.' She set to. When she raised a filter, he shook his head. She finished one, kept it before her while she finished a second, handed his over. Her Zippo was already on the table and he beat her to it, flicked the lid, then the wheel. Bending to the flame, she put her hand on his.

The shock as she touched him. Like the moment he'd laid his lips on her back, as if one of them had walked across thick carpet. He flinched slightly but she kept his hand, drew the flame.

'Thanks.' She pulled away, let smoke go out of her mouth, sucked it up her nostrils, like she'd done on the balcony three days before. He drew on his, felt the nicotine rush immediately. God, he'd missed that. Only realising in the moment how much.

'And what is a day like this, Mr Severin? For you?'

'Is there any way I can persuade you to call me Joe? "Mr Severin" makes me feel like your, I don't know, like your art teacher or something.'

'Maybe. You'll have to earn it, though.'

'How would I do that?'

'Oh, I'm sure I'll think of something.' She looked away then, discontinuing the challenge, sucking at her ciggie, then exhaled hard at the next table, where a woman glared at her, before turning back and continuing, 'Actually, I already have. I'll call you Joe if I like your explanation.'

He swallowed. 'My explanation of what?'

'Oh, I wonder?' She clicked her tongue, flicking it against her top teeth, eyes to the sky. Then she looked down, at him. 'The tequila, Mr Severin. Its unusual method of consumption. Something you do often?'

He shook his head. 'Never before.'

'Never? Not a fetish, then? Like rubber. Or sheep.'

He laughed. 'Do I look like a sheep shagger?'

'I'm not sure there is a look, is there?' She smiled. 'You don't look like a man who would suck tequila from a stranger's back either. And yet, there we were.'

'Well, you don't look like someone who would allow it to be sucked.'

'Don't I? That's interesting. Because I've been wondering ever since if I did. If it was, like a, ah, a vibe I gave off.'

'No. Nothing like that.' He hesitated, covered it with a sip of wine. 'It's just that I . . . saw it. You. Your back. That part.'

'When?'

'When you came to Tufnell Park to check out of the flat. I walked into the room just as' – it came out in a rush now, confession – 'just as you were reaching up into the chimney. Your blouse had ridden up. That's when I saw your—'

He broke off. She pulled a thread of tobacco off her tongue, rubbed it between her fingers. 'I see. And are you normally a back man?'

'I told you. Never before. It was just so,' he sighed, 'perfect.'

'Perfect, huh?' She smiled. 'Well, I've been complimented on various parts of me in my life. Never that.'

'Is that why you . . .'

'Agreed? Naw, not really. I think I agreed because you asked so nicely. And because you so clearly wanted it. Needed it.' She picked up her glass, swirled the wine in it. 'It felt nice to be needed again . . . Joe.' She added his name with a smile, taking a sip. Then the smile left, her brow creased, those wild eyebrows drew together, nearly joining. 'What now, though,

Joe? Now we've established you're not a pervert. Or much of
one anyway. What now?'

'You don't beat about the bush, do you?' He shook his
head. 'I thought we'd meet, have a drink, you know, get to
know each other a little, talk—'

'Why?' She leant forward, fixed him with those eyes.
He'd been so much in the memory of her back, he'd almost
forgotten her eyes, their iridescence. 'What's your limit? Your
line?'

'Line, as in . . . ?'

'Not pick-up. Not coke. Line as in limit. A threshold. One
to cross – or not. Where do you draw your line?'

'With you?'

'Yes and no. More with yourself.' Her cigarette had gone
out and she picked up the Zippo, conjured flame. 'Is my back
it? The sum of your ambitions? That your line?'

He'd thought of more of her, of course he had. Woken hot
in the night with an erection and her scent in his nostrils.
Thought of moving from her back, to her belly, to her breasts,
to . . . but he couldn't say that. Because mostly he'd thought
this. 'Look, I'm married,' he blurted.

'I know. Your ring.'

'Oh yes.' He looked at the thick gold band. 'Should I have
taken it off?'

'Not if you had any hope. Of anything.' She blew smoke
at him, her eyes narrow. 'I hate lies, Mr Severin. Hate 'em
more than anything. I've had enough of them in my life.'

'I thought I was Joe now?'

'You may be again. If you promise never to lie to me. And
tell me your lines.'

'OK.' He laid his cold cigarette in the ashtray, took a deep breath. 'I don't know, longer term. For now, I . . . I just want to . . . touch. Does that sound pathetic? I'm not seeking an . . . an affair. I don't want . . . sex. I mean, I do, but I can't. I'm married. Happily married. Christ, I said that to you before, didn't I? Fuck!' He picked up his wine, drained off his glass. 'That's pathetic. I'm pathetic.'

'No, you're not, you're—' She held up her empty glass to him and he lifted the bottle from the ice, poured for them both. 'Touch is fine. We all need to be touched, I think. It's been a while since a man just—'

She broke off, stared above him, and he saw someone in her eyes, hated him whoever he was, the one who'd put the sadness there. Was simultaneously glad of him too. Especially when she took his non-pouring hand, and tugged it. 'You seem quite far away over there. Why don't you come and sit by me . . . Joe?'

He stood and she thought, *What the fuck? What's going on 'ere?*

It was one curse of her nature, to overanalyse. Seek root causes. Break things down into causative chunks. With Patrick it had been simple. He was gorgeous and pure lust had dictated her actions; love had only crept in later when she'd got to know him, his vulnerabilities, his tenderness, his self-doubts. Lust was still there now; she couldn't deny it. She had desired him even when he was entwined with that Russian beauty the night before, that Sonya. But he was no longer vulnerable, and tenderness was a rare and fleeting thing with him these days. Success had done for it, together with its trappings, money, cocaine.

As Joe sat beside her, she thought, *Do I fancy him?* She'd thought him cute the other day, when he'd first proposed that she occupy his flat in W11. He was still, but how? The thick black hair was short cropped, with flecks of grey at his temples. There was stubble that she suspected would escalate fast into a beard. He had heavy lids over his eyes, hoods which he pulled down to conceal – or shot up to reveal his change of moods, which had happened often in their brief encounters, while he wrestled with his desires, and his conscience. The eyes themselves were a light brown, milk chocolate to Patrick's mocha.

He's more than cute, she thought, as he slid in, as he pushed himself to the corner, as he grabbed his wine glass and gulped. *He's a handsome man. A man arrived, not a youth on the cusp. But he doesn't see it, or he's forgotten it. Remembering hasn't been necessary in the life he lives now. What did he say? He was 'happily married'? And yet here he was. Needing.*

While Patrick? He needed nothing from her now. Patrick knew his own attractiveness so clearly – yet he still never passed a mirror without checking up on it.

Lottie looked at Joe. He looked back, waiting. *He doesn't know what to do next*, she thought, *doesn't know what he wants, where his 'lines' are, though he says he does. Which means I can set them for both of us.*

The hairs on her forearms rose with a sudden excitement. Covering, she reached for the stub of her cigarette again. Lit, inhaled, then swiftly jabbed the butt down just as her fingers burnt. She rubbed it out, pushing the embers around, then slid over to him, turning to fold her back against his chest. He stiffened, pressing out, resisting for a moment. Then suddenly gave and she sank into him, felt him where they touched – his chest pressed into her back, her right arm laid along his thigh. 'Is this alright?' she asked.

'Yes,' he replied, after a second. 'It's . . . nice.'

She looked around the busy patio. 'You're not worried about the people?'

He only left it a moment. 'What people?'

She laughed, and he did too. 'Oh, Mr Severin.'

'Joe.'

'Oh, Joe.' She stretched for her wine glass, snagged it, took a sip. 'Tell me about yourself.'

'Tell you what?'

'Oh, I dunno. Like, everything.'

She felt his hand then, his left hand, she hadn't noticed before but she must have pinned it against the bench back. He lifted it away, paused a moment, then replaced it, curling around her ribcage, to rest under the curve of her left breast. The edge of his finger was in her crease there, where her breast hung pendulous against the bone. She felt him tense, then relax. It reminded her of the feeling of his lips against her spine. Tension, then release.

Leaving his hand there, he began to tell her everything.

CHAPTER 13

Mr Phipps was in the pool.

He didn't like them. He never had. The chemicals in the water, countering the piss in the water. So much of it, at this time in the morning especially, what with all the kiddies. Over-stimulated, screaming under-sixes. Beyond the chlorine he could swear he could smell the urine.

Meaghan loved it, though. Whooshing out now from the end of the flume, shrieking as loud as any. Louder than most. Making a big splash. 'Again!' she cried, as she surfaced. 'Again!'

Phipps glanced up at the pool clock. How slowly the big hand had moved. But it was at 9.58 now. Two more minutes before the switch, the little kiddies leaving, the general public coming in. On another scorcher of a day, he was sure a mob was massing behind the closed doors.

'Last one, Megs,' he told her.

She pouted, but swam to the side. Pretty good form for a five-year-old. But he'd had her in a pool since she was one and a half. He wanted her confident in the water from the get-go.

Not like her dad.

He watched her hoist herself out, run to the line that had already formed for the flume. The kids didn't need the tannoyed voice to tell them they had only one minute left.

He looked around at the other parents, all waiting like him, waist deep in water. Mostly mums, the odd lone wolf dad like himself. He recognised some from the previous times. Regulars, like him, for Friday mornings at Leyton Leisure Centre.

A woman smiled at him. Janine, divorcée, mid-forties. Fit. They'd chatted a few times as they towelled their tots off. She'd admired his tattoos. He'd only told her his surname, though. Didn't like his Christian name, saved that for later, after. Pillow talk. He was pretty sure it was on but he hadn't dealt with Paula yet and he had made a rule for himself: end one completely before beginning the next. Other way was just too bloody messy.

Still, he smiled back. *Leave that one in the bank*, he thought, as the kids whooshed down, and mums began to shepherd them towards the ladders.

He shivered, not because he was cold.

He'd had to be in pools, of course. And rivers, lakes. The sea. To get into the Paras he'd had to swim; it was one of the tests. He was told afterwards that he now held the record for the slowest ever recruit to complete the quarter mile. That they'd only let him in because he was in the top five in every other area, and number one in a couple. It was why he'd never even thought of the Marines. Too much fucking water.

He knew why, of course. Or at least thought he did.

After the incident in Afghanistan that had ended his army

career, when he was on charges, they'd made him talk to a psychiatrist and the bloke, instead of being a wanker, was actually quite insightful. Ex-soldier himself, officer but he'd seen some action, knew the challenges. Phipps had always thought that going over his past was a complete fucking waste of time – *I mean, I wasn't breast-fed, so what?* What did that mean now? Affect his life now, how? But Spencer was old-school, not very touchy-feely. Simply believed that it all came from childhood. So he probed that. Phipps had almost no memories from before he was seven. Spencer had said that was significant. Indicated abuse, he told Phipps on his second session.

'What, some Cub master put his hand down my pants?' he'd asked.

'Not necessarily sexual abuse,' the reply had come. The man had tapped his head. 'Psychological.'

Phipps looked up from the water surface where he'd found himself staring. Meaghan had disappeared up the stairs. One more minute and he could get out of the water.

'Get out of the water!'

He could hear him, his old man, that morning on the beach at Herne Bay. See him, sitting on the shingle on his tatty pink towel, new mates around him, drawn by his plastic bag filled with Carlsberg Special Brew. The more of them went down, the less attention he paid to his five-year-old son in the sea, trying to show him his tricks. 'Look at me, Dad! Look at me!' His dad had told him to get out five minutes before. But Phipps had just perfected a handstand and his dad hadn't seen it yet.

'Look at me, Dad!' he'd shouted, then dived. But somehow

he'd got a little further out, and he couldn't place his hands on the sand to execute the handstand, but he didn't want to give up this chance with his dad looking, and so he went deeper to find it and didn't have the air when a wave came so he swallowed some water, didn't know which way was up, which was bad until it wasn't. Until it was quite pleasant. Which ended when hands grabbed him, dragged him to the shore, up it, knees scraped raw on the shingle. His dad was shouting at him then, even more when he puked on the pink towel. Which drew a cuff and all.

Spencer had called that a 'buried memory'. Told him it was good to have it up and, oh, the tissues are just by your elbow.

Phipps still wasn't so sure. Again, he'd wondered why he needed the memory at all. What use was it? Any more use than the story of his dad's funeral two years later, dead in the Scrubs one year into a six-stretch for handling stolen goods? The open casket? The face looking younger than when he went in? Uncle Frank had told him that was the embalming fluid. He could barely remember his mum, she died when he was three, so that was that. Or did any of the stories of the foster parents, some shit, some OK, help clarify his life? Getting out as soon as he could did for sure. Into the army at sixteen. The Middlesex Regiment, then the Paras.

Staying out of water whenever possible.

A loud buzzer broke his reverie. Simultaneously, doors opened, admitting people and a lot of excited voices. Mostly teenage boys, jostling. Around him, parents were gathering their kids, moving away.

'You missed it, Daddy! You missed my dive!'

Meaghan was standing in front of him, fists on hips, brow

scrunched. Looking the spit of her mum, Sharon, in one of her frequent furies. 'No, no, love, I saw it. It was great. It—'

'Liar!' The brow cleared. 'Doesn't matter! One more. One more!'

'No! Megs, we 'ave to—'

She was gone. That fast front crawl away. Too fast for him. 'Megs!' He went after, walking through the water. But by the time he got to the side wall, she'd already reached the flume. No queue there now, but boys coming up fast behind. She disappeared from sight, lads' legs following her up.

Fuck! OK. One more time.

He moved back to the spot just back from where she'd land. He mustn't miss it this time; it would put her in a strop for the rest of their visit. She could bear a grudge, Meaghan. Just like her mum.

She came. But this time, she didn't come alone. Two bodies shot out from the plastic mouth of the tunnel, too fast to see much, other than the pink of her swimsuit, vivid against a white male chest.

She popped up. Her anger was gone. Replaced by fear.

'Daddy!' she wailed, and swam forward, into his arms.

He lifted her. 'Megs? What is it?'

'He . . . he . . .'

She pointed back. Just come up from the water was a lad, maybe seventeen. Dark hair, close-cropped. Some acne. Crooked teeth revealed in a wide grin. Aimed at them.

Phipps went cold. 'He what, love?'

The words struggled out between sobs. 'He . . . he . . . he wouldn't let me . . . I said, no. Said . . . I wanted . . . alone. He . . . jumped on . . .'

'Fuckin' loved it, she did.' The boy's accent was local, harsh. 'Give 'er a treat, I did. Bitta speed.'

Meaghan shoved her head into her father's neck. Buried her sobs there. Phipps looked at the lad. 'You need to apologise to my daughter,' he said.

The grin vanished. 'You got a problem . . . *old man*?'

He stood taller now, straighter. He only gave Phipps an inch or so. The acne from his face was also on his shoulders, which were broad enough. Amidst the blemishes, a tattooed skull and crossbones intertwined with West Ham's double hammers. Beneath those, initials: ICF.

Phipps knew what they stood for. Before he'd found the army, he'd got into a little trouble, running with 'the Herd', a gang from the Gunners. They'd clashed with the ICF, the Inter City Firm. West Ham hooligans, named because they'd take the trains to matches and fights.

Two other bodies hit the water, making a big splash. Two heads surfaced, bodies following. Bigger, fat to the still-staring boy's lean. Same tattoos. 'Magic,' said one. 'Again, Stan, or the 'igh board?'

'In a moment,' replied Stan, not taking his eyes from Phipps's. 'Once this old cunt moves on.'

The other boy looked from his friend to Phipps. Gave a smile. There was something knowing in it. ''ave we got another problem, Stanley?'

'Nah, don't think so.' He waded a step closer. 'Or do we? Cunt?'

He spat the last word. Phipps broke the stare, looked around. The pool had filled up rapidly. The older crowd pouring in, mums and under-sixes still leaving. One had just

144

passed them – Janine, holding her daughter, Natasha, under her belly as the kid kicked, swam.

'Janine, love,' he called, and she stopped. 'Mind taking Megs here? Just for a second?'

The woman looked back at the four men. She frowned, then nodded. 'Of course, Mr Phipps. Of course.'

Phipps took a few steps towards her, unwinding Meaghan's fierce grip. 'It's alright, darlin',' he murmured in her ear. 'Dad'll be right along.'

'Come on, sweets.' Janine took Meaghan's hand. 'Tash 'ere would love to race ya.'

His daughter responded as he knew she would. Sorrow gone, into the challenge. 'Let's go,' she yelled, and the two kids struck out for the pool's end.

He knew he should just follow. Walk away. With all he had on this week, it would be the sensible thing to do. But his daughter had told this man 'no', and he hadn't listened.

So he turned back. All three of them were grinning now. 'You need to mind your manners, son,' he murmured.

'You fuckin' WHAT?' Stan yelled, loud enough to get people's heads turning. But Phipps could not pay attention to them, as he had already moved, attempting to close the gap as fast as he could. There were ways of dealing with superior odds. Some he'd learnt in the Paras; some he'd learnt on the streets.

The kid may have been a tosser, but he had balls – and two mates to back him up. Stan came at him fast too, as fast as the water allowed each of them. But he started to swing from just a little too far away so Phipps was able to sway his chin back, let the fist pass him, grab the wrist in his right hand, put his left against the kid's elbow, and twist him fast down, shoving his face into the water, as pure an aikido move as you could get. It would have worked too, but for the other lads, moving quickly despite their bulk and though Phipps could use the body he held to fend one off, he couldn't use it on both. The one clear on his left lunged, fingers reaching for Phipps's face, a gouging move. To save his eyes, he had to break his hold, step back.

Stan came up spluttering. 'You fuck!' he screamed, and came again.

On dry land, he could have manoeuvred. Knew tricks and techniques that these lads – scrappers, used to fights in playgrounds and bars, on the terraces at away games – didn't. But Phipps was out of his element, in an element he hated.

Stan had also learnt from his first mistake. When he came this time he came low, letting his bigger friends go high. Phipps got one punch into the cheek of one of them, before they were on him and he was under.

He'd taken a breath. It didn't seem to last him very long. But he couldn't have breathed anyway as there was an arm wrapped round his throat, squeezing hard. Other hands on his arms, his shoulders. Combined weight pushing him deeper down. His face hit the tiled floor, only buoyancy stopping it being a blow. His air soon gone, he suddenly wondered something.

Should I do a handstand? Look at me, Dad. Look at . . .

His hands had slipped off the limbs he'd tried to grip in his turn. They floated above him, untethered. But then he felt his fingers brush first cloth, then flesh. Something pendulous. Something that wobbled.

Knowing it was the last thing he might ever do, he grabbed and then squeezed, very hard, someone's dangling balls.

Far away he heard a shout. Not only one grip was released, two were. Enough.

Phipps twisted sharply against the remaining grip, felt it loosen. Managing to swing his feet down, he placed them on the floor, bent at the knees, and shot himself up and out of the water, fist leading. Breaching like a whale.

It wasn't aimed but it still connected. Wasn't sure what he struck, what with the water in his eyes and his desperate need for air. Bone, though, not just flesh, and another cry came. He threw himself backwards, away, giving himself room for the next round.

Which would not come now. His ears had cleared along with his eyes and there was so much noise. Lifeguards' whistles shrieking, their shouts rising. Kids and mums screaming. He focused on the enemy before him, but it was Stan on whom his lucky blow had landed, Stan with a hand covering his nose, failing to stop the blood pumping between his fingers, the sight of which seemed to have cooled the two bigger boys' fire. One of whom, anyway, had both hands under the water and was whimpering in pain

'Oi! Out! Out, all of you! Out now!'

It was an older man in a jacket and tie doing the yelling, two twenty-somethings in singlets and shorts beside him with whistles in their mouths.

Everyone obeyed, Phipps following tendrils of red to the poolside. He hoisted himself out, and the older man, his cheeks flushed red with fury, ordered him to 'sit and wait there' while all attention moved to the moaning bigger boy, and bleeding Stanley, now staining hand towels in claret. A crowd had gathered, as they will. After thirty seconds, when all eyes were elsewhere, Phipps rose and pushed his way through.

Janine and her charges had only just made the poolside before the eruption. Meaghan was staring at her father, eyes wide. 'Daddy. You . . . you—'

'Come on, Megs. Let's go.' He turned. 'Thank you, Janine.'

She wouldn't meet his eyes. 'It's OK,' she mumbled, turning away. 'This way, Tash.'

She walked off, without looking back. *That's blown Paula's replacement*, he thought. Shame. Still, Leyton Leisure Centre was in his rear-view mirror now anyway. But there had to be other flumes in North London, surely.

He suspected the police may have been called. So he got Megs changed fast, pulling his own clothes onto a body still damp. As they were walking out of the main entrance a squad car pulled in, disgorging coppers, one man, one woman, who ran into the building.

Meaghan would barely talk on the drive, despite his cajoling. Except to say she wanted to go home, which meant Muswell Hill, not his gaff for lunch as planned. Insisted.

When they reached Coniston Road, Sharon was out in the scrap of a front garden, watering some plants. Their daughter ran up the front steps, and threw herself into her mum's legs.

'What's up, sweetheart? What's happened?' She bent. 'Sorry, my love, I can't hear you.'

She shook her head, still uncomprehending, looked a question at Phipps, walking up the drive with Meaghan's swim bag. He shrugged. There was nothing he could say, no explanation that wouldn't reinforce what his ex already felt she knew about him. So he put the bag down and said, 'I'll be by to get her on Monday.'

'What time?'

He thought about the standby call he'd had from the Shadows. He had a gig, place and time and target yet to be determined. 'I'll let you know.'

'Please do that. We have plans.'

He knelt, spoke. 'Bye, Megs.'

She didn't turn her head. Muttered 'bye' into her mum's thighs.

It was all he was going to get. He went back to his car, got in, pulled out.

Spencer, he thought, as he turned onto Colney Hatch Lane, heading for the North Circ. Didn't his psychiatrist say that everything was laid down by the time you were seven? Would this morning play out for Meaghan somewhere down the years? In what way? Her father defending her? Is that how she'd remember it? Instead of leaving his kid to drown?

CHAPTER 14

Saturday 28th July 2018

As soon as his daughter began to sing, Joe began to cry.

He'd been on the edge of tears all morning. A blackbird's call, his wife's fingers on his cheek, his son's giggles as he watched his cartoons, Rachel coming down the stairs in her bat mitzvah dress, each had brought him again and again to the brink. Now, hearing her voice, her clear, beautiful voice ringing with the haftorah verses . . . he went over it.

Vicky took his hand, squeezed it and he glanced at her, saw tears in her eyes too. But his were not like hers, and her touch did not comfort him. She cried only for pride, for love. And though those were in him, too, he knew that most of his tears were for himself. For this life he saw before him, hearing it in his daughter's voice, feeling it in his gathered family and friends, in his community in the synagogue. His life here, spiralling out of control.

He squeezed Vicky's hand, then took his own back, to thrust the heel into his sockets, wipe away the salt tracks on his face, rub at a jaw inexpertly shaved that morning, feeling the rough patches his distraction had left him with, noticing a trace of red on a fingertip where he pulled off a scab. He looked up, away from his daughter because the sight of her would finish him, across to his parents on the other front bench. His mum's attention was fixed on her granddaughter. His father was looking at him, smiling at him, that ironic smile he always had. *You see*, Morrie was saying with it, *they break your heart, your kids. Now you know what we went through with you.*

He looked behind his parents. Two of his brothers there, their wives beside them, the third, Israel, in the land he was named for, his own wife about to give birth to their fifth and so unable to travel, his sister Nomi and her latest partner, David. Behind them, cousins, family, back through friends, some of whom he'd known since primary school, whose bar mitzvahs and bat mitzvahs he'd attended, as they'd come to his, in this same synagogue. Behind the friends, others he knew less well, the congregation. All were staring forward, entranced by the beauty of Rachel's voice. He took pride from their looks, for the efforts his daughter had put in, though much came naturally, for she was the star of Channing School's drama department, had always craved the spotlight.

He felt his tears recede. *It will be alright*, he thought. *I'll sort it. I'll end it. I'll . . .*

Then he saw him, the one face other than his father's not turned forward – because a man he barely knew was staring directly at him. A man who was part of the chaos.

Nate. Nathan. He didn't know much more about him than that. Younger than him by about ten years, recent worshipper at Finchley Reform. Who had approached him six months before and asked him how good he was at old-school accountancy.

The man now gesturing outside with his eyes.

Joe responded with a widening of his own, flicking them to the bimah upon which his daughter still triumphantly sang.

The reply came in a shrug. *Of course. Afterwards.*

Joe turned back, looked at Rachel, didn't truly see her, though it wasn't his tears that prevented him now. It was fear.

The Shadows were back in touch.

'Joe, you take Mum, Aunt Silvie and Esther. Go straight to Mum's. Caterers will already be there but the magicians and disco people will arrive soon after that. I'll bring—'

He didn't need to know the rest, now he had his instructions. He couldn't focus on anything else anyway. He was seeking among the shifting, greeting, smiling crowd for that less familiar face. His attention had been on that through all the handshakes and back claps that followed the ceremony. 'I'll see you later,' he'd kept saying. 'Catch up at the party.'

Then he spotted him. Nate was standing on the other side of the street, beyond the gates, leaning against a BMW, smoking. Removing himself from his brother Dan's embrace – 'I'll see you later, yeah?' – he walked down the long driveway, let himself out through the iron gate, crossed the road.

'Mazeltov.' Nate tipped his head to the synagogue. 'Your daughter's got a lovely voice.'

'Thanks.' Joe raised his hand, anticipating the congratulatory handshake. But one of Nate's hands was busy with his cigarette, and the other was in his pocket.

He drew it out now. It held a packet of Rothmans. 'Want one?' he said.

Fifteen years of instant refusals came. But so did a flash – of Lottie, lying naked next to him in the Portobello bedroom, after the pub patio, after they'd tried again, failed again, and her reaching for her tobacco pouch. 'Nothing that can't be solved by nicotine, I've found,' she'd said, beginning to roll. 'You just need to chill, bra.'

'Sure,' Joe said now. Nate offered the packet, he extracted one, Nate held out his own half-smoked fag, Joe took it, sucked the glow, handed the butt back. He looked over his shoulder to the crowds still milling around the synagogue's entrance, and kept the cigarette low.

'Don't worry, they won't catch you,' Nate said. 'Your family's distracted.'

'Yeah. Uh, so am I. I haven't got long. I should . . .' He dragged deep, felt that buzz, the instant high that regular smokers lost. 'Is there something . . . ?'

'There is.' Nate had taken his cigarette back between his thumb and forefinger, pinching it. He raised it, took a drag, not deep, letting smoke slip out to rise over his face. Then his voice altered entirely. 'You've been a fucking idiot.'

'What?' Joe was shocked. The change in the man, from congratulatory fellow Jew to accuser, was instant, not just in the voice. His whole face was contorted with rage. 'What do you mean?'

'When I approached you about doing this little job for me, you were grateful for the cash. Bills to pay, you said.' He glanced briefly at the crowd outside the synagogue's entrance. 'But that wasn't enough for you, was it? No, you had to get greedy.'

'I don't know what you're talking ab—'

'Cut the shit. You know very well.' He dropped the half-smoked Rothmans, stamped on it, rubbing hard. 'You were paid to do the books. Tot up the figures, that's it. Be handsomely paid for the work too. You were not meant to take the details and use them to make your own investments.'

It was another stinking hot day – and Joe suddenly felt as cold as he'd done on any winter's one. How had they found out? What had he done? 'I haven't. I . . . really, what are you . . . ?'

'I said, cut the shit. I know. *We* know!' He stepped closer, dropped his voice even lower. 'Are the books safe?'

'Of course.'

'At your home, are they?'

The lie came fast, easy. 'No.' He *had* been a fucking idiot. But he suddenly realised that, with the type of people he was dealing with, the books might be the only leverage he had. 'I can get them for you. Anytime you like. I've been busy so they are not quite up to date,' he lied again, and licked his lips. 'There's not a problem, is there?'

'There may be.' Nate stared at him. 'How long will it take you to bring them up to date?'

'A day's work?' He swallowed. 'I can't probably today, uh—' He glanced back to the synagogue's entrance, where someone was laughing loudly. His father.

Nate followed his look. 'Monday. Midday. I'll text you a rendezvous. Oh, and here. I thought of not giving you this, since you've been so fucking stupid. But I suspect you need it. Consider it incentive for speedy work.' He reached into his suit, brought out a plain brown envelope, the kind Joe had collected before from the PO box.

'Thanks.' Joe took it, shoved it into his own jacket pocket.

He felt the weight of it there, even though fifteen £100 notes didn't weigh much. Instead of the thrill he usually got, though, it made him uneasy now. 'Listen, if I give you the completed books, everything will be OK, yeah?'

'Everything? No. But guess what?' He reached over and put his hand on the back of Joe's neck, drawing him near, before whispering in his ear. 'If you keep everything kosher, everything, mind, from this moment on . . .' he paused a moment, then continued, 'I may be able to keep you alive.' He pulled back, and looked at him. 'How's that for incentive?'

He released his grip, stepped away, as Joe staggered. Suddenly, Nate was smiling again. 'Mazel tov once more,' he said. 'Enjoy the party.' He reached into his pocket, and the BMW's door clicked.

Joe stepped away, walked unsteadily back across the street. Turned to watch Nate drive off.

He felt faint. He took a deep drag of his cigarette. It helped; he remembered now how much it used to help him focus.

What had Nate said? 'I may just be able to keep you alive'?

He heard his wife's voice, rising from the hum, calling him. He turned to look at her, saw her with Reuben in her arms. Saw his daughter, laughing in a group of her friends. If he was under threat, so were they. He had to protect them, even before himself.

But he'd been right, in his first thought, when Nate had confronted him: the books were all he had in this mess. They needed them. While he had them, they needed him anyway. He had to get them out of his house, though, away from his family, fast.

There was only one place he could keep them.

He pulled out his phone, dialled her number. It went to voicemail. He spoke. 'Please message me as soon as you get this. I need to see you.'

He didn't say his name. His name suddenly seemed a dangerous thing to him. But she would know it was him.

Lottie would know it was him.

Smiley faces glowed at each teenager's ear; rainbow lights alternated with white strobe, shifting through the thin filaments of the plastic chandeliers dangling from the ceiling like a glowing, inverted forest. The only noises came from the click of one DJ's fingernails as she worked the keyboard of her computer, manipulating the music that played in two of the channels – came also from the soft fall of vinyl onto rubber as the other DJ hoisted records then placed the needle onto the turntable in front of him for the third channel. Behind Joe, back in the house, the loudest sounds of all came from the parents of those who swayed before him, in the clink of ice in their gin and tonics, their whiskies, in the rumble of voices marvelling at technology that allowed them to hear themselves at a party, and not have to listen to what passed for music with kids these days.

The speeches had been spoken, the food inhaled, the magicians had conjured and vanished, the jugglers had put away their clubs and their chainsaws. It was the time of the silent disco, Rachel's request. Joe had worried that the result would trigger an epileptic fit in the dancers, or some prolonged flashback in him, which he'd been warned might be the consequence of all the acid he'd taken during his own clubbing youth. But he had to risk it, because standing there was better than standing inside making conversation, fielding questions or, worse, having Vicky on his arm being all lovey-dovey and teary and proud of what they'd made, their child, now, this day, a woman. And he'd have to listen, and smile and pretend and lie, while most of his attention was on his pocket, the phone there, waiting for it to buzz with the message he needed: that Lottie was back at the flat in Notting Hill, and that he could come round immediately.

He pulled it out, checked 'Settings' for the fourth time. 'Vibrate on Ring' was still highlighted. He wouldn't miss her. He couldn't miss her.

The books were in his car. They mustn't stay there. Keeping them at a flat he owned probably wasn't ideal either but it would do as a standby until he could think of an alternative. The best would be to return them to Nate on Monday and say, 'Sorry, and thanks, but can't do more.' Not that they'd want him to, it seemed.

He'd miss the money. But the fifteen hundred in his pocket would finish off paying for most of the bat mitzvah and the stress of earning it, collecting it, laundering it, the stress of the figures themselves with their codes and their amounts going all over the world for God knows what to God knows whom but he could guess . . . no, it was time to end the relationship. He'd already sold all his shares, and closed his account, deleting the trading app. How had they found out about that?

Who were these people?

The faint tinkle of keyboards bled out of the headphones he'd slipped down to his shoulders. He recognised it, unlike the execrable grime, rap and house that had been in all three channels before. It was Journey's 'Don't Stop Believin' '. He placed the headphones over his ears.

The kids who were listening to that track were telling others. More were switching channels to it. Why thirteen-year-olds were into a song that was already getting old when he was young beat him. But they all seemed to know it and their movements changed from frantic to smoother, contrast to those still stuck in rap. Many were now lifting their arms, reaching up into the forest of lights.

It was actually quite a good song, he recalled now. He let the singer's voice carry him, watched his beautiful daughter raise her hands too, and then his mind jumped back.

'End the relationship.' It wasn't only the Shadows he should part from. He should end the madness of him and Lottie. It hadn't gone too far, after all. What had she talked about at the Union Tavern? The lines? He hadn't crossed any of the big ones, after all. Hadn't broken the Ten Commandments. He'd coveted her, but she wasn't a neighbour's wife. And as for the adultery . . .

He flushed, tried to focus on the music, failed – and he was back for a moment in that bedroom in Notting Hill, the girl beside him, gorgeous, naked, willing . . . and he just couldn't. Wanted to, couldn't, no matter what they tried. The guilt was too much, the fear. It was a relief now, of course. He hadn't committed adultery. The commandments said nothing about tequila on a back. He could live with that. He would end it with Lottie. He'd let her stay there the month he'd promised and then move her on. He'd never see her again.

And then his pocket buzzed. He pulled his phone out.

I'm back. Only for a couple of hours. Come round.

Raising his phone to his lips, he watched the silent teenagers dance.

Joe pulled up outside the flat. He'd been nervous on the drive over, kept looking out for suspicious vehicles – as if he had any chance of spotting a professional tail. Still, he looked around again now. At a road sweeper, a big man with an eastern European face, emptying a large pan into a bin bag. At that same traffic warden, still on the prowl, who scowled at him when he placed the one-hour visitor's parking on the dashboard. At a homeless man outside the bakery café, young or old he couldn't tell, kneeling on the pavement, his forehead to the ground, his arms stretched out before him, his hands clutching a polystyrene cup, its edges frayed, as if chewed. At a dozen other people going about their business under the hot sun. Any one of whom could be a spy for all he could tell.

Bloody idiot, he thought, chewing at his lower lip. *Just get on with it.*

Still, he sat there a few minutes longer looking for things he wouldn't recognise if he saw them, before he finally grunted, got out, grabbed the hemp Waitrose bag from the boot, the books inside it. As he passed the prostrated man, he reached into his pocket for coins. All he had were pounds. He dropped two in but the beggar didn't react, didn't move at all.

Joe went up the steps and pressed the buzzer marked 'C'. As he waited he thought of Vicky, her puzzlement as he told her he had to leave the party for a bit – a tenant with lost keys, all his staff away. Was it because he felt so guilty that he thought she must know he was lying? She didn't reveal that, only her annoyance. 'Make it quick,' her final words.

He would. Drop the books, ask Lottie to look after them for two days. Then tell her that this was his last visit. She'd deal with Oliver from now on. He needed to keep away. He was a family man.

The buzzer buzzed, no voice. He let himself in and went into the lift.

Lottie was standing at the flat door, wearing a sleeveless slip of a primrose dress, one brown arm running up the door's edge. 'Mr Severin.' That voice of hers, the slight husk in it, mockery tinged, made his breath come a little shorter. But he took a deeper one, made his own voice solid.

'Hello. Sorry about this. Needed—'

'No apologies necessary. Do come in,' she replied, stepping aside for him to pass her. As he did, he inhaled, caught her scent, almost the same as when he'd first met her – tobacco, leather from her car, mainly that tanning oil, coconut in it.

It was as if she read his mind as she followed him into the living room. 'Sorry I took a while to get back to you. Been sunbathing in the park. Always turn the phone off.'

'Oh. No worries. I—'

'You look nice,' she interrupted, was looking him up and down. 'Wait! The fancy suit? Isn't it your daughter's thingy today? Already finished?'

'Bat mitzvah. Yeah. No, still going on. I have to, uh, get back.'

She raised one wild eyebrow. 'But you took a break to pop around and replenish my tequila?'

'Eh?'

She nodded to his Waitrose bag.

He lifted it a little. 'This? No, I need to . . . need to leave something here. If that's, uh, OK.'

'Of course it is. Your flat, right?' She gestured to the kitchen. 'Coffee? Beer? Me?'

She'd flopped her hair over one eye on the last word, taken her lower lip between her teeth. She was playing with him, he knew it, and he couldn't play back. 'Sorry, no, got to go. I just need to—'

He'd lifted the bag again. Now he was there, he didn't know where to put it. There was no safe in the flat. And he didn't know her, not really. What if she was to look inside? The figures wouldn't mean anything but . . . would she call someone? Why would she? Who the fuck was she?

'Are you alright?' She'd taken a step nearer, concern replacing the tease on her face. 'You look ill.'

'Oh. No, I'm fine. Maybe a glass of water?'

'Still or sparkling?' The tease back, but she didn't wait for a reply, just went into the kitchen. He heard the tap run as he dropped onto the sofa, bag at his feet. *Get it together, you fucking idiot*, he told himself.

She returned, held out the glass. He took it as she said, 'So if not tequila, what's in the bag?'

'Books,' he replied. 'Not to read. Ledgers. I've been doing some accountancy work, on the side. For, uh, this company.'

'And you want to leave them here?' Her brow furrowed. 'Why not at your office?' Her brow cleared. 'Mr Severin! Is all this not quite kosher?'

The ready lie he'd prepared slipped away. Kosher? It brought it back, all of it. The party he was missing, the synagogue, teenagers gyrating silently, Nate stamping out his cigarette.

161

'Could I have one of your cigarettes please?' he blurted.

'Of course. Special or—?'

'Just . . . tobacco. Please.'

The fixings were on the coffee table. She took her time; her focused movements calmed him as they had before – and he realised, suddenly, quite clearly, that he was calm with her in a way that he wasn't with anyone else now. It wasn't because he'd touched her. The sex had been almost non-existent, and such as there was, a failure. But she had this air to her, this Lottie, as if the world about her was . . . just there, supporting her, something to ease through, not confront. While he felt like he was running into a succession of walls, she was just . . . a breeze passing between hardnesses.

She lit the roll-up, dragged on it, passed it over. He was a smoker again, fuck, fourteen years since Rachel was coming. Well, his daughter was a woman today, and he inhaled again, gratefully.

Lottie rose, then flopped beside him, close to him. 'I think you need to tell me what's going on, Joe.'

He knew he couldn't tell her too much. It could be contagious, what he was up to, and he didn't want her infected. But she'd need to know a little. In case . . .

In case. It was the first time he'd thought that. Everything had been easy before. No 'in case', nothing to go wrong. Until it all went wrong.

He told her his half-truths. Tapped the bag when referring to its contents. Books, to keep the figures out of the cloud. A friend's company, tax evasion, nothing too sinister.

'"Sticking it to the man"? Isn't that what you used to say in your hippie days?'

'Hippie? How old do you think I am?'

'Dunno. Fifty?'

'I'm forty-two! Christ!'

'Ah, but you have an older air, Mr Severin. Especially today. The cares of the world?' She leant down and tapped the bag as he had done. 'And they're all in here, aren't they?'

He hadn't thought of opening the bag. Stash it. Leave. But this Lottie, her ease, her scent, the world out there. *In case.*

'Look, there's something else. I . . . I don't know how to . . . I don't know if I can explain but—' He sighed, and opened the hemp bag.

She saw the plastic bag from Tesco straight away. Her eyes went wide. 'My letters!'

'Yes.'

'You told me they were lost.'

'I know.'

'Did you just find them?'

'No. I've had them all along. Since that first day, when you came to the flat.'

'What? Then why did you—?' Her eyes widened. 'Wait a minute! Have you read them?'

'Every one.' She took a breath to voice the outrage on her face and he rushed on. 'I had to. I became obsessed. As soon as I saw your back. Then I read your words. Your wonderful, angry words. I couldn't help myself. It was like . . .' He looked out the window, into the hot blue sky. 'Like someone had opened a door onto a world I used to know. The one where I . . . where I used to live. A world I . . . I suddenly really missed.'

He looked at her again, tried to read her expression. The

anger was still there, but something else warred with it. Warred and won, and then she spoke.

'The real Joe, eh? That one I've glimpsed, who comes and goes?' She shook her head. 'I'm still pissed off . . .'

'. . . I'm so sorry!'

'And yet' – she smiled – 'you know the problem with "letters never sent", which a couple of those are? If they are never read, what's the point of them? What's the fucking point?' She stood, reached down a hand. 'Come on.'

'What? Where to?'

'The bedroom.'

'Lottie. I—'

'No. Come on. The real Joe's here. About time.' She took the fag, dead now, from his fingers, dropped it into the ashtray without letting him go, then tugged. 'I think we need to take advantage of his visit, don't you?'

It was so different, their lovemaking. The other time, after the canal-side pub, the fear in him, the guilt, had held him back. The lies too, and since these were mostly gone, at least to her, so were his restraints. He didn't rush, didn't feel the need, despite that world out there, its demands. And Lottie was different too. The teaser had left, the role she'd taken on, the tough young seductress with her roll-ups, her hashish, her bravado, had left too. She opened to him, they opened to each other, touch was unplanned, positions unthought. All simply unfolded.

Afterwards they lay there for a while, her sprawled across him as if she would sink every part of herself into him – her toes into his shins, her hip bone into his, her belly sunk into his, her breasts into his chest, her head tucked under his chin. He took strands of her hair and ran his fingers through the knots, untangling them through a long, easy silence. She left only to get her tobacco, sat up to roll one and he watched her do it, fascinated again by the precision. Done, she flopped beside him again, placed an ashtray on his chest. They smoked, passing the fag back and forth, once more in that content silence. *Words*, he thought, *will just draw me back* – like the words on the phone that had buzzed twice in his suit pocket, that he knew without having to read.

Where are you? Get back here!

And yet, for the first time in a long time, he was in no rush.

It was Lottie who broke it. Sitting up, stubbing the butt out, pressure over his heart. 'Listen, sorry, but I do have to get on. Someone's coming over.'

Another pressure, this time within. 'Your boyfriend?'

'I'm not sure that's what he is.' She rolled off the bed, reached down for her cotton underwear, sat back to pull them on. 'But I'm sure it's over. Just need to tell him.'

'Really?'

He couldn't help his smile. Which she saw, and her voice went back to what it had been, London-edged. 'Wassat to you, mate?'

'I . . . I don't know. I—'

She stepped off the bed. 'Well, you and I need to talk. But not now. You have . . . things to do, right?' She sniffed. 'Wow! Smells like people have been having sex in here. Shocking!' She twanged her panties. 'Best these come off again.' She reached down, ran her fingers through his thick chest hair, then picked up the ashtray and placed it on the side table. 'Shower?'

There was a clock on the bedside table. It read 4 p.m. Fuck. 'I . . . don't think I can.'

She grinned. 'I think you should, brah. I assume you're going back to your daughter's party? Probably best you don't walk in smelling like a dead boar.' She raised her hand and slapped his chest now. 'I won't distract you. Go!'

He knew words would screw it all up. Whatever they'd had, had passed. But as he rinsed quickly in the walk-in shower, he wondered if it could pass his way again – and what might be the cost.

He towelled, dressed, went out, found her on the balcony in a silk kimono, smoking of course, staring down at the street. 'That yours?' she asked, pointing down.

He looked. The traffic warden was just slapping a ticket on his windscreen. 'Fuck,' he exclaimed.

'So that's the price of love!' Lottie said. 'Sixty pounds to the Royal Borough of Kensington and Chelsea.'

She laughed and after a moment, he did too. 'Listen, there's something else,' he said, and put the envelope of money into her hand.

'Woss this?'

'Fifteen hundred pounds.'

'Crikey, Mr Severin, I'm not that kind of girl.' She giggled. 'And even if I was, I don't think I'd fetch that much.'

'Can you keep it for me too? Just till Monday?'

She turned to him, serious now. 'Tell me, Joe. Just how much trouble are you in?'

'Not much,' he blurted, too quickly. He took a breath.

'Not too much, anyway. And it will be sorted by Monday, honest.'

'OK.' She took the envelope and threw it onto the coffee table. 'Don't worry. I'll tuck it away somewhere safe. And that bag.' She nodded to it on the coffee table.

'Good. And I'll see you . . . Monday.'

'OK. You'll have to call first.'

He'd lifted his jacket, paused. 'Playing hard to get?'

'I've been got, haven't I?' She shrugged. 'You're not the only one with complications, Mr Severin.' Maybe it was something on his face but she smiled, relented. 'But it would be good to see you. Joe.'

He slipped on his jacket. His shirt was instantly damp again from the heat and clung to him, almost as close as she had. He turned at the door. 'Monday too, we can, uh, talk. About us.'

'There's an us?' She dropped her hair over an eye. 'Thrilling.'

He wanted her again, suddenly, badly, right then, right there. But his phone buzzed in his pocket, and his two lives pulled him, the new and the old. 'See you,' he called, as he walked to the door.

When he reached it, she spoke. 'I'll be expecting the real Joe, mind.'

He smiled as he left.

CHAPTER 15

Sunday 29th July 2018

Sonya had made a mistake.

She knew it immediately, as soon as the second handcuff locked. Saw it in the john's eyes, how they changed with the click.

She'd always trusted her instincts. They had kept her safe, long before she became an escort, before the army even. From her childhood, her father. Unpredictable when sober, he was doubly so when drunk, when his restraints dissolved and the meanness came. The professor of music vanished; the kid who'd starved on the streets of Leningrad during the siege returned. He had only survived the war because when an opportunity came to take what he wanted, he had. Later, in the army, she'd thought her father had been her first and best training course. Unarmed combat. Read the enemy, discover his weakness, use it against him. A few early losses to her father had taught her most of what she'd needed to survive.

Desperation, she thought – as she watched the man's eyes change, narrow, and he went to the end of the bed, to his briefcase on the fold-out stand there, and she pulled against the cuffs, the two pairs that held both her hands against the single wrought-iron bedpost, hoping that one of them might somehow have failed to fully lock or that the post was weak within the frame.

Neither was true.

Desperation had made her careless. His offer had been high – £1,500, and not even for the whole night. A quarter of what she still needed to make for Marusya's operation, which had to happen faster now, her daughter's pain greater, her movements slower, the drugs less effective – according to Georgiy, her husband, on his own cold edge, deciding whether to tumble off it into the warmth of his addiction. So she hadn't tried to read this man deeper, had accepted the softness in his eyes as genuine. He'd also said she'd been recommended to him by Bernard, the one who mourned his wife and mostly only wanted to hold her in the night. She hadn't tried to contact him, to confirm this Eric. You didn't contact clients; they contacted you.

She watched him pull a large, black rubber dildo from his case, complete with straps to attach it around his pelvis. Which he proceeded to do, dropping the white dressing gown from his shoulders, wrapping the belts around his waist, below a small, bulging pot belly, which was streaked in curly, greying hairs.

She tried to keep her voice level, to keep the fear from it, to even make it playful. 'What are you planning, Eric?'

He started, almost as if he'd forgotten she was there. Paused in his strapping, his eyes piggy-small, angry. 'Planning, Eric?' he echoed, mimicking her accent. 'Eric's planning to fuck you up the arse, you fucking whore.'

She didn't mind the abuse. Most of her clients were nice, polite Englishmen. Some needed to be angry with her during the act, perhaps to justify it. Though afterwards they nearly always apologised, and tipped her.

Not this one, she knew, she could see.

They'd agreed a safe word. She tried it. 'Bluebell,' she said.

He only laughed again and came nearer. He banged the dildo into her face.

'Though of course Eric's not my real name. My name's Sebastien.' He smirked. 'Ring any bells? Did dear Bernard never mention me to you?'

It rang no bells. Bernard talked of no one except his dead wife. It did not matter anyway now; there was only one way this was going. Still, she had to try. 'You will stop this!' she yelled at him. 'Free me now or I will call the police.'

'Police?' He shook his head, halting at the edge of the bed, the erect rubber rising toward the ceiling close to her face. 'A Russian whore calls the police on a . . . well-known government servant. She claims assault; he claims blackmail. I wonder who they'll believe? I wonder if your work permit, if you have one, permits whoring? I wonder if you want to risk that, and lose the chance to make the money you need for your brat's operation.' Her eyes must have shown her surprise because he added, his grin widening, 'Oh yes, Bernard told me. Wept as he told me about you, how you hold him in the night, help him forget poor dead Eloise for a while.' He laughed. 'And I clucked, and poured him another whisky, and thought, *Silly cunt, she's a whore, a fucking Russian whore.* But that was before I knew you were something more than that. Or rather, in addition to that. Which is what you are going to tell me about now. All about how you met Bernard and your . . . intentions for him. All about Lottie Henshaw and Patrick Ogulu too. I assume you fucked them both last Thursday, hmm?' When she did not reply, he smiled. 'Though I suppose the first question to answer is this: do I bugger you first, Sonya Ivenetza, and you answer me afterwards, or vice versa? Shall I toss a coin?'

She still didn't say anything. He shrugged. 'Aren't you the silent type? Learn that in the army, did you?' Her eyes widened a little and he smiled. 'Oh yes, I know a lot about you, Miss Ivenetza. Ex-forces, and' – he laughed – 'I discovered this simply extraordinary fact – that you were once the fastest Kalashnikov stripper in the whole Russian Army! Gifted with your hands, eh? Hence my precaution.' He nodded at the cuffs. 'But what I would really like to know first is if you are current KGB – sorry, SVR now, isn't it? Hmm? Any thoughts?' He jammed the dildo again into her face. 'No?' He shrugged. 'Very well, you know what? I've made up my mind. As to the order of things. So why don't you turn around? I've got something for you.'

She didn't move. 'I'll scream.'

'I certainly hope so.'

'The hotel staff will come.'

'What, from ten floors below?' He shook his head. 'And there are no other guests nearby. There are two suites on this floor and I've booked them both. But just in case—'

He went back to the drawers, picked up the remote, turned on the TV. Flicked through the film offerings to the guide, found a classical music station on FM, turned the volume way up.

Schubert filled the room. Her father's favourite. He dropped the remote back onto the console. 'Scream over that, why don't you?' he yelled coming closer.

She opened her mouth to speak, to try, and he hit her, backhanded across her face. She wrenched hard on the cuffs, twisting her wrists, felt a greater pain than on her cheek in the right one. She was frightened now, her breath coming faster, too fast. *Breathe*, she thought. *Think*. This was more than just a bad client. This man, his knowledge of her? But that she would consider later. There was one thing for now, and she would only get one chance at it. For it to work, though, she needed him angry.

So Sonya began to laugh.

It stopped him, even as he bent to grab a fistful of her silk teddy. 'What's so fucking funny?' he snarled.

'You. You are so fucking funny. What are you, a British spy? You think you're James Bond or something? But you can't get it up any more, so you have to put on this thing. No women will fuck you now, because you can't, you are so useless. So you blame them, blame me. You should blame only yourself, you weakling. You coward.'

He stood upright, his face working in fury. Took the step back, the one she needed. 'You ugly—' he began.

Making her toes rigid as a board, she swung her leg hard round and kicked him in the side of the nose. His head snapped around and he went down fast, the bonus for her when his head hit the bedside table, spilling it. Lamp, alarm radio, his phone, water glass all fell to the floor around him.

He groaned, writhed. She knew she only had a little time. If she'd obeyed him, turned to face the iron post where her hands were, she'd never have been able to get any weight into a kick, or twist her hips to the other side of the bed, knowing that the only force would come from their uncurling. She'd been lucky, with the table, but luck would last only until he came to. She could guess what would happen if he did and she was still attached to the bedpost.

She'd seen him drop the keys to the cuffs into his dressing gown pocket. That lay where he'd left it at the end of the bed beside his briefcase. She wriggled her body down the bed, biting her lip against the pain at her wrist. At full stretch . . . she still could not quite reach the dressing gown with her toes. She wriggled back up, levered herself off the bed till she was lying on the floor. This Sebastien was about a foot away from her. He groaned now, his eyelids fluttering. His nose was bleeding.

Her arms stretched high above her, she reached, and just managed to curl her toes into the linen robe, held it, pulled it, lost it, got it back. Slowly, she inched it towards her, then used both her feet to lift it onto the bed. Hoisting herself back up, she probed the pockets, using her big toe and the next one to try and snag the keys. She had them twice, dropped them twice. Third time she had a proper grip. Curling herself round, blessing the yoga she did to keep in shape, she lifted her legs over her head and lowered the keys onto her outstretched fingers.

The angle was hard, and her fingers numb. The two cuffs helped, where one would have been impossible. She could twist her wrists, the right one hurting a lot when she did. Through the pain she turned it, got the first key wrong, just as Sebastien rolled onto his back and started to cough. The second key turned, she had one hand free, and then she swiftly released her second, just as the man sat up, leant towards her. 'What the fuck?' he gasped, stretching his own left hand out.

She folded the serrated claws over his wrist, snapped them shut, then stepped away from him off the other side of the bed.

He was fully awake now, blowing blood out of his nostrils, like a stabbed bull in a Spanish arena. His fury made him inarticulate, and he wasted time trying to jerk his hand free from the bedpost. By the time he realised that was impossible, she was half dressed.

'Let me go!' he bellowed, loud over the music, Mozart now. 'I'll kill you! I'll fucking have your visa revoked, you bitch.'

She finished dressing, then came close fast. He flinched, raised his free hand to ward her off. She seized it, twisted it against the grain to a yelp, lifted it behind him and snapped on the other cuff. He was on the floor where the table had been, his arms bent awkwardly above him.

She got out her phone. The best angle was from the ground so she knelt and snapped some photos, the first couple catching his furious face just above the priapic dildo. Even when he turned away for the second, his identity was clear.

'Look!' He sniffed blood, his voice now conciliatory, though still loud to top the music. 'I am sorry. I made a mistake. Let me get you some money. More money.'

More? Something in the way he said it. She went and looked in the envelope beneath the TV. Fifties only on the ends, tens between. Maybe three hundred quid there.

She looked at him. He shrugged. 'I'll get you more. I'll—'

She raised a hand and he quieted. 'If you contact me. If any immigration people come after me, those photos go to the press. You understand?'

'Yes. Yes, of course. Look, I—'

She tucked the envelope into her handbag, picked up her coat. She closed the door on his yells, which were lost to the Mozart anyway. As she left, she hung the 'Do Not Disturb' sign on the handle.

In the hotel lobby, she raised a hand to cover her bruised cheek as she passed reception. A desk clerk studied her. But what had Sebastien said, about this hotel's discretion? They would not disturb him for quite a while. The sign would prevent them. And they were probably used to moaning. Perhaps later tomorrow morning the maid might knock, or someone would check into the next-door suite and complain about the noise.

The hotel was near Portland Place and she walked to that busy road then up it, north. It was 8.30 p.m., there were lots of people about, and all the black cabs were occupied. She pulled her phone out, pressed a speed-dial number. It was Sunday night but there was a chance. It rang three times before the pick-up.

'Tsarina.' His joke.

'You free?'

'I can be. Where are you?'

She found the street signs on the corner, told him.

'You wanna wait in a bar near there or something?'

She fingered her cheek. 'No.'

'Fifteen minutes,' he said, and hung up.

Sonya leant against a railing and watched the traffic. Two

young men, drunk, tried to talk to her but she pulled out her phone, dialled, and they walked on. She hung up, and resisted the urge to sit down on the steps of the building nearby. She was suddenly tired, near overwhelmingly so. Her face and wrist hurt, and both were swelling. She didn't know which was worse. She needed her prettiness to attract men in bars. And she needed two good hands for what they'd want her to do to them. *Jesus, please, not now*, she thought, *not now.*

She got her phone out again, and pulled up FaceTime, her finger hovering over the name. But it was eleven-thirty in Moscow; Marusya should be asleep and if she wasn't . . . she knew she'd cry if she saw her daughter, and she didn't want that. While Georgiy? If he was drinking, which he would do once Marusya was in bed, it would be bad. If he was doing something worse . . .

She dropped the phone back into her bag. It was a warm night but still she shivered. *What am I going to do?* she thought. *Who was he? Why did he know about me?*

She waited, trying not to think, heard a car horn, a familiar one, looked up to see the four rings of the Audi on the grille of the black car. She walked quickly to it, using her unhurt left hand to awkwardly open the pavement-side rear door. She flung her bag and coat in, and dropped into the seat, reaching across herself to pull the door closed.

'Are you alright, Tsarina?'

She looked up at Tadeusz's reflected eyes in the mirror. His concern was in them as well as in his voice. 'Yes,' she replied. 'No. Just drive.'

'Where to, Tsarina?'

'I don't know. Around. I have to think.'

He turned around to look at her. Jerked his chin at the damage. 'Some fucker did this to you?'

'Some fucker, yeah.'

His eyes narrowed. 'Near here? You want I should—'

'No. Do you have any ice?'

'In the console. There are cloths too.'

The Audi was an A8L. Tadeusz leased it for his chauffeur work. It was luxurious and behind the door that clicked open she found two crystal decanters, a small ice bucket and some serviettes. She took two, wrapped cubes in each, laid one against her wrist on her thigh. Before she raised the second to her cheek, she poured a tot from one of the decanters, took a deep swallow. It was good cognac, and it helped a little.

Tadeusz drove off, turned left, heading north. He was muttering lightly under his breath, curses in Polish. In a way, he was the closest she had to a friend in London. They'd arrived near the same time, eleven months before. He'd been an Uber driver then, had driven her across London from an early gig, another that had not gone so well. They'd commiserated about how the city treated them, how those from the east were regarded by many. When he saw where she lived, how she lived, on the estate in Walworth their bond grew – he was in a similar 'heap of shit' off the Harrow Road. He'd given her his card, said that for her he was always available.

She'd wondered if he wanted something more from her. Until she discovered that Tadeusz, the burly former boxer, was gay, had an old mother and a closeted teacher lover back in Gdańsk, was earning money to bring them both out of there. Even when he graduated from Uber to the luxury service, he was always there for her, had only rarely been unable to get to her after a job. Except for Sundays, most of which he spent at a Polish church, good Catholic that he was, with many sins to confess. No doubt he'd done that earlier that day.

He drove them up into Regent's Park. Her one eye was closed to the cold cloth on her face and she regarded the huge, columned white houses through the other. She'd worked in one of them, couldn't remember which. A prince from the Gulf, a full night, a lot of money. She'd hoped he would become a regular, but he'd gone home.

In her mind, she went through her contacts list, seeking a client she could call, one who cared for her a little as well as for the sex. There were only a few, like Bernard, who'd lost his wife, who wanted comfort. But she couldn't contact him now, now she knew he was connected with this Sebastien. Which government service was he? He'd mentioned the Russian secret service so he also had to be something in intelligence. Perhaps Bernard was too? This close to her goal, she could not afford the fuss. And the others? How could she call them on a Sunday night, on the off-chance? What excuse? Offer them a discount rate for – how did the English say? – 'spoilt goods'?

It was not possible. And unless this ice really took the bruise down, she didn't see how she could visit some of the better haunts, in Kensington, Mayfair, Shoreditch. Bars and clubs where she tipped the doormen and barmen generously so they'd let her in, let her stay. Sunday night and yet many men would still be drunk, lecherous, looking for a good time. They would have on what that man had called 'beer goggles'. She didn't find it so funny now. And she wasn't sure she could be as seductive as she'd need to be. Not if she couldn't stop this shaking.

Focus, Sonya, she urged herself. *Think of Marusya.* Six and a half thousand more, to be safe. A week's double time work. Fly to Moscow, collect her, fly to Baltimore. Johns Hopkins Hospital for first tests. Bring Russian X-rays, lab results, translated reports. An operation required immediately. Have you the funds, Mrs Ivenetza? Yes. On my phone here. Immediate transfer to any account you say.

Her one open eye had glazed. She focused again. Tadeusz had brought them to Camden Town. Traffic crawled down Parkway through the Sunday-night revellers. She was looking at girls in summer dresses, guys in long beards, shorts and checked shirts, drinks in hand on a patio. All laughing, having a good time. When had she last laughed? When had she last had a good time?

She cracked the window. Warm air and music flowed in. She closed her one good eye to both.

Her phone buzzed. It was the sound of hope and she fished it from her handbag. A number she didn't know, but people passed on her number. She thumbed and the screen opened.

L here. Doing anything tomorrow night?

Sonya considered. L? She knew a couple. Leo, the Swiss banker. Larry, from Montreal, the ex-hockey player turned MMA-fight promoter. She hadn't heard from either for a while. Both were big tippers.

She was about to text back her query, when another message came.

Sorry. That's L for Lottie.

Lottie. The girl from last Thursday. The threesome with

the actor. It had actually been a fun night. Mainly because of Lottie. She'd liked her. Funny, tough. Sexy, though she didn't usually think that about women. Though after the year she'd had, she didn't think it about many men either. That Sebastien had known about her, though, and Patrick, about their time together. How was this Lottie connected with him?

No, he'd been following Sonya to her rendezvous, that's all. Why and how she could not think of. Not now. Not with one week to earn what she needed.

What had she charged for the threesome? £1,500? Near one quarter of the way to her goal. She put thumb to keyboard.

Party for three again?

Three replies came fast.
A sad face.

Just us. U n Me.
That ok?

Sonya tapped the phone against her teeth. This Lottie would remember her threesome rate, so she couldn't charge more than eight hundred for one. But if she scheduled it right, she could still get out and down to Mayfair for a bigger payday later. She tapped.

Have to be early. 9 for a couple of hours?

The sad face came again. Then.

Done. Remember where?

She had it in her notes. She texted back a thumbs up.
Lottie responded with an X.

Sonya probed her cheek with her tongue. Still swollen, and the shaking hadn't diminished much. She wouldn't do well tonight. She called, 'Take me home, please, Tadeusz.'

He looked at her in the rear-view mirror. 'Good,' he replied.

She put down the cloth, got a couple of paracetamol from her bag, washed them down with brandy. Then she scrunched down and laid her head against the cushioned seat. But when she closed her eyes she saw handcuffs, a strap-on dildo, a pot belly with grey hairs, so she opened them again and watched London pass.

It didn't seem to take long to reach the Aylesbury Estate. She usually insisted he dropped her on Deacon Street. It was easier to reach her flat via the walkways. This time he insisted on dropping her at her block – and, over her protests, walking her the three floors up to her door, carrying her bag.

He'd never been into her flat before. His glance was neutral. She was pretty sure he looked at the same basic furniture, the same bare walls, saving decoration money for those who needed it more back home.

He saw the photo – of her, Marusya and Georgiy, taken at Moscow Zoo. 'She is pretty, your girl.'

'Yes.' She reached into her bag, brought out the envelope the Englishman had short-changed her with. Peeled off £50 and held it out to him. 'Thank you, Tadeusz.'

He looked at the money, didn't take it. 'Not tonight, Tsarina. This one on me.' He lifted his palm to her, shook his head. 'You be OK?'

'I'll be fine.' She suddenly leant forward and kissed him on the cheek. 'You are a good friend,' she said, her voice thickening.

He nodded, squeezed her arm, left. Wiping a tear away with the back of her good wrist, she poured herself a vodka from the freezer, and went to run the bath.

As she lay in it, her shakes faded. The liquor helped. But she was also planning and that usually calmed her. *One more night*, she thought. *I can't do any more.* About six grand to make. She'd never done that before. But there was the eight hundred promised by Lottie. After her, 11 p.m. Mayfair, the Arabs. Choose carefully, make it very special, earn a very special tip. Then, one in the morning, the Groucho. There was an Australian film director, always there on a Monday. His London residency, he said. He'd been waiting for his new film to be greenlit. 'When it is, Sonya, love, you and I will celebrate,' he'd said, running a finger up one inner thigh under the table. He'd previously mentioned a few things he'd like to do. Somewhat unusual. She'd quoted him the price and he hadn't blinked. And the film had been greenlit, she knew. It was the one that boy, Patrick, had been cast in.

She'd hire Tadeusz to stick around. She could use the speedy rides and, after what had happened with Sebastien, a bodyguard.

One more night in London, she thought, and sank into the hot water till her face, her swollen face, was beneath the surface. The shabby bathroom looked better blurred.

CHAPTER 16

Agony! Sebastien didn't think he'd ever been in such pain. Maybe when he'd had his appendix out. But that was a memory and this was present, real. His nose throbbed where the bitch had kicked him, was still bleeding. The back of his head hurt and he wasn't sure why – until he craned around and saw the bedside table on the floor, with all the things that had been on it. He must have hit it when he fell. He could taste blood and snot, and a burning in his throat.

But the worst were his wrists. The cuffs were so tight his fingers were already numb. The wrists weren't. The wrists were afire, radiating agony all down his arms, into his shoulders. They were thrust above him, he was stretched out; whichever way he moved – and he tried several – nothing eased. He couldn't get himself up onto the bed; the angle was impossible.

'Fuuuuuck!' he screamed. But he knew that no one would hear. Not above the music, blaring some orchestral piece. And though he'd lied to the bitch about everything else – his name, his desires, the money – he hadn't lied about renting both suites. Though she was meant to be making the noise, not him. To be screaming, unheard, and telling him everything he needed to know.

'Fuck!' he whispered. Pain was making thinking hard. But thinking was all he had.

He thrust his head forward, peered around his bicep. His phone was on the floor, screen up. He could see messages on it, though couldn't read them through the sweat that was stinging his eyes. He yelled, 'Siri!' but she couldn't hear him over the music. If he could just get the phone into his hands . . . but as soon as he tried to get his legs that way, double agony shot through his shoulders. He couldn't move like that. How had that bitch managed it?

He sank to the least painful position, still fucking painful. He started to cry, salt stinging. What was he going to do? He'd paid for discretion. He was a regular at the Excelsior. They liked his tips. They'd keep away.

He twisted his head from side to side – and noticed the hotel phone. It had fallen a little further into the room and he thought he might be able to reach it with his left foot. It nearly killed him, but he did. Three flicks and he'd righted it. He could hear the distant *beep beep* of the disconnected line. He was weeping fully now as he angled his foot still more and pushed the disconnect. When the dial tone came, he managed, on the third attempt, to hit first zero, and then the button that read 'Speaker Phone'.

Three rings and a pick-up. A male voice, accented.

'Good evening, Mr Devereux. How may I help?'

He was about to scream, *Get me an ambulance, the police, my wife* . . . but he managed to stop himself. 'I need you to call someone for me.'

'I'm sorry, sir, please to turn down the music—'

'No!' he screamed. 'I need you to call a number for me.'

'You may dial nine for an outside line . . .'

'No!' he yelled again. 'I wish *you* to call this number.' He swallowed. Christ, what was Bernard's number? He usually just speed-dialled him. 'Zero seven nine six six, uh, three six, no, seven, three two, zero four. No, I mean eight!

'Zero seven nine double six, three seven three two zero eight?'

'Yes! Yes, I'll . . . I'll explain later. It's a . . . it's a kind of a joke.'

'I see, sir. I will . . . call.'

'Wait! The call is for Bernard Crouch. Only him. When you get through, tell him to come here straight away. No delays. When he does' – Sebastien shifted slightly and the torture of that almost made him faint – 'when he arrives you are to bring him up' – he bit his lip, tasted blood – 'bring him straight up, I say, and let him into my room. Do not come in with him! Do you understand?' He tried a laugh. 'The joke won't work then.'

There was a silence. For one horrible moment he thought they'd somehow been cut off. Then the desk clerk said, 'I see, sir. Of course. Anything else?'

Sebastien managed to hit 'Disconnect' before he fell back and fainted.

He didn't know how long he'd been out. Woke to an electronic beep, the sound of voices through an opening door. One of them Bernard's.

'Thank you, young man.'

185

'No, thank *you*, sir.'

As the door closed, searing pain surged through him. Bernard appeared out of the corridor, glanced around, didn't see Sebastien on the other side of the bed. Went to the television, picked up the remote, muted the music. 'Sebastien?' he called.

'Here.'

Bernard turned, took a step, saw him, stopped, his face whitening. 'Dear God,' he cried. 'Sebastien, my dear fellow!' He crossed, sat on the bed by his friend's head. His mouth fell open as he took in the handcuffs, the blood at nose and naked chest, finally the huge dildo strapped to his waist. 'What the . . . what the devil has happened here?'

'Never mind that. Just get these fucking things off me.' Sebastien jiggled the handcuffs, even that little movement sending shards of agony shooting from his wrist to his shoulder. He cried out, his groan transformed to a scream of, 'Now!'

'Of course, but' – Bernard looked around – 'but where are the keys?'

'I don't know! Look, for fuck's sake!' Something came back to Sebastien, a small, tinny noise piercing the pain as the Russian left. 'Try the waste basket!'

Bernard went to it, delved – and pulled up two small silver keys. Sebastien yelped relief, closing his eyes for a moment. But when Bernard wasn't instantly at his side, freeing him, he opened them again . . . and saw his friend still over by the bin. He had his phone raised, pointed.

'You . . . you fucker! You're taking a photo?'

Bernard shrugged. 'No, no. A wee video, actually. I mean

I won't share it. Probably. But do you remember, at school? How you once videoed me masturbating in the dorms? What did that cost me? Fifty quid?' He slipped the phone into his pocket, and crossed back. 'Payback, old love.'

Sebastien swallowed every vicious rejoinder and threat that came to his lips. Nothing mattered right then except ending this horror show. He'd deal with the fucker later.

Bernard sat, fitted a key. When he freed the first wrist, the blood surging back into Sebastien's hand nearly made him faint again. The other was a little less painful, and he managed to haul himself onto the bed. Somehow his fingers worked well enough to undo the strap of the dildo, tip it onto the floor.

Bernard had gone, to return from the bathroom with a dressing gown, which he helped his friend slip on. Then he went to the mini-bar and came back with whisky in a tumbler. Sebastien threw it back, the coughing it brought causing his nose to start bleeding again. He wiped a sleeve across it, a smear of red against the Persil white.

Bernard had fetched himself a glass too. Sat on the end of the bed and sipped. Though he was striving to look concerned, he could not conceal the trace of amusement in his eyes.

'Care to tell me what happened?'

Sebastien was an ace away from blurting it all. How everything he'd suffered was Bernard's fault, for allowing himself to be honey-trapped by a Russian agent. How his career in Five was over, once the powers found out. That he'd be ruined. Oh, how wonderful to see his smugness wiped away!

However, the pain had receded a little – only a little, Christ! – and he was beginning to be able to think again.

To remember that he hadn't actually got to the stage of the interrogation where he would have confirmed for sure what *was* the situation here. After all, it was still possible that Sonya was exactly who she claimed to be: a mother working an unusual job to pay for her kid's op. That his friend hadn't been duped – at least not in a security-breach way.

The thoughts moved through his mind as Bernard waited for his answer.

One came. 'I was stupid. Found someone on a BDSM site I occasionally frequent. I mean,' he continued over Bernard's *tsk-tsk*, 'usually it's all fine. But this tart turned out to be a player, and had a boyfriend in tow, huge fucking West Indian. Let him in when I was just getting down to, uh, business. They rolled me.'

'Seb, dear boy, I have to say. When you gave me such a hard time about my friend Sonya—'

'I know!' He raised a hand, grimaced. 'I said, stupid. I'll be more careful in future.'

'I should hope so.' Bernard gestured to Sebastien's still-dripping nose. 'I'll get you a cold compress. There's an ice machine in the hall. We need to tidy you up before we get you home. Whatever will Genevieve say?'

He stood, picked up the ice bucket, went down the corridor, out. Sebastien rubbed his sleeve under his nose again. Stared at the vivid, glistening blood stains.

Sonya, Bernard had said. Well, he would find out much more about her in the next twenty-four hours, beyond the bio he already had. Though facts wouldn't make an iota of difference to what Sebastien would do to her. Whore, spy, a bit of both, he would make her suffer as she had made him.

Worse, actually. Far worse. Her connection to Severin's tart might only be that thing he loathed – a fucking coincidence. If so, it followed that the Shadows and their enterprises weren't under threat from that quarter. Which also meant he could take his time over his vengeance.

A happy thought came. He'd film it. Not just for the memories. For Bernard, who had filmed him, after all, just now.

I'll delete mine if you delete yours.

PART II

ONE LONDON DAY

CHAPTER 17

9.45 a.m., Monday 30th July 2018.
One hour after the hit . . .

There was a park not far from Mr Phipps's house in Gants Hill, between two rough estates. Run-down, with a tatty playground and toilets that saw a bit of action on a Saturday night – drug action, prostitute action – but not much during the day. No CCTV – a camera would be gone in hours. People tended not to bring kids there because of the needles. He always took his white overalls and cap off in a cubicle there, shoved them into a bin liner then put that in the boot. When he'd started in the game, he'd been so scrupulous about getting rid of any possible traces, he'd go to a foundry where a mate from the Paras now worked and had given him the door code. At night, when no one was about, he'd burn everything in the furnace. But overalls cost a shocking amount these days so now he recycled. Figured that with a good hot-water bleaching, any of his or the gig's DNA that might have splattered onto him would be gone. If it wasn't . . . well, if the Old Bill was checking his overalls for DNA he was probably fucked anyway. But he didn't want anyone to see him arrive home in them. The gig's wife would not, he was pretty sure, remember much about his face – but she'd remember the white overalls, the red cap. *Those*, he thought, *she'll remember for the rest of her life.*

There was a parking spot right in front of his house, which was not always the case. He'd driven up and down three times, scoping it, and all was fine – precautions he could probably do without but habits were hard to break. He sometimes wondered if it was like a . . . what was it called, he'd read it in a book recently, a . . . fetish? He'd thought that was only sexual, like being into women's shoes or something; but apparently it was also a way of behaving, like a ritual, to bring luck or some such when you did things like place a bet, or repeat a tricky activity. A bit like the footballers crossing themselves when they ran onto the pitch; though most of the players at the Gunners, who he still loosely kept an eye on, appeared to be Mohammedans these days.

He'd been annoyed to think that he might have fetishes. They would make him easier to track, like spoor on the tundra. Yet he still went to the gym before each gig, did the exact same amount of bench presses, shoulder lifts and sit-ups. Still drove past his place in Gants Hill three times after each hit.

Satisfied, he got out of the car, grabbed his duffel bag and the bin liner, went into the house. Outside, it was just like the others in the terrace – two-storey brick, white windows with lace curtains, slate roof, chimney. But inside, the door opened not onto a narrow corridor but straight onto a whole floor. When he'd bought it, for peanuts at an auction in the 2008 crash, it had looked like all the others in the terrace with their little box rooms, faded wallpaper and dark, cramped kitchens in the back. He'd opened it all up, taken out the internal walls, sunk the living room around a fireplace that he got working again. The kitchen was now bright, clean, functional. Most early gigs he'd bought something new for the place. State-of-the-art, it was, though he despised that term. He still had lace curtains on the back windows, and he'd also planted cypresses; now they topped the brick wall of the tiny garden by a good five foot. In case anyone was sneaking about.

After tapping in the security code at the front door to turn the alarm off, he went to the kitchen, lobbed the overalls and cap into the Bosch washing machine, added bleach and powder. Set it to hot. Then he made himself a cup of tea, crushed an avocado onto some toast with a spray of lemon juice and black pepper, ate, drank and cleaned the Glock. The four spent bullet casings he put into a glass jar filled with vinegar; he'd wipe them, then drop them down different drains later in another part of town.

His phone rang. 'Blue Rondo à la Turk'. Sharon. He let it go to voicemail. It would just be a nag, 'What time you coming for Meaghan?' He thought of blowing her out; he was a bit knackered. He wasn't worried about annoying his ex. There was little he could do these days that didn't. Still, he didn't want to disappoint his daughter. He'd take her for gelato, show her the brochures from the Maldives. Make it up to her for that little unpleasantness in the pool the other day.

When he got back to his phone, he saw that Shazza – as he called her to annoy her – had added text to two, he saw, voice messages.

We need you earlier. Lots to do. Can you please pick up your daughter by noon?

The clock on the stove said 10.25. He could power-nap for forty minutes and, even if the North Circ was busy, still make Muswell Hill by then.

He texted back a thumbs up; then, just in case that tosser Malcolm happened to be looking, added a kiss. Then he went to bed.

He was woken by a beep from one of his pre-paid phones. He went to the utility drawer and pulled the phone out, reading the message through the plastic of the bag it was in.

Coach & Horses W1. 6.30. Work tonight.

He sat in his dressing gown at the computer and looked up the Coach & Horses. Behind Cambridge Circus, famous for drunkards, media world and also, at that time of day, punters coming in for a drink before the theatres – loads of them nearby. Suit, he decided, not fancy. Blue shirt, dark red tie. He could be a theatre lover fresh from an office, or a commercials director.

He'd wondered if they'd be in touch fast. Suspected so, since these books were obviously so important to the Shadows. How important? Well, they'd just ordered the accountant who kept them, this Severin bloke, killed. They didn't want what he'd created for them in the wrong hands, that was for sure. Phipps had wondered, not if he was in the books, he was almost certainly a line of expenditure in them, but how. Knowing these jokers with their love of absurd titles, he was probably Nemesis, or Megatron, or some such crap. But even if he was a number in the books, not a name, it would still be a clue to him. Yeah, he thought, pocketing the phone, he didn't mind being a collector this time. He'd like those books too, just in case.

If I have to live on a hill I prefer Gants to Muswell, Mr Phipps thought, as he pulled up before 46 Coniston Road. When he'd been a teenager, not far away in the Archway, Muswell Hill had been a joke, a shopping area you couldn't even reach by Tube – not that you'd want to. Now it was so lah-dee-fucking-dah, with all the bollocks required for the perfect middle-class life. Gastropubs, trendy cafés, sushi, Waitrose and Oddbins with the few non-white faces serving you your macchiato, and other Europeans speaking some Slavic language behind the deli counters.

Perfect for Shazza.

Still, he thought, unbuckling, it was safe for Meaghan and the schools were better than down his way. He had no nostalgia for his shitty education, was more than happy to pay his share so his daughter's only problems stemmed from a brief shortage of poster paints rather than knives, or learning to cuss in Urdu.

He got out of the car, looked up at the house. Almost twice the height of his, what with the attic conversion. The brickwork a deeper red. The dormer windows a richer cream. It was the only thing he envied, though. Open the door and it was the same poky layout that the Edwardians who built it had craved.

He rang the bell. A large shape loomed through the frosted stained glass. *Fuck*, he thought. *Malcolm*.

'Oh, hullo there.'

Mr Phipps looked up at him. Had to, straining his neck, because even though he wasn't that small – five ten, good height for a Para – Malcolm Potter was probably six four and wide with it. He'd been in the Territorials, so when Shazza had first started up with him three years back, Malcolm had thought that made them comrades. Which was bollocks, of course. There were some OK guys in the Terries but the public school, rugby playing, home cunty officers tended not to count amongst them. So he'd shut down the camaraderie quite fast by mentioning times with 3 Para in Helmand and South Armagh to contrast with weekends on Bodmin Moor and the two weeks spent each summer near Darmstadt. Malcolm tended to go into a sulk whenever they met now, which Phipps tried to keep to a minimum.

Which made the expression on his face now a little disturbing. Not to mention the tone of his voice, thick with plum. 'Good to see you, old chap. Thanks so much for popping round. Do come in,' he said.

Phipps thought of all the comebacks he could make, but it truly wasn't worth his time. He didn't move. 'I'd rather just collect Meaghan and go, if it's alright with you, Malcolm.'

'Ah yes,' Malcolm replied, and coloured slightly. 'Well, um, the memsahib wants a word about her first.'

Memsahib? God in heaven, Phipps thought, sighed, stepped into the hall.

'Come on through, there's a good chap.'

They went to the back. When they were together, Phipps had insisted that Sharon spend some of her divorce payout and open up at the back. So a wide kitchen with marble-top counters gave onto a dining room, which gave onto the garden. *Fuck me*, he thought, *it's a ringer for Severin's kitchen, even down to the primrose paint job. I thought it looked familiar this morning.*

Sharon was at the breakfast bar, on her iPad. 'Ah, there you are,' she said, standing, smiling. 'Cuppa tea?'

Phipps stopped where he was. Usually Shazza began each conversation with no greeting, just a barrage of complaints as to his tardiness, his neglect, his general . . . uselessness. He'd been readying himself to tune it out, as usual. This friendliness made him wary. He looked at her a little more closely. Her make-up was not as carefully applied as usual, her auburn, grey-streaked hair pulled back into a bun. She looked . . . brittle. Her voice was brittle too. 'Where's Meaghan?' he asked, going to his immediate concern.

'She's . . . fine.'

She said it in a way that implied she hadn't been. 'I didn't ask how she was. I asked where she is.'

'Upstairs. Getting ready. She's—' She looked over his shoulder at Malcolm, standing just behind him, slouched against the door that led to the utility room, then swallowed. 'She wasn't feeling very well this morning.'

'She ill?'

'No. She was upset. She—'

The clatter came, fast feet on the stairs. In a moment the whirlwind that was Meaghan burst into the kitchen and ran straight into Phipps's opening arms. He bent to absorb her force – and to try to hear the words his daughter was sobbing into his chest. 'What is it, love? What are you saying?'

She pulled back to look up at him. Her china-blue eyes were liquid, and she had salt and snot trails all over her cheeks.

'He hit me,' she wailed.

'Now look here—'

'That's not what happened at all. She—'

Phipps went cold. There was a lot of explaining going on, but he couldn't focus on any of it. Only the look in his daughter's eyes. Outrage . . . and fear. Just like in the pool the other day, after that last ride down the flume. With that punk, Stanley.

He took a deep breath. Another, then bent down, pulled her close and whispered, 'Meaghan, love, it's alright. Daddy's here. Will you do something for me? Go into the living room and watch *Beat Bugs* for a bit?'

She rolled her eyes, something she'd only just learnt to do. 'Not *Beat Bugs*, Daddy. *PAW Patrol*.'

She wiped her nose and, with one glare for her mother, one for Malcolm, she turned and marched out of the kitchen. It was impressive bounce-back for a five-year-old, and Phipps admired it, even as he turned back to look at his ex.

She started in. 'He didn't . . . Malcolm didn't *hit* her.'

'Of course I didn't. She was being . . .'

'. . . cheeky. No, downright rude, refusing to tidy up . . .'

'. . . I gave her three chances to pick up her . . .'

'. . . then he said she used foul language – which I can only assume she learnt from you . . .'

'. . . three light spanks, that's all it was. She . . .'

Phipps had stayed silent, listening, taking it in. It was kinda like when prisoners babbled under interrogation, especially at the beginning when they were still trying bravado. They always gave away something. 'You weren't there?'

'What?'

'You said, *he* said that she used foul language. You didn't hear it.'

'No, but Malcolm told me straight afterwards. He was totally within his rights—'

'His *rights?*'

'As her stepfather.'

'He's not yet.'

'In two months he will be. We discussed this. Malcolm is here and he must have the power—'

He'd heard enough. He turned about to fully face Malcolm. The man had come away from the doorframe and his meaty hands were held before him. 'I warned you once' – Phipps's voice was low – 'that if you ever laid a hand on my daughter . . .'

He shouldn't have been surprised, the speed with which it all kicked off. Still, he was. They'd been expecting it, he guessed, from the moment he arrived. What their confession might provoke. And though he'd never once hit Sharon, barely ever raised his voice, she'd told him later that she'd always been scared of him. His 'penchant for violence', she'd called it, with no evidence, just his history at war, almost none of which he'd told her.

But scared people do silly things. He heard hers, in the sound of air displaced.

He turned in time. She was lunging for his head, tea mug leading. He got his left hand up, turning to brush the blow aside, letting her own force carry her down and away.

That was when he heard the grunt from behind and turned, just a little too late.

Malcolm had swung and, unlike Sharon, he at least knew how to do it. Phipps hadn't time to deflect it but got his right arm up anyway and took the blow, aimed for his face, on his upper arm. It fucking hurt. But Malcolm was a punch-up artist, all those dust-ups on the rugby field, not a real fighter. So Phipps, bending at the knees, swivelling his hips, drove the heel of his left hand straight up into the bigger man's chin. Malcolm reeled back into the door of the utility room, smashing it in, then crashed into the stack of machines before sinking to the floor.

The dryer beeped, started, as Phipps turned back to Sharon. He could see the fight had gone out of her; she was still clutching the tea mug, holding it in front of her like a shield. He stepped close and she shut her eyes, and he thought of the woman in the hall that morning, Mrs Severin, shutting her eyes when he shouted at her. He didn't shout now, spoke softly. 'If he *ever* touches her again, I will kill him. Do you understand me?' She didn't react so he raised his voice just a little. 'Do you understand?'

She didn't open her eyes. But she nodded, just once.

He looked down at Malcolm, who gazed back, glassy-eyed, trying to pull himself upright. He could have killed the fucker with that same strike, if he'd aimed for the nose, not the chin. Driven the bone up into his brain. But that wouldn't do any of them any good.

He didn't say anything else. Sharon would make the rules clear. Sharon was good at that.

He went out to the living room. Animated dogs were scrapping on the screen. 'Come on, Megs. Grab your stuff. Let's go.'

She pressed the remote. Her bag was by her feet, and she didn't need a coat with this heat.

As he got her into the car, he tried to lift his right arm. It was pretty dead, and he wondered if he had nerve damage. His fingers tingled and they didn't move too fast when he curled and uncurled them. *Fuck*, he thought. *If I need the Glock tonight, I'll have to use it left-handed.*

CHAPTER 18

11 a.m., Monday 30th July 2018

Sebastien parked in a resident's bay on the street called Parliament Hill. This time he'd taken the correct vehicle from the Six pool – an Astra – for the notice hanging from the mirror. This time there would be no kerfuffle with authority. No trail whatsoever. And if any warden observed him walk, they would sympathise. He looked disabled. He felt disabled.

All of him ached. He couldn't decide which part of him hurt worst. They alternated in their claims. When he bent to take his briefcase from the passenger seat, his back protested. When he closed the car door, and put on his sunglasses, his wrist complained. When he entered the gates of Hampstead Heath and began the trudge up Parliament Hill itself, his legs wobbled.

To begin with, he'd thought it was only his nose, shoulders, arms and wrists that had suffered. But this morning he'd woken feeling like he'd played in an especially ferocious rugby match the day before – a sport he'd loathed at school, mainly because thickos he'd mock in the Bedales corridors and classrooms would take such delight in knocking him over and sitting on him. He ached now as he had then. He'd obviously twisted his back in his gyration to try and reach the phone, and bent his legs in ways they were not meant to bend. His wife had always urged him to attend yoga with her. This morning he wished he had.

An aged jogger passed him halfway to the crest, giving him a sympathetic grin. He paused, looked up. There was a bit of a breeze today – hot like everything else about this bloody summer! – so the kite flyers were out. And there, amidst the swoops and dancing tails, stood Bernard. Already there, watching him climb.

It was Bernard who had decided on the venue for the meet. In the Shadows' rotating schedule it was his turn. But instead of a club, pub or restaurant, Bernard had obviously chosen the top of Parliament Hill, and got there first, for this very reason: to see Sebastien struggle up it.

Bastard. Oh, how he'd drunk in the sight of dildo and handcuffs. They'd always mocked each other; ever since prep school they'd sought fuck-ups to use to lord it over the other. Those few seconds had given Bernard the advantage for years to come. And he had that fucking video too.

He was smiling now as he watched his friend labour up the hill. Sebastien knew he had a way of wiping that smirk away. By mentioning one name. Sonya. By telling what he had planned for her. But he would not do that, not yet. Later – afterwards – when all was certain. He looked forward to the moment of telling. It would restore the balance between them. And he'd decided he would definitely film his actions. Tit for tat.

When he finally limped up, the smile was gone; Bernard

was all concern. 'My dear fellow! Here, I've bagsied us a seat.' He moved back to the bench, over which he'd spread a raincoat, and left his briefcase in the middle. He cleared them to the side and they sat, Sebastien with a sigh that he could not restrain.

Bernard noted it, of course. 'How are you feeling?' he asked, with his false solicitude.

'Like shit, thanks. And you can stop pretending you aren't thrilled.'

'I'm hurt, Sebastien. I care about you. You're my oldest friend.' The smile was in the eyes if not the mouth as he continued, 'Though I must say, it's indelibly lodged, the sight of you with that . . . thing.' He held his hand palm down about nine inches above his groin. 'You still don't wish to tell me more of what happened? I mean, are you sure it has nothing to do with . . . us?'

Us. The Shadows. It has everything to do with us, you fucking idiot, Sebastien thought. *You've been sleeping with a Russian whore whose been sleeping with our bookkeeper's mistress.* It was so tempting to confront him with that now, take that look from his eyes. But he mustn't. Because then he'd have to tell him what he had planned for her, soon, maybe even as soon as tomorrow. The softy would object, argue against it, perhaps even muster the votes against him. This was one thing he certainly wasn't going to take to sugar. Sometimes a decision needed to be made by only one of them. He was, after all, *primus inter pares*, whatever the rest of them thought. He'd set up the Shadows. Now he would dissolve it. Besides, though Sonya may have picked up something from Severin's girlfriend, he'd concluded she wasn't Russian secret service.

None of his research pointed to that. She was, as Bernard had told him to his mocking disbelief, a part-timer trying to earn money for her brat at home. Therefore his actions were no concern of theirs. This was personal.

'Really, Bernard? You couldn't have chosen somewhere near the City? You don't think we're busy enough today?'

Sadiq spoke as he arrived, without a hello, and flopped between them onto the bench. Nate was behind him, said nothing, just went and stood a couple of paces ahead, staring at the view, London spread out before them.

Sebastien studied the man, his body language. He had his hands thrust into his suit jacket pockets, his shoulders hunched, folded in. He had received the text like all of them had, once Mr Phipps reported in. His fellow Jew was dead. It annoyed Sebastien, his attitude. 'You know it had to be done, Nathan. No choice.'

'There was plenty of choice.' Nate didn't turn around to speak, kept staring ahead. 'I spoke to the man on Saturday. He knew nothing. He was no threat. He was happy to give the books back. I was collecting them' – he turned to look the other way – 'this lunchtime.' He shook his head. 'It was two days after his daughter's bat mitzvah, for fuck's sake. You had no right—'

'I did. *We* did. We'd already voted—'

'Fuck that. I told you I wanted to be consulted again before—'

'Well, there wasn't time.' It was Bernard who spoke. 'Sebastien found out some disturbing things about your supposed lily-white friend. Confirmed what Sadiq learnt.'

'It's true, Nathan.' Sadiq nodded towards the city, the Shard dominating the jagged skyline. 'The reason we had him do old-school books in the first place was that we didn't want an electronic trail. His buying of the shares we invested in was a mist—'

'Yeah, yeah.' Finally, Nate turned. His face was ashen. 'Can we just get on with this please?'

'Very well. I'm in the chair today. Or rather, on the bench.' Bernard smiled, then put his hand on Sebastien, who winced. 'Our friend here's not feeling so well.'

Sadiq looked down, noticed for the first time the black eye, under the sunglasses, the bandages around both wrists. 'What happened to you?'

'Nothing. Fell over. Get on with it, Bernard.'

'Certainly. And just to let you know, I have Perry's vote in absentia, should we need to decide anything. He had to speed back to Ankara. To solve a crisis.'

'Getting the fuck away, more like.' Nate stepped closer. 'Come on. Spit it out.'

Bernard cleared his throat. 'As you know the, uh, necessary operation was successfully carried out this morning. Through some contacts at the Met, I've managed to contain the news getting out – perhaps until tomorrow morning, certainly till tonight. Which leaves us this day to sort ourselves out.' He glanced at Sebastien, continued. 'We both feel that we've had our fun, made some money, but now we need to cut our, uh, gains and wrap up the Shadows.'

'I agree. I'm out anyway, whatever you decide.' Nate turned away, back to the view. A jogger ran past him, three feet away. 'If I never see you lot again it will be too soon.'

Sebastien leant sharply forward, the pain of it adding to

his sudden anger. 'You're not going to be a problem for us, are you?' he snarled. 'A problem we have to deal with?'

Nate whipped back around. 'Like you dealt with Severin?'

'Wouldn't rule it out.'

'You threatening me, you prick? Do you know who I know? I could—'

'Oi!' It was Sadiq who spoke, loudly. 'Keep it down. We're in a public place.' He gestured behind him to the crest ten feet behind the bench, where two female tourists had stopped to take photos of each other against the backdrop, chittering in Spanish. He lowered his voice. 'And you both know that we are all far too connected to be a . . . a problem for each other. One goes down, we all go down. So the pair of you – just shut the fuck up and listen to Bernard.'

'Thank you.' Bernard leant forward. 'As Sadiq told us the other night, we can wrap everything up quite quickly, if we want. Burn any trail behind us. The one outstanding issue is that lucrative heroin shipment coming through Turkey.' He turned to Nate. 'That's why Perry's not here. Not getting away. Seeing if he can salvage something on the ground. But whether he does, or doesn't, is a separate issue. Our closing bonus, if you like. For the rest of it we just need to finally decide: do we shut up shop or not?'

'Sugar?' Sadiq said.

'Fuck that!' said Nate. 'Fuck all this schoolboy shit. I've had enough. Just vote, will you?' He stuck up his hand. 'I motion we dissolve everything today. As soon as possible.'

'Well, since time presses . . .' Bernard raised a hand. 'Seconded. Those in favour – as indeed Perry is.' He raised his other hand and looked around. 'Carried unanimously.'

'It's fairly straightforward. I've always had an exit strategy ready.' Sadiq frowned. 'I really need those books, though, to wrap it all up.'

'That's in hand. You'll have them tonight.' They all looked at Sebastien. He continued, 'His mistress has them. In Portobello. I'll send someone for them.'

'Who?'

He looked at Nate, then tapped his nose. 'Never you mind.'

Instead of replying, Nate just stared for a moment before turning and heading back down Parliament Hill. 'Wait up!' Sadiq called, rising to follow.

Sebastien caught his arm, though it pained him to do so. 'Will he be alright? You've known him longer than us.'

'He'll be fine. He has as much to lose as we do. Till later. Oh, and my advice? Once the money is in your old offshore accounts, open new ones, and move it.' With that, Sadiq disengaged his arm and set off after his friend.

Bernard and Sebastien watched them go for a while, then Bernard stood. 'I'll be off back to the Box, then, controlling the fall-out.' He took a step, turned back. 'You sending Venom?'

Sebastien turned away. 'See you, Bernadette.'

'Hope you feel better soon.' He walked off, not back to the street but straight down the hill, towards the distant city. Then he stopped five paces away, turned. The look on his face was now unalloyed pleasure. 'You know, since prep school, I've always tried to find a nickname for you that would stick. None have, you always wriggled out of them. But now I think I may have one.' The smile widened. 'Seb *Strap-on*. Like it, old boy?'

He laughed, turned, headed off. When he disappeared

down the path between the trees ahead, Sebastien pulled out his phone, tapped a text.

Coach & Horses. W1. Soho, 6.30. Work tonight.

He hit 'send', then held the phone in his hand while he considered the view. He focused on the sharp spire of the Shard and thought, *One last job for Mr Phipps.*

He felt the pain in his wrists as he levered himself off the bench. *No*, he thought. *Two*.

CHAPTER 19

6.30 p.m., Monday 30th July 2018

Mr Phipps didn't like pubs. Hadn't before, when he was a drinker. Didn't now he was ten years sober.

Clean, he thought, sipping his soda and lime. That was the term. Ten years clean. It was what they called it at the first AA meeting he'd gone to, when he'd made the decision to quit. The only AA meeting. He'd thought it was bollocks, truly, and the people sad. He actually went because he'd heard that it was a good place to pick up women, them seeking some buzz to fill the cravings. But the women there were sad too and he never went back. It was a matter of willpower, and that was something he'd never lacked.

What is it with the English and their pubs? he thought. No matter what class you were, what you did, where you lived, there was a pub for you. Around Catterick, where he'd trained, the pubs were functional booze palaces for squaddies to get arseholed. Beer mugs not sleeves, 'cos mugs were harder to smash and drive shards into some annoying bastard's face. Bruises, broken bones, no blood, corporals and landlords agreed. A jukebox, cheap beer, strippers. A boozer made in heaven for most. But he'd grown up in pubs like that, watching his dad, and never liked them. It was worse in Belfast, 'cos then they weren't allowed to drink off base, for fear of death. And the bars on base were horrible, clinical, controlled. It was when he'd first cut back on the boozing, and really started to read, rather than waste his money.

This one, behind Cambridge Circus? As his research had told him, Soho media types – commercials directors, editors, sound engineers. The odd boho artist. With a better-dressed crowd arriving, getting a few in before going to the theatres nearby, no doubt. There was a photograph of that actor Peter O'Toole on one wall, he'd played a part in some play set in this pub, apparently. There were framed cartoons, in which some oafish man yelled, 'You're barred!' The worst, though, was that the place claimed to be London's only vegan public house. Vegan! Something called 'tofush and chips', for fuck's sake.

He'd liked the bars in Cyprus, when he'd been briefly stationed there. Mediterraneans knew how to drink. Not the British mad rush to oblivion. A gentle slide to sleep. Good food, too, not beans and chips – or tofush. Calamari. Taramasalata. Salads with feta, tomatoes, peppers and olives. After he'd left the regiment, on the proceeds of his first gig, he'd gone back and put down a deposit on a piece of scrub. Not much, but a view and a path down to the sea. Next year, if the work kept coming, he'd break ground. Didn't need much, something simple. He could build that himself. He'd spent time with his uncle Frank when he was ten, eleven, and Frank was a builder.

Mr Phipps checked his phone. 6.40. Sebastien was late.

Perhaps deliberately so, giving his contact time to check for irregularities. For observers. Understandable, given that he'd killed their accountant that morning, and the books were still missing. There would be unease in the Shadows. Their rogue op had probably been rumbled. It didn't bother him too much. He was just a freelance employee, not a manager. If his current employers went down, another set would pop up and take their place who would also need his skills. It would be a pity, though. This association had been lucrative. No guarantee that the next one who took over would be as generous. Then the shovel into Cypriot soil would have to wait.

He went back to doing what he did, what his tardy employer was expecting. He observed, using skills he'd acquired when he'd briefly worked at Six, recruited the year after he left the Paras in 2007, after the fuss from 'the incident' in Kabul had died down. For a year there'd been a salary. NIC. Pension scheme. He'd learnt things but he fucking hated it, went freelance as soon as he could. His kind of work, you didn't post a CV on LinkedIn. But 3 Para, the stint at Six, and word of mouth as to his efficiency meant that offers came fairly regularly. He'd done alright. Then, when the Shadows found him, he'd done very well indeed.

He saw immediately why Sebastien had chosen this pub – anonymity. In the City, there'd be too many of his mates from Eton, or Harrow, or Balliol, or wherever the fuck. Anywhere close to 'Legoland' – as MI6 headquarters at Vauxhall Cross with its weird stacked architecture was known – and there'd be a good chance of running into some boys and girls from Six. And they'd notice Mr Phipps; it was what they were

214

trained to do, after all. Notice his suit, decent off-the-peg, not Savile Row like theirs. Notice the way he filled it, perhaps a little too much, muscles from a life in proper gyms, not spin classes and Pilates. Notice his stillness, and the way he was looking around the pub, noticing them. They might take him for muscle, a bodyguard, which he had also been from time to time. But if they recognised Sebastien, they'd probably guess Phipps's profession and both of them could do without that. It wasn't what either of them needed. The department that Sebastien worked for was hidden. A secret within a secret – within another secret perhaps. Hence their stupid name and the meeting in this Soho pub.

Speaking of … do what you do, Phipps. Locate potential threats.

He'd snagged a table in the corner, near the loos, for the purpose. Good view of comings and goings.

Soon he had it narrowed down to three – two men and a woman.

One man was on a stool at the bar. Phipps had spotted him straight away, ordered his drink next to him, noticed that he was halfway through the *Telegraph* crossword puzzle. Seven across: 'Catching sight at an Austen rave.' He hadn't filled it in yet, but it was pretty obvious: 'espying'. Life was funny sometimes. He'd have smiled if the man hadn't looked up at him.

He'd found the seat. One minute later a woman joined the man, fraternal-style kiss and hug. They could be a team, not siblings, but they looked alike and he'd never heard of brother and sister operatives.

He scanned on. Another man at the bar, but across the

divide that separated the pub into two halves. He was on his phone and out of place in overalls, a plasterer by the detritus. A little too obviously 'hide in plain sight' for Phipps, with his fags on the bar and a betting slip from Joe Coral's. He ruled him out.

Which left the woman at a table. Black, Caribbean he reckoned. Nondescript, which wasn't an insult but an advantage if she was in the game, not on it. Neither pretty nor plain. Regular features, shoulder-length hair, curly, well-styled. Hard to pick out in a line-up. The occasional glance over at him, occasional enough so it wasn't suspicious . . . which made him suspicious. She was also on her phone – and he noticed there was a bit of swiping. All to the right. Tinder as cover? Why not? She had a raincoat; there'd been a couple of showers early afternoon, a short break in the heat.

In one pocket, a paperback bulged. He wondered if it was one he'd read. He read a bit of so-called women's fiction, along with the Tom Clancys and Lee Childs. If he could catch a glimpse of the author, he could google it, work out some pick-up lines. That was how he'd picked up Paula, because she was reading Jodi Picoult on a park bench near Highgate ponds.

Paula. He still hadn't called her back. After that ridiculous fracas with Malcolm – he lifted his right arm from the table, still fucking painful – and a rushed visit with a whiny Meaghan – 'Daddy's working, sweetheart!' – he'd had to change, arrange some things before this meet. To be honest, he knew he and Paula were done. A lovely body, pretty good shag and all but, oh, the grief! Just have to do the deed.

He looked at the woman again – who'd stopped swiping,

and was now looking at him, and holding the look this time. He felt a tightening in his scrotum. She was up for it. He wasn't usually that into black women – there'd been that one in Berlin in '99, Mina, which had lasted a few weeks but aside from that? – but this one interested him. He might go over afterwards and chat about the latest Amor Towles.

She looked away, to the opening door – which admitted his current employer, who paused in the entrance, flicking his head around, scanning, through dark glasses. Phipps raised a hand; Sebastien saw him, cocked his own hand with an imaginary glass, Phipps shook his head and Sebastien went to the bar and ordered, sliding in beside Crossword Man, who shifted on his stool without looking up, still in conversation with his sister. The plasterer drained his pint and left, as Sebastien picked up two glasses, a pint and a long drink, and crossed to the booth.

'I said I didn't want—'

'Not for you,' said Sebastien, putting the glasses down, sitting. 'Spritzer for the wife.'

'Your *wife* is joining us?'

The younger man laughed. 'Fear not, Mr Phipps. She'll text before she arrives. She knows the score.' He took a long swig.

Does she? he thought. 'And does she also know my name? Since you're so casually mouthing it off.'

'Oh, sorry!' came the reply, not sorry at all. 'But surely we're safe here, aren't we?'

Phipps glanced at the woman at the table. She was swiping again. 'We're not safe anywhere,' he replied.

'Ah, ever cautious, Mr . . .' He smiled. 'One of the things

we like about you.' He drank off some more beer. 'It was just convenient. Meeting here. Genevieve and I are going to see the new play at the Shaftesbury, and we needed to grab a bite first. The steak and kidney pie here is quite acceptable.'

He enjoyed telling him. 'Not any more it's not. Place has gone vegan.'

'What? Nonsense!'

Phipps nodded at the menu on the wall next to the bar. 'See for yourself.'

Sebastien rose, peered, then shook his head. Phipps looked at him as he came back. At his black hair, groomed with expensive product. The eyes, under the glasses, a little too close together, the long nose and almost translucent skin. Centuries of cousin fucking – or worse – leading to *him*. To 'fear not' and 'ever cautious' and 'acceptable pies'. He'd had officers in the Middlesex like him, before he'd transferred to the Paras. Prats. Certainly not stupid, though. His brains bulged out of his dome forehead.

But as he returned to the table, Phipps noticed something else, which he hadn't before. The Shadow was moving a bit gingerly. He glanced down, saw tensor bandages over the man's wrists. Wondered now what was behind the sunglasses. 'What happened to you?'

Sebastien grimaced slightly as he sat. 'Slipped on the pavement,' he replied and Phipps thought, *Like fuck*. He couldn't give a toss about any injuries the man had, nor how he got them. But there was an air of grievance about him today, and an edge behind the nonchalance. The meeting was unusual, too; he usually avoided the face-to-face. *Careful here*, he thought, as he sipped his lime and soda.

'Well, that's bloody annoying. The food. We'll have to go somewhere else.'

'Better be quick, then, hadn't we?'

'Indeed.'

The brochure that came out – for sun holidays in the Aegean – was not the usual bang-up job. They'd been in a rush, given what he'd told them after that morning's work, in a brief text conversation on a new mobile, now disposed of. *The sewers of North London are awash with phone bits today,* he thought.

'We found the mistress quickly enough. You got the first letter right anyway. "L", not for Laura or Lorraine but Lottie.' He opened the brochure to the Cyclades, to a pasted-in, professional shot of a smiling young woman. 'Lottie Henshaw. A pianist, classically trained but earning a living in jazz orchestras and playing in the pit for, uh, musical theatre.' He gave a brief shudder. 'She was a tenant of Severin's in Tufnell Park, a one-bedroom. Then five days ago he moved her to the flash pad he owns in Notting Hill.' He shook his head. 'Honestly, we are very disappointed. The reason we chose this man to be our accountant was his normality, his regularity. Family man, North London Jew, synagogue, cap thingy, the lot.'

Phipps knew that Sebastien knew that what Severin had worn on his head was a yarmulke, even if he himself had had to look it up. Didn't say that, but had said 'Jew' with such low-key emphasis. Dismissing him as 'other', not quite one of us, old chap. The casual anti-Semitism of the English upper classes. Made his murder easier. *Well, whatever lets you sleep at night,* Phipps thought.

He leant over the brochure. Pretty blonde, cheeky grin, wild eyebrows. The photo was taken from some rag of a mag, part of the article pasted below.

From Lieder to Alan Jay Lerner: it's all in the ivories, says lovely Lottie.

He looked up. 'You sure she has the books?'

'Oh yes.' He turned a page. 'Here's the print-out of one text exchange, from this morning. Just before he actually called her – while his wife was still there. And before you, uh, you know.'

He tapped the screen, and Phipps read the texts:

Severin: *They still in the house?*

Lottie: *Nah. In the car.*

Severin: *Did you get the residents' pass?*

Lottie: *Not yet.*

Severin: *#&*! L! You'll get towed!*

Lottie: *Nah*

Severin: *Bring them in. I need to know where they are. I'll pick em up today.*

Lottie: *Lol! Teasing! I have them.*

Severin: *I'll call when the fam have gone. About 10 mins. Like to hear your voice.*

Lottie: *k*

'You sure it's the books they are texting about?'

'What else?' Sebastien shifted on his stool, frowned. These stools weren't the most comfortable at the best of times. Which this clearly wasn't for him. 'Also, there was a call that he didn't answer from an untraceable number shortly before the texts. Naturally, we traced it.'

He looked away, licked his lips. It was what in his poker-playing days Phipps would have called 'a tell'. For all his attempted nonchalance, the man was bricking it. 'The call came from within MI5. We suspect that they were onto him. And so eventually onto us.'

Shit, Phipps thought. He picked up his soda and lime, sipped. 'They must have seen these texts too. If they are onto him, why aren't they kicking her door in?'

'We have a . . . a friend in Five. He's suppressing her info. For now.'

'Won't she run squealing when she hears about his death?'

'He's suppressed that too. At least for now. May make *News at Ten*.'

'So we have . . . ?'

'Tonight. A few hours.'

'I see.' Phipps sipped again. 'And why's your *friend* doing this?'

Sebastien took off his glasses, rubbed his left eye, which Phipps saw was indeed bruised purple. 'Well, he's, uh, he's also in the books.'

There was something in the way he said it. Phipps put down his glass. 'Am I in the books?'

'Of course.' Sebastien picked up his pint, drained another quarter off. He was nervous as shit. 'It's all in code, though.'

Phipps damped down his anger. 'Good code?'

'Took one of our best boys a week to create it.'

'So one of theirs will take at least that long to crack it? Fuck.' It was the first time in a long while he'd fancied a real drink. A week? He had contingencies. Bank accounts and bolt holes. His Cypriot land was in the Turkish enclave and extradition was tricky.

Sebastien was watching him. Reading him, which wasn't easy but for once he got it. 'But as I say, we have tonight. Now. To make this go away. Go and get them. Then give them to me.'

'Why don't I get them and burn them?'

'No. He may have been an idiot, but Severin was a bloody good accountant. Since we're rumbled, there are . . . assets we need to divvy up. To fund our . . . re-emergence. When we can rise like the phoenix, eh?' He finished his pint. 'There'll be more work for you down the road, Mr—' He cut himself off again.

Phipps looked down again at the girl. 'Her?'

'We don't know how much she knows. It's unlikely a pianist, if she's read the books, could make sense of them. But besotted men do tend to blab, don't they? Pillow talk. Can you use your judgement? We'd prefer not but we'd also prefer to be safe.'

'Ten grand.'

'What? Nonsense. She's a bystander.'

'A bystander with the ability to bring you down. And I want half in advance.'

Sebastien's narrow eyes narrowed further. 'I'm afraid I've only brought you the remaining five for Severin. I'll have to give you the rest next time.'

Phipps looked down. A second brochure – the Algarve – was on the seat between them. It bulged. He reached in, grabbed the envelope with his left hand – he wasn't going to show this man that he'd also had a tumble – then, with a little difficulty, tucked it into his right inside pocket. 'Next time, but full rate. I also want another five grand for the books, not two, now there's been this fuss. Besides, I'm not a bailiff.'

'Very well.' Sebastien's voice, his face, were sulky now. But he was fucked and Phipps knew he knew it. 'It's Flat C, 45 Clonmarle Gardens, W11. Know it?'

'Why do you always ask me that? I'm not a fucking cabbie either. I'll find it.' He glanced at the picture again. 'You sure she'll be in?'

'She's expecting Severin, isn't she?'

His reply was testy. Phipps couldn't care less. 'Anyone else likely to be there?'

'No, but' – sulk switched to concern – 'but she does have an on-off boyfriend.' He pulled out his phone from his pocket, went online, tapped. 'Here he is. Patrick Ogulu.' He held up a photo, handsome black dude. 'Know him?'

'Should I?'

'He's an actor. Successful. That Netflix series, *The Trail*? No? The movie about the Yardies, *Payblack*?' When Phipps shook his head again, Sebastien continued, 'Genevieve and I saw him last year in a Jacobean revival at the Donmar. He was—'

'Don't matter.' Phipps studied this Patrick's face. 'If he's there, do I—?'

'Again, we'd rather you didn't. I tell you, he's well known.

The press would make a huge fuss, tie it into Severin, since it's his flat. Besides' – his lips peeled back over his less-than-perfect teeth – 'he really is a rising British talent. Be such a shame.'

'Oh well, in that case . . .' He would deal with what he had to deal with and leave the Shadows to deal with the fall-out. 'Anything else?'

Sebastien slipped a piece of paper across. 'The new number for you to call. The old might be . . . disconnected.'

Phipps took the paper, tucked it into his breast pocket. 'Anything else?'

He'd asked because the man looked like he had something else on his mind. 'I . . . don't think so, no.' Sebastien licked his lips again, looked away. 'Don't want to keep you from your work.'

Phipps nodded, stood, stepped around the table. He stopped, laid his left hand on the younger man's shoulder. Was gratified to feel the wince. He leant down, spoke softly. 'Think about this, friend. If you do rise like the fucking phoenix, choose a number for the department, not a comic-book name. You're not at Eton any more.'

'It was Bedales, actually.'

Phipps heard the mumble as he turned away. At the door, he remembered and looked back. But the woman with the book in her pocket was gone. Perhaps Tinder had come through. He felt a little disappointed as he headed towards the NCP car park on Brewer Street. 6.55 p.m., and sultry warm. He didn't know West London that well, being an Archway boy. And he never used GPS. But he had a tattered *A-Z* in the car. There was a good gym in Shepherd's Bush, though he

224

didn't think he had time for a second workout today. Besides, his arm still fucking hurt. Two gigs in a day, though, possible bystanders to deal with. The collection. Forty grand plus.

He grinned. Definitely business class to Mauritius after all.

CHAPTER 20

Sebastien watched the door swing shut behind Mr Phipps, and thought, *Cunt*. He hated to be disrespected by that oik. He'd had sergeants like him when he'd been in the army, with their scarcely veiled contempt. Just because he'd been born into better circumstances, hadn't had to fight his way out of a slum. Spoke proper English.

He texted his wife, threw down his phone, thought more about Mr Phipps. What was more disturbing than the insolence was the greed – and the ingratitude. The Shadows had put more than £150,000 into Mr Phipps's pocket over the eighteen months of their existence. Now the man was arguing every toss, rather than just accepting and obeying. From that aspect at least it was good that the Shadows were disbanding and so would not need to avail themselves of his services anytime soon. See how he liked short rations.

Or did he need even more than that?

Sebastien considered. In the hierarchy of risks, their assassin placed quite high. He knew quite a bit of the Shadows' operation. He knew *him*, for God's sake. And he'd shown again, just now, how he didn't respect his employers. He was a killer after all, a mercenary, available to the highest bidder. Or to someone who would make his life impossible if he didn't roll over and betray all he knew.

Someone like that black bitch Bernard had uncovered at the Box. Ellerby.

He recalled the other two candidates he'd interviewed for Phipps's position. One of them, a chap called Simkin, had a good CV. Public school also, albeit a minor London day one. Still, a little less *comme les autres*. When he'd been told they couldn't use him, for now, he'd taken it well – and had assured Sebastien that, if he ever changed his mind, he'd drop everything to be available.

After tonight, he thought, *I may just give him a call.* He knew he'd rather give him the rest of the payment for the books, and this Lottie, than to Mr Phipps . . . and in addition *for* Mr Phipps. Get a discount too, probably. A trial offer.

A man on his way to the toilets stepped aside to allow a woman out, and banged into him. The instant pain it brought! The instant fury. He was glad now, given these recent thoughts, that he hadn't shown Mr Phipps Sonya's photo, as he'd thought he would, hadn't commissioned him for that job too. Though she was connected to all this, through Bernard, through this Lottie, his research had shown him she *was* who she professed to be – just another Russian tart on the make. So his revenge on her would be personal – and he would pay for it himself.

There was also that other reason he'd held off mentioning her to Mr Phipps. A simple shooting wasn't enough. He'd suffered, so she must too. He owed her that. He suspected that this Simkin would be as deft in kidnapping as he was in murder.

He opened his phone, scrolled to one of the shots he'd downloaded, of her outside the Portobello house. She truly was a beauty.

I'm going change that, he thought, just as the door opened and his wife walked in.

It was a choice, and Ellerby had to make it sharpish.

She'd been following Sebastien Grant all day, alternating with a young man from Six, Duncan. But she'd been the one on Parliament Hill when the Shadows convened. Sat on a bench about sixty yards away, 'birdwatching'. It had been interesting to watch their faces through her telephoto lens. She'd recorded it on video, and a lip-reader was transcribing it all for perusal later tonight. There'd be gaps, of course, when they turned away. But you didn't need to read lips to read the body language. Stags, battering at each other. Nathan Goldberg's shoulders up in his ears from the get-go, before he stormed away.

All was not well with the Shadows.

And now, she thought, watching the pub door swing open from the dark shelter of a Cambridge Theatre doorway opposite, *do I stick with Grant . . . or follow* him?

She watched the man's burly back moving west down Romilly Street. He wasn't hurrying so that gave her a few moments to decide. 'Desmond Phipps,' she murmured. She'd snapped and sent his photo from the pub to the Box, and a brief bio had come back within five minutes.

Former paratrooper. Helmand, Belfast. Award for bravery,

distinguished . . . until he, together with another Para, Wesley Milligan, had shot two Afghans in a street market. A drug deal gone wrong, apparently. It had been covered up, the Paras quietly getting rid of them both. Phipps had also worked low-level at Six for a year, mainly as muscle for ops. Left ten years before. Bodyguard to Arabs for a while. Now claimed his profession was 'bricklayer', which couldn't really account for the expensive holidays he took, the Mazda MX-5, his property portfolio.

The only thing that could would be plenty of stuffed envelopes like the one Grant had just slipped him in the Coach & Horses.

There was no doubt in her mind that she'd been looking at the Shadows' hired assassin.

He was about twenty yards short of the bottom of Dean Street when she made her decision. She jerked her e-bike off its stand and followed. Pulling out her phone as she walked, she thumbed two numbers and the hash sign.

Jenny answered in less than three seconds. 'Yes?'

'I'm following Phipps.'

'Duncan to take over Grant?'

'No. He wasn't making a secret of it. He's going to the theatre. We'll need Duncan. I'll be in touch.'

She hung up, hurried up. He'd turned up Dean Street, wasn't across the junction further up it when she reached the corner. Speeding slightly, she looked right, then left at Old Compton. There he was, still heading west. Zigged briefly up Wardour, zagged onto Brewer. Two hundred yards down, he entered the NCP car park.

There was only one way in and out – for cars or people.

229

So she waited, watching the entrance's reflection in the comic book shop opposite. Soon enough, the Mazda appeared. Turned up Lexington Street, heading north.

Popping the bike off its stand, Ellerby followed.

CHAPTER 21

8.45 p.m., Monday 30th July 2018

Lottie sat at the table, playing an imaginary piano.

She had an audition the next day, to take over second keyboards in the pit for a West End musical, now in its fourth year. But that wasn't why she played. The MD knew her; they'd worked together before. It wasn't exactly a formality but unless she blew it somehow, the producer would just go with the recommendation. If she'd thought it important she could have driven out to Bicester and picked up her Casio keyboard from her mum's. But that would have involved . . . well, Mum, her problems. And, really, her daughter had problems enough of her own.

So she played to ease them. To distract herself. She often found silent music preferable. Never made a mistake, her rhythm impeccable, her transitions superb, her touch light but firm. In the silence, she could bring in other instruments too, other players. Because that was really the buzz; she'd never wanted to be a soloist, to sit at a grand in a hushed hall and dazzle. That was Peggy's dream, never hers. She loved to be part of something – in jazz, funk, in the pit of a musical. So now she went through parts of her repertoire, her fingers gliding over the polished cherrywood, brilliantly blending with her colleagues or taking the solo improv, a fiendish escalation in some sweaty cellar bar. While the other great thing about playing silent and alone was that she could switch it up, slide from Bruckner to Bach to Lloyd Webber with no one questioning her, no one but her controlling anything.

Silent and alone, she thought, lifting her fingers, wiggling them to ease the stiffness. She was out of practice. Hadn't felt like playing much lately. Didn't now – but she needed the money.

And she needed something else.

The writing pad was beside her on the table. She'd begun the letter several times, balls of paper around showing her failures. She just couldn't get the tone right.

She picked up her pen, held it above the page. The trouble started with the salutation. She recalled how she'd begun some of those other letters, the ones Mr Severin had returned to her. *Dear Fuckhead. Dear Tosser.* The fury of their beginnings had swept her along to their conclusions. But anger didn't work here, nor sadness, nor lightness. Too casual had been . . . too casual.

She owed him more than that. She supposed a letter was a bit of cheat, but he'd blown her out the other day, when she'd have told him to his face. *Better just say what I need to say, simply*, she thought. She laid the nib to the paper again, and began to write.

Dear Patrick,

I was sorry to hear you in that state when you called Saturday night. Sorry you lost the gig, of course, but even sorrier to see how you dealt with it. You were pretty fucked up, so I know you didn't mean half the things you said. Have you considered how the fucked-up-ness and the firing are connected? It's a different world now, too corporate for the mavericks and the mayhem artists you admire so much. They can't get away with it any more and, I'm afraid, neither can you.

But I don't want to lecture you, baby. You're twice as smart as me and you'll figure it out, once your brain's clear enough to do so. I hope that's soon. I hope this . . . sobers you up. And I'm not being righteous here; you know I like to play as much as the next girl. We've had some fun, crazy times, haven't we? I just didn't like it when the games became life, instead of a break from it.

I've been thinking and thinking – and to be honest it hasn't made things any clearer. I'm really not sure how much use thought is in these situations. There's a part of me that wants to hang in and help. I still love you and it hurt to hear you, that angry, that certain you were right and every other fucker was wrong. But what really hurt was the . . . self-pity beneath it all. The 'poor me' stuff. That wasn't the Patrick I know. That was the drug, and whatever you're using the drug to cover up. It's not working. I saw that and then I realised – not with thought, with instinct really – that if I did hang in, I would do what I have been doing for a couple of years now, even since

233

before LA: giving you sympathy, giving you forgiveness, giving you nothing that helps you, only helps you carry on.

So I'm done. It's hard to write that, especially as I know, unlike in other letters I've sent, and in ones I haven't, that this time I truly am. Fully, finally. So sad to see that truth. So . . .

Lottie jerked her head back, just too late to stop the tear. It slipped from her eye, ran down her nose, landed. Landed on the word 'honest', which bloomed. She sniffed, got out a tissue from her pocket, blew her nose, gently damped the tear on the paper. The word smeared more and she wrote it in again above, before taking a deep breath, and continuing.

But I need you to know this. This is not all about you, your problems, your behaviour. It's not only my reaction to what's gone on. This is about me. What I want, what I don't.

We were great, baby, for quite the time, weren't we? A show romance that lasted? Blimey, they should put up a plaque! Now, though, I need someone who needs me. Really does, not just to listen and applaud. There's no one, btw, that's not why this is happening. But there will be. I have to let myself be ready.

I'd say, let's stay friends. People always say that, yet it never seems to work out. Anyway, I don't think I'd be any better a friend than I was a lover. Maybe. Maybe someday. I mean, we're in the same business, right? Maybe we'll work together again. See you on the Mamma Mia! *international tour?*

And now I'm getting silly. Always more comfortable with laughter than tears, weren't we? So I'll leave it there.

Don't ring for a while, eh? I need the space.

Take care, love. You know I wish you nothing but the best,

Lots x

She leant away again, letting her tears fall onto her blouse. Then she wiped her nose and reached for her phone. She loved letters, the sending, the receiving. Handling the paper. But she wanted this done. She needed to move on now, tonight.

With her cramped handwriting, she'd got it all onto one page of A4. She pulled up WhatsApp, hit the camera icon, lined up the page till it filled the whole screen, clicked. Two more taps, and it was gone. They were done.

She checked. No more texts from Joe, which she thought a little odd. There'd been those morning ones, to bring the books in from Daphne's boot. She'd only been teasing him; they hadn't left the bedroom. Then when she'd come out of the shower and answered her phone, he'd been so insistent that he had to see her, sometime after eleven, he'd said.

And she admitted it, she wanted to see him. He'd been so lovely when he'd finally chilled, let go. The love-making had been nice too, so different from Patrick, which was always an adventure, or like he had some camera on him all the time. Joe had been simply . . . into her. Grateful too, sure. You could tell the bloke hadn't been well laid in a while. But it was like he'd just stripped off all these layers he'd built up. He'd actually laughed afterwards, when he lay back. Twenty years had dropped away. He was married, of course. And she wasn't really mistress material. Though she was in his flash flat for free and he had left fifteen hundred quid with her. Perhaps she was? Blimey!

Hey you, she texted him. *Still coming?*

She put down her phone. On the table before her, the imaginary keyboard lay. She began to play, not knowing what – and then found it was the song she'd played for Patrick in the show where they'd met: *My Fair Lady*. Freddy's song. So she continued and murmured it as she played. Hearing his voice as she did, the beautiful, simple way he'd always sung it.

She began to riff on it, changing it, jazzing it. Soon she was lost in the improv, the tune a distant thread, there and not. Her fingers moved faster and faster, other instruments in her head, taking up her idea, running with it. She reached the point where she could pull her fingers away and still hear them. Hear the clarinettist taking over, soloing for a few bars, going higher into a series of shrieks. It took her a while to realise they were car horns. She got up, went to the balcony.

In the street, a jam. A delivery van was in front of the corner shop, rear ramp down. Its driver, ignoring the chaos he was causing, had picked up another tray of baked goods from the stack, and headed into the shop. A black luxury Audi was duelling to pass through the gap with another car, she didn't recognise what, snazzy too, coming the other way. She watched with more than simple curiosity as the white van had stopped right opposite her MG – and she perhaps had not parked it quite as flush to the kerb as she might have done. Not that Daphne would mind another scrape to her paintwork. The old girl was as battered as haddock. But both cars involved in the duel were new, black, fancy. She doubted they'd like a smear of Daphne's rusting red on them.

The other car surrendered, reversed. The Audi slid through, missing the MG by inches, then pulled into a parking space just beyond. For a moment she wondered if the loser driver was going to lower his window and shout a few words. Perhaps he changed his mind when he saw the size of the man in the black suit who got out of the Audi, gave him a look, then went to the pavement side and opened the rear passenger door.

And then the other car was gone, with Lottie's mind anyway occupied by who the driver – chauffeur, had to be – was helping out.

The Russian escort.

Lottie stepped away from the balcony, so Sonya wouldn't see her.

She'd completely forgotten her, in the words, in the music. In the farewell to Patrick. In the hello to Joe. She'd texted Sonya on a whim the night before because she'd drunk too much gin. Now she wondered, *What have I done? The fuck have I done now?*

Sonya looked back into the rear seat of the Audi. She'd forgotten her bag, with its accoutrements, the tools of her trade. Though most of those were for the clients she hoped to meet later in the evening, an unknown-as-yet Arab she would find in Mayfair, that film director who'd confirmed in a text that he'd be in his 'residency' at the Groucho after midnight. What this girl, this Lottie, would want from her, she couldn't know. Nothing too different, she suspected. Amidst the whirlwind in her brain, a moment of tenderness from the week before was all she could remember of her.

She leant in for the bag. But her legs suddenly felt weak, and she knelt on the seat.

Tadeusz was standing behind her, holding the door. He took her arm. 'You OK, Tsarina?'

'I'm fine. I need just a minute.'

He glared. 'That bastard client last night. The one who make you trouble.' He gestured to her cheek. 'I would like to fuck him up.' He shook his head. 'You take your time.'

He helped her in, closed the door, looked up and down the street, then climbed back into the driver's seat. He studied her again in the rear-view mirror. The concern in his eyes was still there, had never left them. When he'd picked her up in Walworth as soon as he'd seen her, the swelling around and below her eye, her bruised wrist, he'd tried to get her to abandon the night's plans and rest. But she couldn't. If she didn't get out tonight, she wasn't sure she would again. And then? It was unthinkable. Everything she'd done, this whole year of whoring, a waste. Bad for her. Death for her child.

'Just a minute,' she muttered again.

He tried to distract her. 'You see that fucker in the Mazda, Tsarina? Coming onto my side of the road, wanting *me* to back up? Ha! It was, what do they all this? A Cuban standoff, eh?'

'Mexican. Mexican standoff.'

'Mexican. Is right. And me, I am . . . Clint Eastwood! My Audi is my six pistol, yes? "Feel lucky, punker?"'

She smiled. It actually hurt slightly, up the left side of her face, but it felt good. She was glad she had booked Tadeusz for the whole evening. £300 from her profit. But if she didn't have his car to slip into and shelter in between the gigs she had planned, she wasn't sure she could make them.

She took a deeper breath. Reached for the door. And her

238

phone rang. She hoped it was a client, a regular. She could do with the certainty. Then she realised it was the Signal sound, not the regular phone. It was her husband's name that came up. When she clicked 'accept', though, it wasn't Georgiy's face that appeared. It was his aunt's.

'Ludmilla, what's wrong? Is it Maria—'

'No, no, Sonechka. She's here, she's—'

The screen was shifted over, to Maria at the table. 'Marusya! Are you alright?'

She heard her daughter's cry of 'Mamochka!' but didn't see any more as Ludmilla pulled the phone back to her own face. 'It is not her. It is Gosha. He's . . .' She hesitated, and the pause was filled with terrors.

'Tell me.'

Ludmilla swallowed. 'He's gone.'

'Gone?'

'Not here. Gone. Not—' The older woman swallowed. Her face, grey as a winter morning in Moscow, creased up. 'He left this morning. He didn't get Marusya from school. They called me. He hasn't come back.'

'Have you phoned everyone? The family?'

'Of course. Went to the club he likes. Some bars. I could not—' Tears came to her eyes, overflowed. 'And I have his phone. Why does he not take his phone?'

I can guess why, Sonya thought. 'Have you tried Artem?'

Ludmilla sniffed. 'Who is Artem?'

'Artem Solyansky. He is an old' – she wasn't going to say it – 'drinking buddy. From the army. He may be with him.'

'How do I find him?'

'His number will be in the phone. Call. Leave a message.

And try Petya too. Petya Igorovich. Yes, try him too.' *Petya might be a better bet*, she thought. He was a drinker, like them all. But he wasn't into the smack.

'I . . . I will call.' Ludmilla sucked back the tears. She was tough enough, had spent time in a gulag with her parents when she was a child. 'But little Marusya is very sad.'

'I know. Put her on.'

Her daughter's face appeared. Sonya kept her own turned half away, only showed the good side. Maria was upset enough. 'Marusya. Dumpling. Everything will be fine. Daddy's fine.'

'He was very angry, Mamochka. I don't know why. Maybe I was slower than usual to go to school. He left, even before the bus came. Left me at the stop. He never does that.' Tears ran from her eyes. 'Will he come back soon? I want to tell him I am sorry for being so slow.'

Sonya focused hard, held back her own tears. They would not help – neither her daughter, nor her own looks, already compromised by men. 'Listen to me, it is not your fault at all, my doll. Poppa is fine, he just . . . just needs to hang out with his friends sometimes. He'll be back soon.'

Maria wiped a hand across her eyes. 'Promise?'

'I promise. And here's something else I promise.' She brought the screen closer to her face. 'I will be home next week.'

Maria's eyes went wide. 'For a visit?'

'For good.' She raised her voice over the gasp. 'And then you and I will take a trip. A wonderful trip together.'

'A trip? Where to?'

'America.'

'Am . . . er . . . ica?' She dragged out the word in her wonder. 'And Poppa? Poppa comes too?'

The truth was not needed. 'Of course.'

'Oh, wonderful.' Maria beamed, tears forgotten. 'Auntie says I do not have to go to school tomorrow. I will make a big drawing for you and Poppa. A drawing of us at Disneyland.'

'Do that, sweetheart. Lots of colours, eh? America has . . . lots of colours.'

'Of course! I'll start tonight. Just a little before bed. I'll start now.'

'Do that. But not for long. You need your sleep.'

'Yes, Mamochka.' She leant in, and they did the three-kiss thing, each side, last one on the screen. Then she ran off.

Ludmilla reappeared. 'Call those numbers,' Sonya told her. 'You will find him, I think. If you do not' – she ran her tongue over her lips – 'try the hospitals.'

'I will. Right now.'

Without a goodbye, Ludmilla hung up. Sonya held the phone to her mouth, stared at the leather seat back before her. It was even more dangerous now, the drug scene in Moscow. Anywhere. Before there were the dirty needles, the uncertain quality of the heroin, the crime. Now there was a super-drug; she forgot its name. Too strong, and people died all the time, and fast.

No, Gosha, she thought. *Not now. Not when we are this close.*

She still didn't allow her tears. She had more reason to cry them – and even more to keep them in. She had this night to make the money they needed. It all came down to her.

'OK, I go.' She grabbed her bag. Tadeusz was out in a moment, holding the door open for her. 'Wish me luck.'

'Luck, Tsarina,' he said. 'I can't stay here, fucking traffic warden is giving me the funny eye. I park up, close. You call, I be here in minute, yes?' He leant in a little closer, his concern clear. 'You sure you are OK?'

She was, now. 'Yes. I'll call. Two hours, at most.'

He nodded, got back in the Audi. She let him pull away before crossing the street and walking up the front steps of number 45.

CHAPTER 22

Mr Phipps sat at the window of the pub, watching the beautiful woman walk up the steps of the house opposite. One of the other tenants, he thought. Richly dressed, as suited the area. He remembered when the Portobello was still scruffy, market stalls with a load of old tat. Decent boozers, not this gastro rubbish.

Not tenant – visitor, he realised, as he watched her press a buzzer and, after a moment, be admitted. When he'd parked his Mazda down the road – residents' bay but it couldn't be helped – he'd quickly walked up the steps and snapped a photo of the door entry system. He looked at that now – three names, one English, one Greek, one he didn't know what 'cos it was in a Middle Eastern script. One just said 'Flat C'. Her flat, this Lottie Henshaw. Who he was collecting from.

Another light went on in the flat above C, the penthouse. The beauty had gone there, no doubt. And she'd got out of the car that had blocked him earlier, the flash Audi. Was a time when he might have stepped out of his car to *remonstrate* with the driver. That time when he'd have been drinking more than the lime and soda in front of him. But now, he needed to keep everything on the downlow. Besides, the Audi's driver, who'd pulled up and opened the door for the beauty, had been a wide fucker. Eastern European by his pudding face. Filling his black suit. Malcolm wide. He could be tasty, and Phipps, even if he'd been interested, knew he wasn't at his best. His right arm was still numb, the fingers tingling when he flexed them. The paracetamol hadn't made so much as a dent.

Besides, attracting attention was the last thing he wanted. He needed to be in and out fast. The girl was in the house; she'd appeared on the balcony once since the duel with the Audi. Still, he'd sit and wait a little longer. He wanted to be sure – sure! – because what his daughter would call his Spidey-sense had been tingling ever since he drove out of Soho. Sebastien had said they only had tonight, that the Shadows had been rumbled and only a 'friend' was giving them even this amount of time. But he didn't trust Sebastien or his fucking friends. Too many people knew too much. He'd driven strange routes to get to Portobello. No one car had followed him, he was sure. But lots of cars had been behind him, and spotting tails wasn't a big part of his skillset. He could kill. He could collect. And he'd probably need to do both tonight pretty sharpish.

Still, he sat. He'd learnt during his Para days that before you went in – to a suspected IRA farmhouse, or a compound in Helmand Province – you always made sure there was a good line of retreat, with none of the bad guys astride it. So he'd sit, watch a while longer.

He glanced up at the TV in the corner. Sports on, but not the usual football. Swimming meet, European something or other. How much time did those guys have to spend in a pool? Years.

He saw it then. A blood trail in water. Some stupid bloody kid, full of the same piss and wind that he'd had at sixteen, who'd decided to challenge him, just as he probably would have done.

He wished he hadn't hit that Stanley now. Wished he'd just waded away. It wasn't like Meaghan would be scarred for life.

He stared at his empty glass. The last drink had tasted even blander than usual. That coating of artificial lime in his mouth.

Fuck it, he thought, and went to the bar.

'Another, sir?'

'No. Whisky and ginger.'

'We've a special on doubles.'

Mr Phipps shrugged. 'Why not?'

By the time the lift pinged its arrival on the third floor, Sonya had herself together. The conversation with her daughter, and Georgiy's aunt, had done that. She'd learnt as a young recruit in the army: deal with what's here, right now, right in front of you. Actually, she'd known that going into the army. Her father, his behaviour, had taught her that. Rely on no one but yourself.

She'd been playing a role for a year now in London. One more night, with some good luck, and the acting was over.

She pushed the lift door open – and there she was, standing at her door.

'Hello.' Lottie stepped aside to let Sonya into the flat.

It was strange. Unless they were regulars, she would forget people quite quickly. Forget the places where she'd met them, the samey hotel rooms or the service flats in mansion blocks that were her main arenas. But step back in a second time, see that same face, and it all came back. This Lottie with her crazy eyebrows and her perfect figure, in miniature. Sonya had her fuck-me heels on, an essential for later and the Arabs who always wanted tall. So she guessed she was nearly a foot taller – especially as Lottie was in her bare feet.

The room, too, the memories came fast. Three people, leaders and followers, taking turns. Here was the deep sofa. There, through the back, that comfy bedroom, and lovely walk-in shower. One of the items in her bag was the simplest – a shower cap. She'd need to clean Lottie and whatever they made off her before she moved on to Mayfair. Again between there and Soho. And she wouldn't have time to wash and restyle her hair.

She looked all around before dropping her bag behind the sofa, moving around and sitting. 'Anyone joining us?'

'No. I told you. Just me here. Patrick is—' Lottie came around, sat herself, but on the short end of the L, a distance away. 'Patrick is . . . no more.' She frowned. 'I don't mean, you know. I mean he and I are . . . over.'

'Oh?' Sonya raised a thin eyebrow. 'Should I be sorry to hear that?'

'Not really, no.'

'He was very beautiful.'

'He was. Is. He is also a bit of a dick.'

'I see. It happens. Especially when . . . he liked this quite much, yes?' She tapped her nose, left the finger there.

Lottie nodded. 'Too much. But it wasn't just that, there was other stuff—' She broke off, leaning closer, peering. 'Are you alright? That's quite a bruise you have.'

Sonya dropped her finger, leant back. No make-up totally covered up such a thing. But this room was quite well lit, with all its gleaming white, metal and glass. She could only hope that the lighting in the bars she'd go to later would be . . . kinder. 'Well' – she shrugged – 'I met a bit of a dick too.'

'I'm so sorry. Men, eh?'

'Men, yes.'

Lottie turned away, to the balcony, but not quite quickly enough to hide the tear that ran down her cheek. 'I'm sorry.' She gave a little laugh, running the heel of her hand up her cheek. 'It's all a little new. A little complicated. There's . . . someone else too.'

'Would you like to talk about it?'

As she asked, Sonya glanced at the clock on the cooker she could see through the kitchen hatch. 8.49. In her plan she'd allotted two hours for this visit. She didn't mind how it was spent. In fact, if talking ate up much of the time, that would be fine. Sometimes, more often than she'd have believed when she started in the trade, talk was what many of her clients wanted most. Bernard, missing his dead wife, was only one.

She patted the sofa beside her. 'Why don't you come over here and tell me about this man.' She raised one eyebrow. 'If this someone else *is* a man?'

'He is. He . . . owns this flat. He's—' She broke off. 'I'm sorry. I don't think I can go through with this.'

'Go through? I do not know what this means.'

'Uh, you know. Like the other night. The sex.'

247

'You do not wish to make love with me?'

'No. Yes but . . . I mean, it's not really my thing. With a woman. It was Patrick. I think I thought it was a way to hold him. Fuck!' She shook her head. 'Stupid.'

Sonya looked at the clock. 8.50. Already the plan was going wrong. Fear made her angry, and with her, anger was always cold. 'I do not do this for fun, Lottie. This is my business.'

Lottie sat up to the edge of the sofa. 'Oh, I know. I'm sorry. I was drunk when I called and—' She shook her head. 'I'll still pay you, of course I will. Eight hundred, yes?'

'Yes.'

'The man he . . . he left some money. I'll take it from that.' She stood up. 'I'll get it now if you like. You could go. If you need to, that is.'

Sonya looked at the clock. 8.51. The earliest the Arab millionaires would be hitting Shepherd Market would be ten, but realistically closer to eleven. She could sit in Tadeusz's car and wait. But then she'd only have her thoughts for company. This sofa, this girl, this was better, for now. 'No hurry. Maybe we just talk, for a while?'

Lottie nodded. 'Sure, I'd like that.'

Sonya lifted her left arm, her good arm because her right wrist still hurt. Opened it wide. 'But why don't we talk with you over here?'

Without another word, Lottie came over, sat – and immediately folded herself into Sonya, whose arms closed around her. 'There, little one. There. Better?'

And then Lottie began to shake, making a sound deep in her throat, part moan, part sob, part cry. And Sonya put her right hand, even though it was a little painful to do so, to

Lottie's hair and gently began to stroke her head, murmuring as she did. But she was not murmuring in English; she only knew the terms for her trade in English, the jokes, the innuendoes, the 'ropes'. She murmured in Russian, because she knew those endearments.

'Milaya,' she crooned. 'Lyubimaya, malyshka.' *Darling, beloved, baby.* Holding Lottie as she would hold Maria, as she had missed holding Maria all this time; not holding this English girl as she held her English men, but as her daughter, her daughter in pain, different but still pain, not just because of a man or men. For being alone in the world.

Yet as she whispered those words, other words – *solatka, latachka* – the words moved from the body she held into her own body, loosening the tightness she used to keep everyone else out. Lottie sank deeper; Sonya took her in. Until she was shuddering too, crying too, tears running down her face, her words dissolving into sobs that grew louder fast, and were soon louder than those of the girl she held.

Lottie felt, heard, pulled back and saw – that beautiful face, distorted by pain, saltwater and snot, and . . . and something else in eyes that had been cool emptiness before, filled now with fire, hurt, a desperate longing. And seeing, she sat further back and knuckled her own tears away. 'Please,' she said. 'Please tell me.'

So Sonya did. Stilled her sobs enough to tell her everything. Marusya's dissolving spine. Georgiy slipping back into the warmth of his oblivion. The man who'd hurt her last night, hurt more than her body because her confidence was gone when she needed it most because she only had one night, this night, to do the impossible, because what she planned would usually take a week, and a good week at that. One night because it was all she had; she knew she'd never be able to rouse herself to it again.

And when she'd said it all, she realised that the positions had changed, that it was Lottie holding her now, enfolding her, murmuring her endearments – 'Sweetheart! Angel! Little one!' And she let her. Let Lottie soothe and caress her. Until Sonya sat up, moved away so she could look this English girl in the eye.

Which was when the door buzzer went.

A few minutes earlier . . .

Mr Phipps had barely felt the first double whisky. The second, without the ginger this time, jingled a little, literally sounded like a bell somewhere in his head. His arm felt better too. The numbness was still there, but more distant, didn't bother him so much. He thought of a third but decided against. A third was what an alcoholic would go for, and he wasn't one. He'd proved that by quitting before, cold turkey, no counselling, no twelve steps, simply willpower. Willpower stopped him ordering a third now, and sensible thinking. He had work to do. Taking the incriminating books from the girl in the flat across the road.

He would prefer not to kill her. Use his judgement, Sebastien had said. He'd wear a balaclava, posh up his voice a bit too. It wouldn't be a long conversation. She wouldn't remember much about him. All would depend on her answers. Though it was probably safer for them to kill her.

For him too. He was in the books. Under some fucking prattish alias, no doubt.

It was a pity about his suit. He'd have to burn it, couldn't risk the dry cleaner. It was one of his nicer ones too. But overalls would have stood out at nine o'clock on a Monday night in Portobello, and there were a lot of people about.

Like this fucking traffic warden, he thought, watching the large black woman walk by. Bitch had probably ticketed him, parked as he was in the residents' bay down the road. She had that sort of smirk. He supposed they were on some sort of bonus scheme, else why was she working at this time at night? He was no kind of socialist but, really, it was a crying shame that councils were so strapped for cash in these days of austerity that all their employees had to compete.

Hmm, he thought. *Maybe the whisky* has *had a bit of an effect. I might have another later. After.*

As he'd sat and drank, he'd observed. And really noted nothing out of the ordinary. People came and went; cars parked, took off. A couple sat in one and argued for ten minutes, him waving his arms about, her weeping. Could be an act, but then they drove away to continue elsewhere. Apart from the patrolling warden, no regular caught his eye. There was a kid, begging. Every street in London now. Delivery men arrived on bikes, in cars. Pizzas, Uber Eats. He was a bit peckish himself but he never liked to eat before a gig. It's why the whisky had had even the minimal effect it had, he supposed.

Time, he thought. He tapped the Glock in his left armpit. He hadn't bothered to change the holster around, even though his right hand was still pretty fucked. But he'd found he could still draw it with his left. Not so graceful perhaps. Not so fast. But he wouldn't need to be fast with Lottie Henshaw, pianist.

He swirled the last of his drink, knocked it back, just ice water now, Scotch flavoured. Then he heard the bartender say, in his Latvian-English accent, 'Fuck me!' and he turned and saw what the man was looking at, the TV above the bar. The swimming was over; it was the news now, and on the screen was a house he recognised, because he'd been at it that morning. Though then, of course, it hadn't been wrapped in yellow tape.

The headline read:

Gangland slaying in suburb.

He stepped to the bar. 'Turn it up, mate?'

The bartender grabbed a clicker. The volume dial went up. A woman was speaking.

'. . . shattered the silence of this quiet close in Finchley. The victim was Joseph Severin' – an inset picture came up – 'a forty-two-year-old landlord and property manager. Police are baffled as to a motive, as Mr Severin was unknown to them, and early investigations show a happily married family man with a successful legitimate business. Our reporter, Darren MacArthur, is outside the house now and files this report. Darren, is there anything you can tell us?'

The feed cut to the house, two uniformed plods at the door, a forensics guy in white overalls and booties going in, and the reporter with an officer, again in uniform, beside him. 'Yes, thank you, Amrita. I am with Chief Superintendent Chambers of the North London Division.

Chief Superintendent, have you identified any possible motive for this murder yet?'

The senior plod shook his head. 'We are working on a number of theories – not least that this may be a case of mistaken identity. The victim, Joseph Severin, had no known connections to crime, was a pillar of both the Finchley and the local Jewish community. It is a particularly nasty crime, in that the victim's wife and young son were there when it happened.'

'So you have witnesses?'

'We do indeed – though the boy is only two and his mother is, understandably, severely traumatised. We hope to have a longer conversation with her when she is feeling better, perhaps as soon as tomorrow.'

'No clues yet, then?'

'I didn't say that. We are working on some promising forensic evidence.' (*Tosh*, thought Phipps) 'We also know that the killer was male, Caucasian, probably in his forties, of average height and build, wearing white overalls and a red cap.' He looked straight at the camera. 'And we appeal to anyone who may have been anywhere in the Finchley Central area this morning between 8 and 9 a.m. to check their dashcam or camera-phone footage and call the number that will appear later. Any call will be treated in strict confidence and with the greatest respect. Please call, no matter how innocent your observation may seem. Thank you.'

He walked away. The reporter said, 'And that's it from a shocking scene in Finchley. Back to you, Amrita.'

The screen switched back to the anchor. 'Thanks, Darren. And that number to call with any observations is . . .'

Phipps turned away. It was nearly all bollocks, and he still doubted that the wife would remember anything much more about him. It was annoying about the overalls. He'd probably have to find a better covering for future gigs. *I probably should have killed her*, he thought. *And that decides it. Fuck the balaclava; I'm killing the girl, and have done.*

He bent and picked up his duffel bag. He'd forgotten to grab a pillow from the supply he had at his house and hadn't wanted to stop and buy one. Good choice, seeing as forensics would be all over the one he left in Finchley, much good it would do them. So he'd brought the large felt alien doll he'd won for Meaghan at the Heath funfair. It wasn't ideal, but it would do.

He stood, looked across the street to the house – and saw a figure running up the steps. He bent into the window, peered – and saw that it was a black man, in shorts, straw hat. He paused before the door, took off his hat, rubbed hard at his head, then turned and looked around before turning back and ringing the buzzer.

The one look had been enough. He'd seen the man before. Earlier that night, on Sebastien's phone.

Patrick something. Actor. It changed things, a little, and he sat again to think it through. He'd been an advisor on a film set when he was first out of the army. Actors, in his experience, were OK at the on-screen violence and useless in real life. But Sebastien had said this bloke was quite well known, that his death might bring heat they could all do without.

Fuck, Phipps thought. *I'll give him fifteen to bugger off. If he isn't out by then . . .*

He licked his lips. He fancied another whisky.

CHAPTER 23

'Who is it?'

Static crackle. Then, 'Lots, it's me. Let me in.'

'Patrick? What the hell?'

'Let me in, please. Please! I really have to talk with you. It's important.'

Lottie took her finger off the intercom and looked at Sonya. 'Shit. I could really do without this now.'

'But he is no longer your boyfriend, yes?'

'He's not. But I only sent him the letter earlier tonight. It's over.'

'A letter? So he will not have received yet. You have to tell him again.'

'No, I sent it on my phone.' She jumped, as the buzzer went again, one long loud whirr.

Sonya stood up from the sofa. 'You want I should go?'

'No. No, I really don't.' The sharp sound came again, and this time didn't stop. 'Fuck! He's probably high as well. Look, could you . . . could you just wait in there? It will just confuse him if he sees you.' She gestured to the bedroom. 'I'll get rid of him.'

'Of course.'

Sonya went into the bedroom, closed the door behind her. Lottie pressed the intercom. 'Fuck's sake, Patrick, stop it. Come up.' She pressed the latch.

She left the front door ajar, went back to the sofa, sat. There was a faint trace of Sonya's expensive perfume in the air, but Patrick was never one to notice scents. *Be normal*, she thought. *One of us has to be.*

Reaching for the clicker, she turned on the television. It was the sports news, football, switching to swimming. She muted it. *Ciggie*, she thought, and started to roll one, as the lift arrived on her floor.

He came in the door hard, and it banged on the corridor wall. *Fuck*, she thought, but carried on rolling.

'Lots!'

'Hello, Patrick.' She gestured. 'Please have a seat.'

She was sitting in the middle of the sofa. 'You alright?' He flopped down on the left end of the stunted square U. When she didn't reply, he continued. 'That one of your specials?'

'Nah. Need to keep a clear head.'

'Why start now?'

He laughed after he said it, on a high note, some vibrato in it. She glanced at him, confirmed what his manic buzzer pushing had indicated. His face was sheeny, but not just with summer heat, though it was still hot, beyond English hot. There was a slickness to his skin, like from a fever, skin that wasn't its usual smooth glossiness, full of little bumps. His eyes, those beautiful mocha eyes, were not sunken under their heavy lids but were prominent, over-bright. He smiled, but he forced it, like he was trying for his best headshot look.

'So, I got your letter.' He tried to say it casual but like the rest of him, the voice was still off balance.

'I only sent it half an hour ago. You must have been nearby.'

'Paris!' He laughed again. 'Nah, Notting Hill. With Danny, some of the old Central crowd.'

'Oh.' She picked up the paper, licked the edges, did the twist. Putting it between her lips, she reached for her Zippo, struck, lit, inhaled. Put the Zippo down. All her movements were slow, deliberately so.

'Can I have some?'

Instead of replying, she leant down and pushed the fixings towards him. He did not reach for them. She knew why. The actor could nearly always control the voice. His hands would be another matter.

He must have read her mind. 'Lottie, what you said in the letter? The coke? I promise. I'm stopping it. It's fucking stupid, I know it, it's cost me. I'm not talking about the job, though that's—' He swallowed. 'I'm talking about you.'

'It's not just that. If you read—'

But he wasn't listening to her. He'd prepared this scene, she could see, wouldn't be distracted. And it came with props.

He took off the straw hat, courtesy of Venice Beach, California. The wrap was in the brim, another trick he'd learnt there. He extracted the folded paper with two fingers, and dropped the hat on the table. 'It's the last of it, Lots.' He shook the wrap. 'I swear. Done. Where's the bin here? Under the sink?'

He rose as he spoke, strode to the kitchen, vanished through the door and appeared again in the rectangular gap that gave onto the living room, above the dining table. It was like a screen, and he moved into the centre of it for his close-up. 'Done!' He waved the wrap for emphasis. Then he bent.

'Patrick!'

He rose. 'What?'

'I'm a tenant here. I don't want coke wraps around, even in my rubbish.'

'Oh! Of course, love. Silly me. I'll, uh—' She could watch his brain ticking, as he considered how to keep his gestures grand. 'I'll do this, then.' He unfolded the origami. 'Voilà,' he said, and tipped the powder – she assumed, she couldn't see – into the sink. What she could see, though, just before he reached for the tap with his left hand, was his right dipping . . . out of frame. Didn't need to see the finger scrape up some of the white powder, nor what he did with it after he turned on the tap to wash the evidence away. She knew, in the moment after he disappeared from the rectangle and the one before he reappeared by the table, that the finger had brushed over his gums.

He returned, sat, rubbed his head. 'There you go. Done. *Basta!*'

He made a chopping gesture with his right hand. It reminded her of her dad. Keith had given up the ciggies half a dozen times. He usually did it with a flourish too – crumpling a packet with three left in it and throwing it onto the fireplace, or some such. The following week, though, he smelt of tobacco again. It was a good smell. Why anyone would ever think of giving up fags was beyond her.

Speaking of, hers was out. She bent, but Patrick was quick, coke quick, and beat her to the Zippo. 'My lady!' He struck, held out the flame. She took his hand to stop it shaking, and drew. They were close, as close as lovers. 'Baby,' he crooned, his voice shaking again. 'Please. Don't. I can't make it without you.'

She looked into his eyes, those eyes she'd so loved. Moments of looking into them this close came back in snapshots – a tatty dressing room, a hill in Shropshire, a County Durham beach at a winter sunset. She loved him. She had loved him. She'd always love him. But she'd written all she had to say in a letter.

'You'll have to,' she whispered, and blew out the flame on the lighter.

He started, pulled back. His eyes narrowed. 'Is there someone else?'

Her reply was a fraction slow. 'No.'

'There is!' He pulled back, dropped the Zippo, still open, onto the coffee table. It bounced, skittered over the glass. 'There fucking is! I knew it. I knew it wasn't . . . anything else.' He ran his tongue around his gums, jumped up, went to the balcony, looked out, did not stop there, moved to the table, then around till he was looming over the sofa, over her, his back to the short corridor and the front door. 'Who is it? Who?'

She dropped her roll-up into the ashtray, closed the Zippo, rose to face him. 'It doesn't matter. What matters is—'

But Patrick was beyond listening. 'It's not this wanker who put you up in this place is it?' Something in her face must have changed because he shouted, 'It is! It fucking is. I thought there was something funny about the whole set-up. You're selling yourself. And you . . . you get onto me because

259

of . . . you . . .' He leant forward, and stumbled slightly. He looked down, and puzzlement replaced the fury. 'What's this?'

'What?'

'This.' He reached, straightened. He had a red bag in his hand, a beautiful, soft leather bag. 'But this . . . this belongs to . . .' He looked at her, and then turned and looked at the closed bedroom door. Wonder displaced everything else in his eyes. 'You are shitting me,' he breathed.

He took a step towards the door. 'Patrick!' Lottie snapped, so loud he halted. 'It is not . . . she's not. She needed a friend.'

'A friend?' Fury was back. 'Bullshit!'

He crossed to the door, flung it open. Sonya was standing in front of the bed, her hands clasped in front of her. 'Hello, Patrick,' she said.

Her words froze him. 'I don't . . . I don't understand.' He looked back at Lottie, shook his head. 'What the fuck?'

There was no way to explain it. She wasn't even sure she could explain it to herself. 'Patrick,' she said softly, 'you need to go.'

'I need to . . . go?'

'Yes.'

'Wait.' He stuck the heel of his one hand into an eye, rubbed. 'If she's here, you're paying her. If you're paying her' – he dropped his hand, and grinned – 'we can have some fun.'

Lottie actually gasped. 'You're not serious?'

'I am.' His grin went wider. 'The letter? It doesn't matter. You write one thing one moment – and do this' – he jerked his thumb towards Sonya, still unmoving in the bedroom – 'the next. You don't know what you want, any more than

I do. Only she does' – the thumb went again – ''cos she's clear, it's her job.' He took a step back, reached out his hand. 'C'mon, Lots. I mean' – his grin widened – 'if this really is goodbye, then we may as well go out with a bang.'

He laughed then, and Lottie saw it all. Who he was, who he actually was now. The drug magnified it, of course. But it magnified what was already there. And when she saw it, instead of the anger that had been waiting to burst like a bust dam over him, she felt the surge recede. So when she spoke again, her voice was calm. 'I'd like you to go now please.'

'Oh, come on.'

'Now, please.'

'Why should I?'

'Because she asked you to.' As she spoke, Sonya took a step forward.

'Really?' He looked up at her. She was maybe an inch taller than him. Lottie could see his shoulders set. The male challenged. Sonya must have noticed too, because she took a step back.

'Patrick,' Lottie barked, loud enough to turn him. 'Go now, please.'

Something went out of him. The fight, the fury. The shoulders dropped as he turned. Though he tried for cool. 'Well,' he murmured, 'I will leave you ladies to *it*.'

There was no mistaking the emphasis. He crossed to the front door, paused there. Lottie could almost hear the whirling thoughts. One of the problems of living with an actor, she'd discovered, was that they were always 'on'. And this was, after all, the famous final scene.

He surprised her a little, when he turned, when he spoke,

looking straight at her. 'I'll miss you lots, Lots. I love you so much. And I always will. You are the best.'

Then with the dignity he'd discovered, he left, leaving the door open behind him.

Bastard, Lottie thought, as tears brimmed and ran. *I'd have preferred a slap.*

CHAPTER 24

Mr Phipps checked the time on the pub TV.

21.12. He'd decided to give the actor till quarter past to leave. Otherwise he was going in. It was the balance of risk and probability. Two people to deal with was more of a risk, especially as he had to find the books before he killed them. One, the girl alone, put the odds on his side again, for a successful mission and a swift exit. But the probability after that was that, whatever Sebastien said about his 'friend' in the other department suppressing information, too many people now knew about Severin. Sebastien had also said that the hit wouldn't be on telly till *News at Ten*. He'd been an hour out. Anytime now, internal investigations or whatever they called themselves would be all over Severin's properties. Though the plods might beat them to it. They weren't stupid, most of the time.

He was ready. It might take him a minute or so to get in. There were methods. The voice of authority usually worked – fire, police. He had some false ID in his suit front-right pocket, in case.

He tapped it, and felt the bulge underneath. Fuck, he'd forgotten to leave the envelope with the five grand in the car. It was too late to go back. Glancing around, no one looking, he slipped it out of his suit and dropped it into the duffel bag at his feet.

9.14. He stood, picked up the duffel. 'Have a good night, sir,' the barman called in his Latvian-London accent and Phipps just grunted without turning around. He'd engaged too much with the bloke as it was. Three rounds of drinks, getting him to turn up the telly when the news of the morning's hit played. Stupid, that. Especially given what was about to happen across the road. *Hope for your sake your visa's legit, mate,* he thought, as he left the pub.

He stopped, looked up at the house. Lights on top three floors, only the ground one dark, so people in, more options for entry. He looked around. Quick shufti, no one that worried him. Monday-night drinkers, local flat dwellers getting snacks from the shop, that young beggar sitting with his back to the shop front now, clasping a polystyrene cup. That fucking traffic warden. How many tickets could he get in a residents' bay in one night? It was a trail, though, paper and electronic – and that meant the car was toast. Mehmet, his Turkish mechanic over Turnpike Lane, would take it, spray it, plate it, flog it and give Phipps a quarter of what it was worth. He knew he should never have splurged on a Mazda MX-5.

Looks like Meaghan and I will be flying economy to the Maldives after all, he thought as he stepped off the kerb, *because I'll need a new motor.* Then stopped – because the black kid was running down the steps. Crying. Lovers' tiff? Didn't stop, just took off at a fast lope towards Notting Hill. He hadn't left the door open behind him, which was a pity. But at least he was one less thing to worry about.

And then Phipps realised that this was going to be one of those blessed gigs, where it all slipped into place. Because a blue Sentra pulled up right outside the house, the driver put his blinkers on, stepped out, holding two white plastic bags, logo of some Indian restaurant on them, and walked up the stairs.

Phipps let him press the button, top floor, penthouse, where that beauty had gone earlier, heard her faint voice, the buzzer go, the door lock release, all while he was running up the stairs. 'Perfect timing,' he said, which was true, reaching past the startled Bangladeshi fellow to push open the door and go in. He raised the duffel. 'I have the beers to go with that.'

The man looked at his receipt. 'Mr Singh?'

Phipps laughed. 'Obviously not. But my sister is Mrs Singh. What do I owe?'

'Thirty-two.'

Phipps put down the duffel and pulled out his money clip from his trousers, peeled off two twenties. When the man jangled coins in his pocket to make change, Phipps said, 'Nah! Keep that. You're a life saver.'

The man shrugged. Bit of a surly bastard; it was a great tip. 'Just put the bags there.' Phipps pointed at a mirrored alcove where flyers and some letters sat before a vase filled with dried flowers.

The delivery man went, leaving the door ajar. Phipps took

a quick look outside then closed it. Food smells rose from the bag and he was suddenly ravenous. When had he last eaten? That Big Mac with Meaghan at noon. He hated fast food, usually had a smoothie for lunch after a gig, avocado, kale, creatine and berries. But Shazza had rushed him and then there was the fracas. No wonder he'd felt the whiskies. Empty stomach.

He pulled a poppadum out, munched it, while he looked at the letters in the alcove. One was from the local council addressed to Severin Properties.

Flat C. Third floor.

He hadn't had time for his usual pre-gig workout. But at least he could climb three floors. Quickly, because the penthouse beauty would be wondering where her curry was soon. This had been his favourite sort of op in the Paras – a fast in and out. What they called a shoot and scoot.

Picking up his duffel, he took the stairs steady, like a StairMaster at the gym.

'When did you last eat?'

Lottie was staring at the door to the hall. The one Patrick had just gone through, leaving it open. She should close it. Somehow it needed to be closed. To shut him out, finally and for ever. But her legs didn't seem to want to move.

Sonya was speaking.

'I'm sorry, what did you say?'

'Eating, Lottie. Have you eaten today?'

'Uh, not really. Perhaps that's why I feel so funny. My legs feel odd.'

'Have you food here?'

'Some in the fridge. Bits and bobs.'

'This is a dish?'

Lottie smiled. 'No. An expression. I think there's some M&S soup. Butternut squash. There's a microwave. Bread too. I'll get it.'

'No, you sit. I get.'

Sonya went to the kitchen. Lottie heard the fridge opened, various cupboards, bowls brought out and placed. She got her legs going, wobbled to the door. When she reached it she heard the front door buzzer, someone let in, distant voices coming up the stairwell. She shut the door, leant her forehead against it. *Done*, she thought. *Finally done.*

She went back into the living room. On the muted telly, the news continued, somewhere in Africa. In the kitchen, the microwave hummed; she heard bread being sliced. Then a plate was put down, the cutlery drawer pulled out. All sounds were sharp to her hearing.

Sounds. She needed some music. She grabbed her phone, hit Spotify, went to one of her jazz playlists. Clicked on a song. Ella Fitzgerald began to sing from the Bluetooth speaker on the coffee table. 'Easy Living'. Late Ella, her voice not as crisp as her younger one, but better, in her mind. The wisdom in it. How she'd been a fool for love, though it had been fun while it lasted.

She shook her head. *Thanks, Ella*, she thought. It had been fun. She had been a fool. No more.

Ella sang on – and there came a knock at the door. Lottie looked down at the table, realising what she'd seen and not seen there – Patrick's straw hat. *Fuck*, she thought, picked it up, stood. *We have to do take two on the exit scene?*

As she walked towards the door, in the kitchen the microwave binged.

The door opened and there was the girl from the photograph. Small, petite really, not a whole lot bigger than Meaghan, who took after her mum, big-boned Sharon. Wild eyebrows, which nearly joined now as she looked at him, puzzled. She was holding a straw hat.

'Yes?' she asked.

He was holding the duffel in his right, numb hand. Which meant he grabbed her by the throat with his left, so she could not make any noise, marched her backwards into the room, gave a good squeeze and threw her over the back of the sofa. She landed hard on a glass table there; he heard a crack, and some woman singing. 'Do not fucking move.' His voice low and hard. 'Move and I'll fucking kill you.'

He dropped the duffel. The sides parted. He hadn't zipped it up since dropping the money in, and the alien from the funfair grinned up at him. He put both hands on the sofa back, leant far over it, till his face was about half a foot from hers. She was sprawled, trying to sit up, despite his warnings. Didn't matter. Just one thing did. 'I need the books. Severin's books. Get them for me or you are fucking dead.' He raised his voice to a bellow. 'Now!'

He'd squeezed her throat pretty hard. Words came, strangulated. 'Yeah, I will. I will! Don't—'

She tried to right herself, like a beetle on its back.

It was then Phipps noticed that there was someone else in

the room — a woman, standing at the dining table about six feet away. She was holding a plate with a bowl on it. Steam came from the bowl. He recognised her; it was the sort of face you'd remember. The beauty from upstairs who could not, of course, be Mrs Singh.

'Oi.' He started to rise. All he could manage before she chucked the bowl of soup at him.

Sonya had not heard the front door open. She had only heard the noise from the room, a man's voice low and nasty, the crash of something heavy onto glass. She'd been coming from the kitchen anyway, the soup steaming in a bowl on a plate in her left hand, a glass of water for herself in her right.

Lottie was lying on the broken glass table, trying to get up. A man was bending over the sofa, glaring at her. She heard him say, 'you are fucking dead', then saw him notice her. As he straightened up, she dropped the glass of water, took the bowl of soup in her right hand, grabbed its hot edge, and threw it at him. It wasn't a powerful throw; her right hand was still sprained from the night before. But she stepped closer to throw, he was only about a metre and a half away, her aim was good and the soup was hot.

It covered his face. The bowl hit him on the chin. He yelled, fury and pain, staggered back. Sonya saw him wipe his eyes with his right hand and reach, strangely, with his left hand into his left armpit. It was then she saw the holster, all she saw because she dropped the plate and she was moving fast towards him, reaching both her good and her bad hand to the gun he was pulling out.

With her right hand she caught his wrist, twisting it hard,

though not too hard as her own wrist hurt but the angle was bad for him, and he grunted. At the same time she grabbed the plastic – *plastic*, she thought, *Glock* – butt of the gun with her other hand, and slipped her thumb behind the trigger just as his forefinger closed over it. She felt the pressure as he tried to pull.

She shot her hands above her, taking him high, twisting as she did. Then she spun around, dropped low, shoved her back hard into his chest, and threw him over her shoulder.

They were of a height. He was heavier, but not that heavy. He had to let go of the gun, otherwise his wrist would have snapped. It fell to the floor, the sound lost in the one he made as he landed hard on his back and neck, half against the wall.

She thought she might have broken her bad wrist now, it hurt so much. There was blood too; the Glock trigger guard had ripped off half her thumbnail as she threw him. He was now trying to get to his knees, yelping as he did so, his left arm at a bad angle. Still, he looked down, and lunged for the gun at her feet. She heeled it backwards, under the sofa. His lunge had fallen short anyway, and he glared up at her, fury and pain in eyes that peeped from a yellow crust of soup.

She'd had no time for thought, only reaction. But now a moment came, and a realisation. Whatever this was, it was not good. For Lottie. For her. She could not get caught up in some crime now. Be held for months before a trial. All her affairs looked into, how she actually made her money. Thoughts flashed, then all were lost to one thing only, one image: her daughter's face earlier that night.

The man was breathing heavily, clutching his left shoulder, still glaring. But he was not moving, so she did, stepping back. 'Go!' She waved at the door. 'Now!' she shouted, when he did not move.

He looked like he was going to say something. Lips parted over teeth bared in a snarl. And then he just stood, swayed and staggered down the corridor and out the door.

She followed, slammed it shut. There was a chain and she put it on, came back. Lottie was just getting onto the sofa. Sonya reached into her bag for her phone, hit speed dial.

His voice came immediately. 'Tsarina?'

'Come now. Fast.'

There was a growl. 'Your client? Is trouble?'

Sonya looked at Lottie. 'Yes.'

'I come now.' Another growl and he rang off.

Sonya dropped the phone back into her bag then went around and sat on the sofa. She leant forward, tapped pause on Lottie's screen, cutting off the music. 'Lottie,' she began, taking her hand.

Mr Phipps stopped in the entrance hall.

The stench of curry filled it. Earlier, the contents of the bags in the alcove had made him hungry. Now they made him sick. Or perhaps that was the butternut squash – on his lips, in his eyes, up his nose. Or the pain he felt all over, but especially in his left shoulder. The bastard was dislocated. It had happened once before, training for parachute jumps.

That bitch! She had thrown him over her back. How had she done that? Who was she? Bystanders were meant to . . . stand by. Like the gig's wife that morning, Severin's wife, face down on the floor. They were not meant to come on like fucking Wonder Woman.

He held up his left arm with his right hand, which wasn't hugely better. Looked in the mirror behind the alcove. He was covered in orangey yellow. Face, hair, suit. *Think*, he ordered himself, lowering his arm, taking the pain, wiping the worst of the muck away with napkins he found in the top of the curry bags. *Think*, he thought again, and did.

If a mission goes wrong, adapt, that's what he was taught in the Paras. Can't achieve the primary objective, go for the secondary. In the limited time he had before it all kicked off again – no doubt those bitches were even now calling the police – he should go back. He'd left too much evidence – prints, probably from when he pushed himself off the floor. His Glock! Worse, his duffel . . . with the fucking money! Why had he put that in there? Because he couldn't be arsed to go back to the car. Where he should go now. Get his back-up – the Beretta he kept duct-taped to the wheel arch. Return, kick in the door . . .

He knew, even as he thought it, that it was all just adrenaline and bollocks. He didn't have the strength. And truly? He didn't want to see Wonder Woman again.

Alright, Plan B. He'd long had it formulated: his line of retreat.

You have to go. Not home. Straight to Heathrow. There was an 11 p.m. flight to Larnaca; he'd taken it before. He had one of his passports in the car, Cypriot credit cards. He was in West London; Monday night he could make the airport in half an hour. No bags, zap, on. He'd have to hit the toilets first. He had gym stuff in the car; he'd change into that. This time of year, this weather, half the tossers who went to Club Med in Cyprus dressed in singlet and shorts anyway. The

Shadows would be no help. They were busted. Sooner he was far away from that set of wankers the better.

His breathing had slowed. Plan B it was.

There was a long, linen cloth with decorative string knots on its ends, under the vase with the fake flowers. He eased it out, pinned it down with his bad arm – fuck! – then jury-rigged a sling. Slipped it over his head, and his left arm into it. It helped. Ready, he opened the door.

There was a man standing there – bald, squat, hefty. His hand was over the buzzer bank, and he jumped when Phipps appeared. Then his piggy eyes narrowed as he took in the mess.

'Hey! You the client?' he asked, his Eastern European accent thick.

'You what?' Phipps shook his head. 'Just stand aside, please.'

As he stepped forward, the man put a hand into the middle of Phipps's chest. 'I think you client. You trouble. You hurt my friend.'

'What? Listen, step aside, you Latvian cunt, or I'll—'

'That's Polish cunt,' the man said, and swung.

He swung right-handed, which meant that Phipps couldn't get his dislocated left arm up to block, could only duck, enough not to take it on the jaw, not enough to get out of the way. The blow landed full on his ear, and had weight behind it; the bastard knew how to throw a punch, unlike Malcolm this morning. There was a popping sound, and he thought, *That's my eardrum fucked.*

His duck had made him stumble forward. The man let him pass. As he staggered down the stairs, he heard some words, Polish no doubt, being called after him. He turned briefly when he reached the pavement to make sure the bloke wasn't following. But he'd stayed at the top, one hand holding the door open. Muttering another curse, the man spat, then went in.

Phipps shook his head. It hurt. Once, in civvies in Catterick, he and two mates had been set on by a gang of locals over some birds. He'd bust some ribs, fractured a cheekbone.

This hurt worse. On top of everything else he now had a constant high-pitched ring.

'Plan B,' he mumbled and set off towards his car.

After about fifty yards, he bent over and puked, thinly, whisky, ginger and flecks of poppadum. A couple stepped wide around him, muttering their disgust. He kept walking. He'd left the Mazda so far away! Finally he saw it, in the residents' bay. And standing beside it, machine out . . . was that same fucking traffic warden!

'I don't believe this,' he cried, staggering up. 'Haven't you got someone else to screw over tonight?'

He expected her reply to be in a West Indian accent, or maybe African. She was a big black woman, after all. So it took him a while to get it when she said, in a voice that could have come from some Oxford college, or from one of those newscasters off the telly, 'No indeed, sir. Tonight you are my sole concern.'

Then someone else spoke, from behind him. Another woman, not as posh. 'Good evening, Mr Phipps,' she said, and he turned to her. Knew he knew her though it took him a moment to place her.

She was the black woman from the pub earlier that night, the one he'd fancied, the one who he'd thought was on Tinder.

Beside her stood the beggar who'd been outside the shop.

He might have done something if he hadn't been grabbed then, by the beggar and some other people he didn't see coming. They pulled his arms back and the agony of that nearly made him black out. He might have said something, if a hessian sack hadn't been put over his head.

He didn't know what, though. He had to admit, he wasn't at his best.

CHAPTER 25

Lottie was shaking so much, she had to use two hands to bring the water glass to her lips. She was also numb, couldn't get out much more than 'yes' or 'no'. Sonya recognised shock, had seen it often enough before. Even though it was a hot night, she fetched a wrap from the bedroom, a thick patterned wool one, and draped it over Lottie's shoulders. She squeezed one, and Lottie bent her cheek to the touch.

Sonya picked up the remote, placed it in Lottie's hands. It was important to give her a task, some focus. The station was still tuned to the news, and who needed that? 'Find something to watch, Lottie. Something funny maybe?'

She noticed the gun. She had kicked it nearly all the way through under the sofa. She grabbed the protective shroud from the sofa's corner, picked up the Glock using that, went and dropped them side by side on the dining table. She turned back, spotted the man's bag next to hers on the floor, went to it, knelt and looked inside. There was a horrible, cheap stuffed toy, an alien. Behind its head she noticed something else and she reached in and pulled out an unmarked envelope that bulged. Slipping her fingernail into the join, she opened it.

'Holy Maria,' she murmured.

She didn't count it. In a riffle she saw that they were all £100 notes, and that there had to be around fifty. She was holding about £5,000 in her hands.

A knock at the door. She dropped the envelope into her own bag, then went to the door. 'Who is it? Tadeusz?' she called.

'Yes, it's me.'

She unchained, opened, let him in. He walked into the room, took it all in – the gun, the broken table, the shaking girl with the clicker in her hand, watching the news with no sound on. 'What happened?' he asked.

'A guy. He attacked, he—'

'The client? I fucked him up, downstairs. For you, Tsarina. Pow!' He swung a punch. 'He don't hurt anyone for a while, I think.' He looked around again, whistled. 'What we do?'

'We go, fast. A minute.' She came around the sofa, sat. 'Listen, Lottie.' She took her hand. 'I have to go. I can't be here when—'

There was no reaction. Lottie just stared at the screen. She hadn't changed channels. 'I need to call someone for you. Who can I call? Maybe Patrick back? Your mother? Is her number on this?'

She picked up the phone. Ella Fitzgerald's face was still locked on it when she lifted it up. 'Lottie? Do you understand me?'

She heard her voice, Sonya's voice. It was as if it was coming from a distance away, though, through static, like a poorly tuned radio. She tried to bring it into focus, but it was hard; the images on the screen were more interesting.

And then she managed to tear herself away from them, to look up into the face, that beautiful, bruised face. What had she just been asked? She swallowed, and her throat hurt. That horrible man had hurt it.

She looked down at the table. It was cracked, a fissure running its width, like the fault line on some seismic map. She supposed the landlord would take it from her damage deposit. Then she remembered she hadn't paid one because Mr Severin had wanted her to live there. That made her remember what the terrible man had asked her. Perhaps it was what the beautiful woman had asked her too.

'I'll get them.' She stood, moving quite fast, on wobbly legs, to the bedroom. They were on the top shelf – the books, an envelope, still in the hemp Waitrose bag. On tiptoes she brought them down, and back to the main room, placing them over the crack on the table. 'Here's what you wanted,' she said. 'The books.'

Sonya peered in the bag. 'Lottie, I do not know this. I must go but I must find someone to take care of you. I think the police will come soon. Listen, do not let in anyone but them, yes?'

'Uh-huh.' Lottie turned back to the TV – and let out a yelp of delight. 'Look! Look, it's Joe.'

She lifted the remote, put on the sound. The newscaster's voice filled the room.

'. . . recap of our main story. In Finchley, North London, this morning Joseph Severin, a well-respected businessman, was brutally murdered at his home in what police are calling a targeted hit. There is speculation that Mr Severin was the latest victim of the assassin known as "the Doorstep Killer".'

Lottie clicked off the sound. Up to that moment, she had been numb. But seeing Joe's face on the screen, hearing of his death, instead of plunging her deeper, it roused her. She felt a surge of energy – sadness, of course, but also . . . the need to do something. To not just . . . stand by.

She turned back to Sonya, the concern on her face. 'I know. You have to go. Don't worry, I'll call my mother. Then the police. I'll be careful.' She bent to the table, reached in the bag, pulled out the envelope. 'But listen, you need to be paid.'

'No, Lottie, it does not—'

'No, listen. I was . . . I was going to pay you anyway, from Joe's money.' She nodded at the screen where Joe's face still was, though it was replaced even as she looked at it. 'His money.'

'What? Lottie, you are still in sho—'

'I'm not. I mean, I probably am but it doesn't matter.' She held out the envelope. 'Take this. It's fifteen hundred pounds.'

'What? No, no. Much too much. Besides I didn't . . . work. I—'

'But it's not for you.' Lottie thrust the envelope into Sonya's open hand. 'It's for your daughter.'

There was a moment, when they were joined by paper, both holding, neither taking. Then Sonya grasped it, took it and dropped the envelope into her handbag on the floor, next to the other one. 'Thank you,' she said.

''s OK.' Lottie's legs suddenly felt very tired so she sat again, turning away. 'Now you should go.'

Her half-finished roll-up was in the ashtray, next to Mr Severin's books. She picked it up, and her Zippo, struck, inhaled. As she did, she felt Sonya's hand once again on her shoulder. She reached up, laid her own hand on top. A squeeze, both ways, and then the Russian, and the man who'd come, were gone.

She'd rolled another and was halfway down it, when the buzzer went, loud, long, insistent. She took a last deep drag, before stubbing the end out, standing and walking. Pressed the intercom button.

'Hello?'

CHAPTER 26

Three days later . . . Thursday 2nd August 2018

Ellerby looked at the remaining five pieces of paper on her desk. Ten-by-eight black-and-white photographs.

She'd taken one of them. Or rather it was a still-capture from the video. Picked it up now – Nathan Greenberg, on top of Parliament Hill three days ago. Behind his head, out of focus, something long and frilly dangled. It had taken her a moment to remember the kites that day, an especially resplendent dragon. In the video, it kept swooping in and out, as if about to fall on his head and devour him.

Nathan Greenberg. He'd been so angry that day, you could even see it in the photo, the set of his jaw. Said some angry things too.

She pulled the lip-reader's transcript from the file. His words were colour-coded an appropriate red. Incomplete because of his head turning. Still.

'. . . plenty of choice. I spoke to the man on Saturday. He knew nothing. He was no threat. He was happy to give the books back. I was collecting them . . .' He'd turned away then, turned back for '. . . days after his daughter's bat mitzvah, for fuck's sake. You had no right—'

He'd been talking about Severin, of course. The books, which had been extensively studied, decoded, ever since she'd collected them from that girl's flat.

She looked at him for a longer moment. Wondered which high-end Tel Aviv seafood beachside restaurant he'd be in on Saturday night. *Enjoy your last fancy meal,* she thought, putting the photo back in the file. *Last one for . . . quite a while?*

She hoped so anyway. When Five's Israeli colleagues went through his door at 4 a.m. on Sunday it would only be the beginning of his journey to jail. And there'd be some bumps along the way. Even the preliminary evidence she'd amassed against the Shadows was pretty solid. And yet, as Wolfden had said the first time she'd met him, these were clever men. Adept at covering tracks.

She slipped his photo in the bulging folder, tapped another. Perry Lascelles. Would he be at some diplomatic soirée on Saturday night? Maybe the champagne he'd be drinking there would make him a little groggy when, early next morning, Six's agents in Ankara rang his doorbell?

She put the photo away, picked up another. Sadiq Khan. A trickier grab as he was in Dubai, and Gulf States policemen were less obliging than some of their colleagues elsewhere. But Wolfden had told her he was calling in a favour. From the way he said it, it didn't seem like one that would be refused. Except tomorrow, Friday, was Yawm al-Jum'ah, the Muslim day of prayer, and they wouldn't engage in all the preparations required so Saturday at 4 a.m. was out. It had to be Sunday, for all of them. They had to be taken simultaneously.

He joined the others in the folder. Then Bernard Crouch was in her hands. As he would be in three days. She'd be part of the team at his Knightsbridge mews house. No cafetière, croissants and *Sunday Times* in bed for him that morning.

She put him away. There was only the one photo on her desk now. She didn't pick it up, just stared down at the face. At the only one – so far – whose door would not be kicked in that Sunday.

Why? What made Sebastien Grant the exception? Was he cleverer than the other four? Probably not. He'd only attained a 'Gentleman's Third' at Oxford while Khan and Goldberg both got Firsts. Better connected? Perhaps. One cousin was an earl, after all. Slightly less greedy, which meant his tracks were just a bit better covered? Possibly.

She'd also read all his entry interviews for Six, taken while he was still a lieutenant in the army. He'd taken the usual tests. Scored very highly on all of them . . . including the PCL-R: the Psychopathy Checklist, Revised. At twenty-five points they'd have diagnosed him as a psychopath and that would have ruled him out. Grant had scored twenty-three. One of the examiners had scrawled on the bottom of the sheet that the service should look for more recruits who scored so highly. She didn't think the man was actually joking.

Ellerby scratched her chin. Such an assessment would lead him to make more mistakes, not less, surely? Or was it the opposite? She sighed. She often wished she'd studied psychology at uni rather than law. More useful in this job.

She slid him in with the others and tapped the folder. She'd spent the day reading and re-reading her preliminary report, seeking something – anything – that somehow she might have missed on Grant. Some field observation she hadn't dwelt on enough. Some piece of computer intel that would wrap it all up. Enable her to nab the whole shebang, instead of just four-fifths of it.

'Perfectionism,' she muttered. Ever her curse, listed in most reports from primary school to the LSE. In most evaluations since she'd joined Five. They always said they preferred it to its opposite, slackness. Just pointed out that if she relinquished a little control, intuition might be allowed more space.

Which she thought was bollocks, truly. Control had four of the five Shadows waiting to be charged in three days' time. Would any intuitive insight have made it five for five?

She sighed again. Her team, gathering now in the Morpeth Arms down Millbank, were quite happy with four out of five. She was expected there. She was already late. They'd cheer her as she came in, no doubt. She'd have to put aside her perfectionism, and take the win. As well as pick up the tab, no doubt.

One last thing to do first. One last chance.

Gathering the bulging folder, she pushed back her chair.

Mr Phipps was sitting in the chair. Again.

It wasn't a comfortable chair. Wouldn't have been, even if he could have adjusted a little, almost impossible with his wrists chained to the table before him. Besides, even if he wasn't hurting all over still, there wasn't an angle that eased him. Which he knew was the point.

He'd waited for about two hours, he thought, on this the

third day of interrogation – though he couldn't be sure of that since he hadn't seen daylight since they'd brought him in. They'd also kept the light on in his cell all night, if night it was and, of course, they'd taken his watch; the rotating bunch of interrogators never wore theirs.

He'd been tortured before. It was part of the training in the Paras for Belfast, learning what a man could take, the varying levels of physical and mental. There had not been much of the former so far beyond denying him painkillers for his dislocated shoulder, which at least they had finally and painfully put back in. Nothing for his ear either, which had cauliflowered and still rang like a mofo.

He'd knew he'd been more forthcoming on that first day. The pain but also the realisation that they knew almost everything anyway, as they revealed in a series of photos and papers to try and provoke him. Despite his condition, he'd handled it all pretty well. He only knew a limited amount anyway. He'd been the sharp end of the Shadows' operations and as a knife was a tool only, knew nothing of why it was wielded.

Most of their questions had focused on Sebastien Grant – of course, since apart from his first interview for the job, he'd only ever dealt with him. And he knew he'd blabbed a bit about him. But the second day, even through the mist of agony, he'd realised there was something about the questions. Some . . . desperation? They didn't have Grant yet. They wanted Phipps to give him to them somehow.

Which he wasn't going to do, even if he could. It wasn't a question of not wanting his employer to go down. He'd happily wield the knife on him, free of charge, the supercilious cunt. But if they didn't have him, perhaps he could not be had. In which case Phipps would probably last less than a week in the Scrubs if he'd grassed him up.

Yet it wasn't so much himself he was worried about. He had Meaghan to think about. Grant had proved again and again that anyone was a target if it helped him. Kill Severin's wife. Kill the piano player. Kill the hitman's daughter.

No, he thought, shifting, wincing. Whoever came through that door today he would give them nothing more.

The first person who did was the muscle, a vast and silent man with a face like a cliff. Phipps had dubbed him 'Lurch', from the Addams Family, and he said nothing, ever. Just stared at him – rather glumly, Phipps thought. The second was her, the same woman who'd nicked him, who he'd briefly admired in that pub however many days ago that was. 'Ellerby' she called herself, just once, no title with it – could be her first name, her last, or more likely an alias.

This time, she was followed by someone new. Older bloke, quite old in fact. Thick, long grey hair swept back. Nice suit. Lurch stepped behind the table, Ellerby sat in the chair in front of it, the new bloke went and leant into a corner, just out of the light spill of the single bulb over the table.

Ellerby placed a folder in front of her. 'Mr Phipps,' she said briskly, opening it. 'Do you know how deep in the shit you are?'

It didn't seem like the sort of question that needed a reply so he didn't make one. She looked at him for a long moment then down to the top page before her. 'This is a list of all the hits we believe you made for the rogue department who employed you over the last three years.'

'Contracted,' he said.

'What?'

'I was contracted. Freelance. Never employed.'

She frowned at him, then reversed the list and shoved it across. 'Can you confirm these are all down to you? And that none are missing?'

He looked down. It shocked him, actually, the amount. Nearly filled the page. Double spaced, of course. Still.

He read and saw that two were missing, which was nothing he need talk about. One on the list wasn't down to him, but again, it wasn't worth mentioning. What was he going to get, a lighter sentence because he'd killed only nineteen and not twenty? The names swam up. About a quarter of them were collateral. He couldn't put faces to many. Except the last: Joseph Severin.

'Looks about right.'

'About?'

'It's right.'

'Well, haven't you been the busy little worker bee? Sorry, freelance bee.' Her voice rang with contempt, then switched to cold anger. 'All these lives destroyed. Not only the dead. Their families too. Parents, children, sisters, brothers. Do you feel any guilt at all? Any remorse?'

He considered. Spoke. 'Will it get me a few years reduced if I am . . .' He looked to the ceiling for the word, a good crossword-puzzle word. 'Penitent?'

She didn't reply. Just pulled the sheet back, replaced it in the folder, lifted another. 'But this last one. You call them "gigs", yes? Perhaps you can explain why you so grievously cocked it up.' She went on without giving him the chance.

'According to other testimony you were sent to retrieve some ledgers. These "books". The ones that this Joseph Severin was keeping for the rogue operation. Fetch them from a young woman who, I presume, you were going to kill afterwards, yes?'

Again there was no point in replying. He didn't even shrug.

She continued, 'I repeat: why such a cock-up from a man who has carried out as many operations as you? Who we found on the street, beaten, smelling of whisky and' – she glanced down – 'curried butternut squash?' She leant forward. 'What went wrong this time, Mr Phipps?'

He hadn't mentioned the beauty. They hadn't asked much about that night yet, being more concerned with the Shadows. He might have told them, when he was feeling weaker. Now, though, he didn't want to. Pride, he supposed. And a certain respect. That fucking ninja had done him, good and proper. 'Bad luck. An accident as I walked in. I tripped over the carpet and she was on me, that girl, like a banshee.'

She stared at him, then her mouth curled. 'You expect me to believe that ridiculous story?'

He leant, as far back as the handcuffs let him. 'Believe what you want, love. It's the only one you're getting.' He looked for the first time to the man standing out of the light at the back of the cell. 'Now, I assume he's the Old Bill. So how's about him giving me my caution and let's just crack on.'

She put the paper back in the folder, bound it with the elastic. 'Before we do that, one last thing. I'd like you to tell me why we should believe your assertion over that of Sebastien Grant.'

'My assertion?'

'Your claim. On the first day here. That he was the one

who contracted you to kill Joseph Severin, and many others. Him and him alone. When he says he was merely running you as an agent. That he was unaware of your murderous sideline.'

'I never said that.'

'You did.' She tapped the file. 'It was recorded and transcribed.'

'I was delirious. It was made under duress. I won't sign that statement.'

'Mr Phipps, you know what you are looking at here. A whole life sentence. Never to see your daughter again except through glass. But if you were to help us? Give us one bit of proof?'

'Are you offering me a deal?'

'Not as such. But it might help you. Judges like it when people are helpful.'

Phipps stared at her for a long moment, then shook his head. 'Mr Grant is obviously a very clever man. Oxford degree and all. I left school with two O levels, one of them in woodworking.' He smacked his lips together. 'So if you haven't got it in that big folder of yours already, love, I'd suggest it isn't there.' He leant back in, lowered his voice. 'And I'm signing nothing.'

She looked as if she was going to say something more. But that other man spoke first, softly. 'It's alright, Ellerby. I'll take it from here.'

She sat back, picked up her folder, stood. Lurch came from behind Phipps to stand with her. She said, 'Mr Wolfden, I would like—'

'I said, I'd handle it.'

The voice was still soft, but now it had steel in it. Ellerby nodded, and left. Lurch made to follow, but the older man delayed him. 'Leave the keys,' he said.

Lurch obeyed, handing over a set, then left the cell, closing the door behind him.

Ellerby stood outside the cell door for a moment. 'So, shall we?' the tall agent, Frobisher was his name, asked.

'Shall we what?'

'The Morpeth?'

There was a small glass window set in the door. The glass was thick; she could only see the vague outlines of the two men in there. They looked identical. In a way they were. Men cut from the same cloth. Not like Sebastien Grant at all. Except perhaps in one way . . .

Suddenly she smiled. More, gave a little laugh. Because she'd had an intuition. She'd relinquished control. At last. Got what she wanted.

'That's five out of five,' she murmured.

'Ma'am?'

She looked up into Frobisher's puzzled face. 'Yes. The Morpeth. Let's go.'

The old man in the cell sat. Looked at Phipps for a long while. Phipps looked back. Finally, the man spoke. 'She was right, of course. You really cocked it up.'

It wasn't said with any venom, and just as softly as he'd spoken before. There was even a touch of a smile in his eyes, and Phipps thought, *'ello, 'ello, what's happening here?* 'I did . . . sir,' he replied, adding the title as an afterthought, sensing something.

The man nodded. 'Three Para, weren't you?'

'Sir.'

'I was First. Before I went to the SAS. And then came . . . here.' He waved a hand and Phipps knew he wasn't referring to the cell but to the service. 'They thought my skills might be useful. Though it's mostly admin now, of course. Don't get out in the field, *much*.' The emphasis was clear. He sat back, scratched his nose. 'I'm torn about you, Phipps. You were good, and then you suddenly and spectacularly weren't. Which would you be, say, tomorrow?'

Phipps tried to keep the hope down, and out of his voice. 'Good again, sir.'

'Would you? Hmm.' He raised the keys, jangled them, stared at them while he spoke. 'As I say, torn. You've created a fuss. You've left a mess. Neither good. The sensible thing might be to throw you to the wolves.' He stared at Phipps. 'But something I've never understood is how so-called society expects to be protected when it trains its protectors to kill – and then is surprised when they do. It seems . . .'

He broke off, looked up at the ceiling for a moment, then down again. 'If you came to work for me, there'd be no freelancing. You'd be employed. You'd have an NI number, bi-monthly cheques, sort of thing.' He grinned. 'And we'd want our money back, Phipps. It wasn't the Shadows' and it's not yours. It's all in those books of course, every last penny they paid you. Think you could live with that?'

Ten minutes before, he'd been contemplating the rest of his life in prison. Besides, Cyprus wasn't in the books. Nor the account in Dominica. 'Yes, sir. I think I could live with that quite well.'

'Alright.'

The man rose. For a moment he was closer to the light bulb – and Phipps noticed dandruff on his collar. 'May I ask, sir? The department I'll be working for? Does it have a name? Like, a nickname?'

'Certainly not. What do you think we are, a bunch of tossers?'

He reached into his pocket, drew out a brown envelope. Placed it on the table, just out of Mr Phipps's cuffed reach. 'First assignment.'

He went to the door, turned. 'Name's Wolfden,' he said, and then threw the keys back onto the table. They slid all the way up to where Phipps's hands rested. Then, without another word, he left the cell.

Phipps snagged the keys with a little finger and pulled them into a grip. It took a while, what with his bad shoulder and arm. When he was free he rubbed his wrists, then reached for the envelope. Opened it. It contained nothing but a single photograph.

Which made him smile.

CHAPTER 27

Saturday 5th August 2018

It was very hot, the day they buried Joe Severin.

Lottie stood quite far back in the Jewish cemetery in Golders Green, part hidden by a tomb. If one of the funeral party, who hadn't noticed her before in the chapel, happened to glance her way, they might dismiss her as one of 'those' people – she'd heard of them – who liked to attend other people's funerals. But no one paid her any mind. They were, understandably, focused on what was before them – the hole in the earth, the coffin beside it, the rabbi intoning. She'd got a few odd looks when she'd slipped into the back of the chapel – she wasn't dressed like them, in uniform black and grey; she didn't think Joe would have liked that – but wore a knee-length, sleeveless blue dress and slingback sandal wedges. She had covered up with her red shawl, too hot for the day, but she'd guessed that bare shoulders might draw too much attention. She did share one item with them all – a kindly older gentleman, an usher, had pinned a small back ribbon to her shawl, the ribbon torn halfway down its length.

He'd accepted her brief explanation: a happy tenant come to pay her respects.

It was, of course, partly true.

She touched the ribbon now and looked back to the gathering. She'd googled 'Jewish funerals' before she came, so knew a little of what she was seeing – and hearing. Psalms were being chanted, a rise and fall of mainly male voices, almost Gregorian. It was beautiful, and she found she was listening while staring up into the clearest of blue summer skies. She wasn't religious in any way. But she wondered if Joe's spirit, that lovely spirit she'd glimpsed as he unravelled before her, was soaring up to the skies, carried by those chanted words.

English was being spoken now, an older man who looked a little like a grey-haired Joe – his brother probably – starting to talk about him. She walked away. This was the eulogy and they were going to praise a man she really didn't know. She didn't need to hear about that man. She had her own Joe.

Daphne was parked just outside the gates on Hoop Lane – illegally of course, but for once she hadn't got a ticket. Result! All the stuff she'd had at Portobello was crammed in – not that much, truly; she'd not been there that long.

She'd had to clear out that morning. That letch from Severin's, Oliver, had come to collect the keys and see her out a couple of hours before. He'd been subdued, though, un-letchy, in his funeral black with ribbon pinned, and his black skull cap. When he saw the broken table, he'd just shaken his head. He knew the story, part of it anyway, the part that had been allowed to be printed and broadcast. Everyone did. But the first person through the door on that one London day had been a well-dressed black woman and she only stayed a little because she got what she came for – Mr Severin's books. She'd gone by the time the police showed up. They'd talked to her for a few hours, and then again the next day, but realised quite quickly that she didn't know much. She told them what she did, all she did, no point in lying. One female officer had sniffed her ashtray like a hound, and given her a knowing grin at the whiff of one of her specials in there. But she hadn't made a fuss. Portobello, after all, and more important things to deal with.

Vapour trails streaked the blue sky. Lottie suddenly wondered if Sonya was on one of the planes that made them.

She lowered herself into Daphne, the old girl greeting her with her usual chorus of leather squeaks and moans. Her mum's for a few days, then back to town. She started in the pit at the Cambridge on Tuesday, second keyboards. Her friend Saar was in the Alps, so she was house-sitting for the first week in Dollis Hill. After that? Something would show up.

Something always did.

Sonya was finally able to settle back into her seat. She'd sorted her daughter out. Maria had her big headphones on, her big glasses, her big eyes fixed on the cartoon story unfolding on the screen before her. On her daughter's other side, Georgiy was already asleep, his face pressed into a pillow that he'd wedged against the cabin's wall. He was unshaven, grey and black stubble stark against his pasty skin. He'd also slept most of the way on the connecting flight from Moscow to Heathrow. Would sleep perhaps all the way on this last to Baltimore. Which was fine. She was happier to watch him sleep here than to imagine him awake back in Russia.

They'd been lucky, all of them. Another week and they might not have been. But that one London day had changed everything. The money, of course, almost the exact sum she'd needed, found in those few strange moments. More fortune following the money – her husband had only just slipped down the slope of heroin, and her early return pulled him back up. A sudden slight rise in the pound, on some rumour of Brexit, a drop in the ruble, both added a few hundred to her stash. A day's sale on flights to America meant she could buy three tickets for the price of two. She couldn't leave her husband in Moscow. Without her, there was every chance he would not be there when she got back. But now, perhaps none of them would go back? Maria's operation at Johns Hopkins, then the post-operative supervision, would take some time. Time to figure out how to stay on, perhaps?

For a long time now, her daughter had been researching America, making a scrapbook of all the places she wanted to visit. New York was number one. She had pasted in a photo of the Statue of Liberty. Sonya remembered studying it in school, recalled its inscription: 'Give me your tired, your poor, your huddled masses yearning to breathe free.' She was certainly tired, not rich. Perhaps there was a way. America welcomed immigrants, didn't it?

She looked beyond Georgiy, to the window, out into the evening sky. A beautiful night, cloudless, the sunset a mauve wonder. She glanced down, reached and tucked Marusya's little silver crucifix back under her T-shirt. Her daughter caught her wrist, held it, squeezed it tight. It hurt a little, under the bandage. But this was a good kind of pain, and she didn't mind.

CHAPTER 28

Same day. Evening.

Mr Phipps was in the gym.

It was one of his favourites, a plush one in Holland Park. He'd go there sometimes even if he wasn't working, which he was, today. It was always busy, with a clientele that suited the neighbourhood. Elegantly kitted out, the mainly younger men and women ran, and rode, and elliptically skied, and pumped. No headbangers here, like in the rec centre in Gants Hill, which was mainly blokes his own age. The tattoos there were blue, smeared, old-school, anchors, girls' names and the like. Here, roses and skulls peeked from singlets, grapevines and snakes writhed up arms. He'd noticed one lady, older than the kids, perhaps thirty-five, well fit, though. She had a phoenix, its head on one shoulder, its feet resting in flames on a shapely bicep.

He didn't talk to ladies in gyms. There was an etiquette and he never wanted to be noticed. He didn't stare, for the same reason. But a swift glance now and again? It helped power his workouts.

Not that he could do much. His shoulder was still fucked

from before. So he did the aerobic stuff, the StairMaster, and lots of sit-ups and crunches. He probably should have taken another week off. But it was his first gig tonight for his new employers and he was superstitious, had his rituals. His 'fetishes'. They'd said it was West London, nothing more yet. He was expecting a text with the address. Around six, they'd said. Three quarters of an hour. A few last crunches, then a shower before . . .

He hit 'stop', the treadmill slowed, he stepped off it. Fetched the cleaner, sprayed the machine, wiped it down, all a bit tricky one-handed. The sloping bench was free, but as he crossed to it, he noticed a phoenix flying in from the west.

They arrived at the same time. 'Oh, after you,' she said.

'No, no. Please.' He refrained from saying, 'ladies first'. He'd been told by Paula, when he'd dumped her in Costa Coffee that lunchtime, that it made him sound like a prat.

She had brown eyes with little wrinkles springing up around them when she smiled, which she did now. She had short hair, a slim physique, toned. 'It's my last set. Uh, want to alternate?'

Do I, he thought, noting the voice. Low, not too posh, a hint of Midlands. But all he said was, 'Absolutely.'

She did a set of twenty, impeccably. Uncurled her legs, slid off. She looked at his arm, still in the sling. 'Looks awkward. And painful.'

'Both, yeah. Bike accident. Some idiot didn't see me.'

She nodded, now noticing his swollen ear. 'Do you need a—?'

'No. I'm good.'

He did his set, impeccably, despite the sling. They alternated in silence but she didn't move away when he lowered himself for his last. When he stood up again, he thought he'd risk it. 'Lovely bird.' He pointed at her arm. 'Phoenix, right?'

She glanced down. 'Oh yes. Though this is the Persian one, the simurgh.' She blushed a little; he wasn't sure why. 'Not quite finished, though.'

'Is the Persian one still about rebirth? Moving on?'

'It is. I am.' This she said firmly; whatever the blush was, gone. She looked at his bare arms. 'None for you?'

'None that I dare show in public.'

He smiled at her. She smiled back. There was a moment – and then his phone dinged. He looked at the text, and grinned.

'Girlfriend?' The challenge was clear in her voice.

'Nope.' He clicked the phone off. 'I've moved on too.'

He gave her his number. Always the best tactic, he felt. Her name was Melanie. She didn't give him her number. But he had a feeling she would call.

Sebastien zipped up his suitcase, rubbed both his wrists – still painful after a week, though the rest of him had largely recovered – then looked around, doing his final sweep. His phone was in his coat pocket, his charger in his carry-on along with the passport he was going to use; his other two were in the bag he'd check.

His Aran sweater was still on the bed but the case was already full and he'd have had to part unpack to squeeze it in. Too much hassle. It was cold in New Zealand this time of year but he wasn't going to stay there long. Once he'd collected his money, he'd move on to Polynesia. From there? Who knew?

He glanced at the bedside table. He'd thought of taking the

photo of him, Genevieve and Toby in Antibes last summer, out of the frame and packing it. But now he decided he couldn't be arsed. What was he going to do, sit on a beach in Bora Bora and pine for his London life? Not likely. That one was over. It was time to begin anew. Besides, Toby was two and full in the tantrum stage, a royal pain in the backside. While Genevieve was clearly as bored of him as he was of her.

I'm like that bird, what is it called? A . . . phoenix, that's right. Rising from the flames. Funny, he thought, Mr Phipps had mocked him for using the image last week in the pub. He'd heard that their killer was going to be charged with twenty murders. Shocking what monsters walked the streets of London.

Flames, he thought, lifting the suitcase, taking it downstairs, dropping it in the front hall. Bernard had said they were licking at the door. Best to leave before the house goes up. He was going to stay, brazen it out, the tit. Perry was back in Ankara; Nate was already in Israel. Both had routes out planned.

His own grilling at the Box had lasted a day and a half. But the clever thing the Shadows had done from the very beginning was to conduct operations in areas that had legitimate British interests involved. Refugees smuggled by truck from Germany, or boat out of Libya? Infiltrate, organise a few shiploads, ultimately to halt the flow. A sting operation involving heroin to squeeze the last lifeblood out of ISIS funding?

He could see that they weren't believed. That fucker Wolfden – the Wolf! – had been especially sceptical. But it was hard to prove them anything other than over-enthused patriots. For now – though perhaps not for long. The money of course was scattered all over. Take a while to pull that info together, since the electronic trail was almost non-existent. Clever again.

They'd need Sadiq. But no one knew where the little brown chap was, including his fellow Shadows. It was a little worrying. Even without the books, the man should still be transferring close to half a mil into each member's account. Necessary funding for the life he had planned.

They'd put Sebastien on gardening leave and taken his British and diplomatic passports, but he rarely travelled on those anyway. While just last night the watchers outside had been withdrawn. Find Sadiq and all might change, of course. If the dark-skinned little bastard could be persuaded to roll?

No, it was definitely time to leave.

He'd ordered the limo for six. Fifteen minutes. The BA lounge at Heathrow had quite an acceptable wine list. His flight wasn't till ten but better to hang out there than here – he might even get sentimental, change his mind about the photograph.

He poured himself a Highland Park, sat on the sofa, looked around. The room was Genevieve's taste, not his. Or truly, it was Jasper Conran's. He doubted she'd be able to keep up the mortgage payments. Well, her dad was loaded, one of the main reasons he'd married her. The old man would bail her out.

At 5.55 his phone gave a distinctive ding in his coat in the hall. Sadiq, at last. Be good to know that other half mil was secure.

He went and fished out the phone. Sadiq's number – but

no message. At least not in words. Because on his screen, two black cue balls, with eyes and grinning mouths, were jumping up and down.

He was puzzling over them when the doorbell chimed. He glanced at the security screen. It was fuzzy, white lines shooting across it. On the fritz again. He'd have to get it fixed . . . no, Genevieve would. He stepped up to the spyhole. The limo driver was a blur, turned away, and standing too close to the door.

He unlocked, opened.

A man in white overalls and a red cap was standing there. He had a sling over his left arm.

'Mr Phipps!' Sebastien exclaimed.

'How many times do I have to tell you?' Mr Phipps replied, as he raised the Glock. 'Don't use my name.'

Mr Phipps will return in

ONE BERLIN DAY

Read on for an early extract...

CHAPTER 1

8 a.m., 7th September, 2019
A forest on the outskirts of Berlin

Stanley's phone pinged. He checked the message.

Are you here?

He texted back.

Close.

He switched to Maps.Me. According to that, the clearing was about 100 metres ahead. The path they were on ended at the rendezvous. He turned back, called softly. 'Nearly there, boys.'

He heard his crew doing what he now did: phone away. MMA gloves on. Zip up the black Stone Island composite jacket. Hoodie up. The one thing they didn't do that he did was reach to the mount on his chest and switch on the GoPro.

'Fuckin' love this, Stan, fuckin' love it!'

Rodge was at his left shoulder now since the path had widened. Stanley glanced up at him, noted the shimmer in his eye, bright yet also cloudy. 'You 'ad a bump? You twat, I warned ya—'

'Just the one, Stan, just the one! Wake me up.' Rodge sniffed, ran knuckles under his nose. 'Fuckin' 'angover fuckin' nailed me. German beer, eh?'

Stanley glanced right. Todge had moved up too. As massive as his twin, his eyes looked clear. 'You 'eld off?'

'Yeah.'

It was all Stanley would get. The one brother did the talking for both. And the snorting, it seemed. 'Good. Glad someone listens to me. 'old up.'

The path had ended between two oaks, like a doorway into the field beyond. The arena. Stanley held up his hand, and everyone halted, watching him. When he rotated his wrist, they spread out either side of him, staying beneath the edge of the canopy. Fifty metres across what was a grassy oval, it was like looking into a mirror: dark shapes within the treeline.

'Fuckin' love it,' muttered Rodge.

No signal was given. Two men took one step out from under the trees, and nineteen men followed each of them.

Stanley assessed. Germans, he thought. Big bastards. Not quite as big as the Dutch or Belgians or Croatians. Bigger than his English lads. Didn't matter. It wasn't the size, it was what you did with it. He and his crew had been in the Canning Town gym all week. No booze. No bumps. Working some moves.

The silence held for a few moments. It was sunny, quite warm, birds were singing away. Nice place for a picnic, he thought.

Silence broken by a call. Sing-songey, like on the terraces. *'Englander. Scheiße. Englander. Scheiße.'*

They'd obviously practised. So had his lot. It had been

hard to settle on one, but the classics were usually the best. 'Now,' he called, then opened up with the others.

'Have you... ever seen a German win a war?
'ave you ever seen a German win a war?
'ave you ever seen a German
ever seen a German
'ave you ever seen a German win a war?'

It was enough. They hadn't come to chant, after all.

It kicked off. No running, both sides a steady stride, meeting in the middle.

Stanley selected his victim. He liked them big, and there was no shortage of that on the German side. He also liked to use tactics. He'd learnt some when he was briefly in the Army Cadets. Head on, big fuckers, good chance of losing. Move in with the Twins and double-team the enemy flank. Left some of his crew exposed. But he'd be back for them.

The big bloke stopped and swung a fist the size of a serrano ham. Stanley didn't stop, just ducked, planted his left foot, kicked hard with his right. Tungsten-toed boot caught the German's knee, and he screamed, went down. You weren't allowed weapons in an arranged fight – but no one inspected your footwear. Todge followed up, ran over him, trampling. Rodge had taken a couple to the boat – *smack smack* – from a wiry little sod but it didn't faze him, he just kept windmilling away, missing most, connecting with some. He was like a fucking combine harvester when he got going, especially after the dickie he'd had.

Stanley moved on. There were two blokes still on that end of the enemy line, unengaged as yet. Stanley changed that by grabbing one by the front of his leather jacket and pulling him into a hard nut. Didn't get it quite right, caught as much forehead as nose which meant he was a little blurry and didn't see the fist that caught him on the ear. Rang his bell, hurt like a cunt, and he followed the force of the blow away, raising arms which was wise as blows followed blow and he took them on his forearm, his biceps, his elbow. That last one must have hurt the puncher because he yelped, pain distracting him, for the moment Stanley needed to step back and one-two him, gut, uppercut. Bloke went down as if he'd been shot. Stanley put the heel of his boot into his face just for luck and left it at that. One of the rules – one of the few rules – was that once someone was out, you left them. No one needed death on their hands. The authorities frowned on death.

Before moving on, he did take the time to slip a card out of his pocket and lay it on the German's lad's chest. *Congratulations*, it read, *you have just met the ICF.*

It was one of the very few relics of his dad's days in the same West Ham crew, the Inter City Firm. You left your victim a keepsake to go with the scar. But his old man would have been baffled by the world of the arranged fight. The group on the Signal app, the even numbers. The fucking rules. Back in his day you ambushed visiting fans at the railway station or outside the ground and if you were tooled up and outnumbered the oppo three to one, so much the better.

Stanley crouched, ready. No one was close so he glanced left – to where Rodge had a bloke down and was pummelling him again and again in the mush, yelling, 'Cunt!' the while. The bloke was clearly gone so Stanley slapped the big boy around his ear. 'Stop!' he yelled.

'Fuck's sake, Stan.' Rodge, eyes bright with dickie and violence, looked up at him, and rubbed his ear. 'oo's side are you on?'

To his right, Todge rose from his own victim, out cold and now with an ICF card held between bloodied teeth. 'Next?' he grunted, looking at his leader for a cue.

Stanley assessed. About half the Englishmen were out, half the Germans. The rest of the fight had degenerated into a series of *mano a mano*, rapidly tiring men swiping at each other, mostly missing. It had lasted about two minutes, which was about average, fighting was fucking exhausting. Unless they wanted to start chasing each other through the forest, it was probably about long enough.

His gaze fell on one German at the opposite end of the line of bodies and swaying fighters. He was also just standing there. Had a boot on a squirming body as if pinning him down – Davey, the youngest of the ICF crew, the least experienced, his fair hair streaked in blood. Stanley recognised the German's face, because they'd had a couple of Signal conversations. One was about arranging this fight. One was about something else entirely. His name was Wolfgang. He looked around, then back at Stanley. Shrugged. Stanley shrugged back, then both men whistled, the German with his fingers, Stanley pulling his referee-dad's Thunderer from his pocket.

It took a few moments for those still fighting to hear, to realise. Some half-hearted last blows, some cusses before the lines separated. Steam rose from bodies vertical and horizontal. Then those standing helped those not, up. Young Davey was out cold, so Rodge and Todge went and picked him up, carried him back to the treeline where they'd started from. Excited whispers, re-lived moments, already ballooning into myth. Stanley would puncture some of them when they screened the footage from his GoPro later, though some reputations would be enhanced. He looked back into the clearing. The Germans had also retired. Wolfgang, however, had not moved – and he beckoned Stanley now.

''old this, Rodge.' He unclipped the GoPro, passed it over. You weren't meant to record fights, but he couldn't resist. He'd never post them, but they were a laugh to look at over a few beers.

Stanley crossed to where the German waited. He'd only seen him on camera, so hadn't appreciated how big the cunt was, at least 6'4" to Stanley's 5'11". The white-blond hair was in the same razor cut, though, the scar beside the left eye still making it droop. The other eye was clear, blue, keen.

The man waited till Stanley was beside him, on a slight rise so that their eyes were level, before he spoke. 'What do think, English?' He glanced at the treeline before him, then back at his own. 'Draw?'

Stanley shrugged. The two crews would probably put up different stats on Telegram, where rankings were followed as closely as the football results. But there was no point in arguing. There were more important things to discuss. 'Seems fair.'

Wolfgang nodded, pushing up his lower lip. 'Good. Now, as to the other thing—'

'You brought it, right?'

'No, it's what I tell you. A little delay from the east.'

'How little?'

A shrug. 'Three days?'

'Day after the game, then?'

A nod. *Fuck,* Stanley thought, and looked away, back to his boys. Young Davey was on his feet, which was good. Spitting blood, which was not. Stanley was supposed to collect the ketamine straight after the fight, go to the U19's England vs Germany on Wednesday, then return home by train direct from Haiger, where the game was being played, with what he'd picked up today hidden among all the England supporters. Coming back to Berlin, almost 300 miles away, and then going home without the cover? It was not ideal, not at all.

The German must have noted the struggle in the Englishman's eyes. 'Look, it's not big problem. Tonight, you come,' he reached into his pocket, pulled something out, 'here. We work it all out, yes?'

He reached out what he held – a beer mat, blank side up, with writing on it. Stanley saw that it was a Berlin address. 'What's this?'

'This?' Wolfgang smiled. 'This is, how do you call it? Here we say *klubhaus.*'

'Clubhouse. Same word in England. English word.'

'Maybe German word first, *nein?*' His eyes sparkled. 'You come, maybe nine? We drink beers. Everything work out, yes?'

'OK. All of us?'

Wolfgang glanced at the English crew. 'I think, no. Beer, maybe something else,' he tapped his nose. 'Kids, eh? They like to fight.'

'Yeah, well, we all like that.' Stanley nodded. 'OK, just me. I'll see you,' he waved the beer mat, 'here.'

He turned away, took a step. Wolfgang's words halted him. 'You need to bring this,' he pointed at the beer mat. 'Security at door. Special *klubhaus*.' He stepped forward, took the beer mat, flipped it.

The reverse side was a swastika. The classic one, black on red. Across the bottom a date was printed in numbers: 20.04.1889, Stanley read. 'What's that?'

'The Führer's birthday.'

'I see.' Stanley knew that many of the German crews were fascist. But loads were in Europe. Some in England too. Personally, he didn't think about politics much; though that bloke Farage said some interesting things. All this Brexit bollocks. Just fucking get it done.

He tried to take the beer mat back. But the German held on, and they were joined by cardboard. 'How did you get this, English?' Wolfgang asked, jerking his chin, using it to point at Stanley's face.

There was no question of what he was referring to: Stanley's nose. Broken, broken again to reset it, which it hadn't truly done. It still splayed left, with the bridge out of proportion to the rest.

He was often asked. Had a story which he varied a little depending on the audience. 'Fight, of course.' He looked down at the swastika they still shared. 'Domzale. My first away match with the ICF. Slovenian Ultra. Fucker was even bigger than you, Wolfgang.' He grinned. 'But I promise you, his face will still look worse than mine three years later.' He pulled the card and the German released it. 'I'll see you tonight.'

He started to walk back to the lads. Took it slow, breathed

deep to get control, as he always needed to do after telling that particular lie. Because as he told it, he always saw the man who'd broken his nose. Not three years ago. Last year, and not in Slovenia but at the Leyton Leisure Centre, East London. He even knew the cunt's name, because a woman had used it in the pool. A name, along with a face he'd never forget.

'Mr Phipps,' he muttered. 'One day. One fucking day.'

CHAPTER 2

Same day. 2 p.m., 7th September, 2019

As the 07.03 from Amsterdam pulled into the Berlin Hauptbahnhof, Mr Phipps wrapped the West Ham scarf around his neck again and shook his head. He knew why he was wearing it, part of his cover for this op, blending in. But he'd been an Arsenal fan since birth, born into a Gooner family, so wearing another team's colours ticked him off.

CHRIS HUMPHREYS was born in Toronto and raised in London. His acting career has taken him from the West End to Hollywood with stops along the way for *The Bill* and at the Rovers Return on *Coronation Street*. His debut novel, *The French Executioner*, was shortlisted for the CWA Steel Dagger and more recently *Plague* won the Arthur Ellis Award for Best Crime Novel. After a dozen years on a remote island in British Columbia, he is now living in Totnes, Devon.

www.authorchrishumphreys.com